HOPE'S DEBT

Sever Squad

Book 3

A.R. KNIGHT

ONE

Hard Rock World

FRAMED IN THE COCKPIT, Wexer looked like a char-covered star. Giant, milky white rivers split the world's blackrock landscape, their chemical glow radiating out to the space-ship Aurora rode in, one heading in for a landing on Wexer's main, and only, true city.

If you could even call the squat, industrial building collection ringed by docking berths a city.

It'd been a month since Aurora had worn her power armor—recovered from Lani, a DefenseCorp agent, who'd borrowed it on Dynas and returned it when Aurora made clear the suit's codes could kill Lani whenever Aurora wanted. One month since Sever had docked anywhere except a small trading outpost for food supplies, and Aurora's patience with the ship's other passengers had run out. Except the one tapping Aurora's knee right now, her insistent pecks demanding attention.

"Hey Kaia," Aurora said, reaching down and picking up the little girl. "See that?"

They stood behind Eponi, occupying the ship's lone pilot's chair in a bridge big enough for several, the broad space committed instead to a viewing couch and walking room, as if cocktail parties ought to be held while watching landings, take-offs, and nebulas. Despite the space, the former kart racer and Sever Squad pilot approached the landing without excitement. Eponi had been opposed to Wexer at all, claiming there was nothing there that'd help them. Nothing that would bring Sever a contract and, crucially, some cash.

Seeing as they were now deserters, Sever Squad found both cash and contracts in short supply.

"Kaia?" Aurora asked again, the girl looking towards Wexer. Kaia tended to take the cautious approach and stayed quiet if she didn't know the answer. "What do you think?"

"I dunno," Kaia said, her hand gripping Aurora's smooth skinsuit.

The clothes weren't exactly made for whiling away the days in space, but skinsuits were all Sever had. Anaskya, the ship's owner and a renegade scientist with a taste for finer things, had refused to donate any spare outfits from her closet, and her two guards had taken theirs when they'd jumped ship at the trading post, along with Lani, who'd agreed to stay quiet about Sever's desertion in return for keeping her life. Minus some brief time in makeshift bed sheets while their skinsuits spun through the laundry, Sever had worn nothing but the tight, combat-ready outfits.

"It's a chance," Aurora said. "One for you and your father to finally give real life a try."

"And for us to do the same," Eponi said. "Though I still think somewhere closer to the core would—"

"Would get us killed," Aurora interrupted and Kaia gasped. "Not you, Kaia. Don't worry." She set the little girl down. "Go tell your father we're about to land." Kaia rushed off, and Aurora put her hands on the back of Eponi's chair. "You know damn well we can't go to the core."

"You keep saying that," Eponi sighed. "Like Defense-Corp will kill us or something. Don't know why you think we're so important to them."

"Not us, but what we know," Aurora replied.

Sever had been sent off to Dynas, run through a simple mission that'd turned into one disaster after another once they'd discovered the remote planet served as a testing ground for a species-altering virus. Anaskya had been leading the project, which sought to transform humans to match the worlds they'd work on, rather than the far more expensive efforts to change the worlds to match the humans.

Bio manipulation, though, went against just about every galactic norm. For all the wonders of technology, the power armors and the space ships and life-extending therapies that pushed human lifespans into the centuries, putting a person into a blender to make them something else lingered as an affront. Alien species echoed the sentiment too, perhaps because humans might see their DNA as fodder for experimentation.

Aurora hadn't considered all this, hadn't considered how many contracts and recruits DefenseCorp might lose if its funding for Anaskya's diseases became public until they were flying away from Dynas. Until Sever Squad voted on ditching the company that'd sent them into a do-or-die mission with zero information, even though DefenseCorp had known, had people on Dynas involved in the work.

"Oooo," Eponi made the ghostly noise. "So scary. A little drug that's going to make a few soldiers live on lava. What's so important about that?"

"Ever hear about the Raiders?" Aurora said. "It's old now, so I get if you're too young to know."

"More like I've got so many important things to think about that I don't have space to keep it in my brain."

There'd been a time when Aurora held the youngest label, had been the newest recruit on Sever Squad. Eponi wasn't quite that fresh, but the pilot still seemed to spend half her flying time digging through frivolous crap that didn't matter. Eponi could've been reading up on briefings, could've been learning about Wexer, or the Raiders. Instead, Aurora would have to teach her.

"Short explanation?" Aurora said. "Early days of our expansion and we get in a fight."

"Like humans do."

"Like humans do, exactly. Except this time, the struggle wasn't about an island or a city, but a whole cluster of planets. Back then, we didn't have so many ships, didn't live so long, didn't have a lot that we do now."

"Sounds rough," Eponi said, her hands pushing the flight stick to adjust their descent ever-so-slightly.

Wexer engulfed the viewports now, those cream rivers bright enough to make Aurora squint. They ran like veins across Wexer's skin, jagged and splitting. Some dried out, leaving lingering canyons, scars across the landscape. A hard world.

"Making new ships took time. Training new soldiers took time," Aurora continued, falling back on old training DefenseCorp no longer bothered to give its recruits. Given Dynas, those cuts now had a nefarious edge. "What didn't, was hitting them up with all kinds of drug cocktails to power our people through. Make them super soldiers."

"So not strange, moldy creatures that would die after a day or two?"

"These guys lasted longer," Aurora said. "They did

well. The mutations kept them strong, kept them burning from one fight to the next, until there weren't any fights to have."

"Let me guess, they kept on fighting anyway?"

"You got it."

"Your story's predictable, Aurora," Eponi said. "Unlike Wexer's damn docking crew. These guys keep changing my bay number because they've got so much traffic. I thought you said this world was a dump?"

"I thought it was?"

Aurora didn't take much offense at Eponi calling the story's conclusion. The Raiders hit their predictable end when the super soldiers came back home, the ensuing wreckage prompting the backlash that'd pushed Dynas into total secrecy.

"You gotta change your definition, captain, because this place is humming," Eponi said. "Don't think we're going to be hiding from anyone here. Want to abort?"

Aurora leaned over Eponi's shoulder, looked at the scanner and the blips crowding around. Wexer had some action, and for a group of deserting soldiers, that wasn't good. And yet, they were low on food, on cash, and if Aurora had to share the ship's small kitchen with Gregor's barbarian manners and bulk for much longer, she'd lose her mind.

"Take us in," Aurora said. "Just do it quietly."

"Since when does Sever do anything quietly?"

"Since we left DefenseCorp's protection," Aurora replied.

Sever's captain left the ship's bridge and headed back past walls covered in artist's depictions of molecules—Anaskya had unique passions—towards the large lounge area. Aurora spent most of her time on military ships, ones with a hard bent towards function over form, so seeing digital paintings and swirling color schemes painted over metal threw her every time.

Kaia's animated squeals marked Aurora's approach to the ship's main space, a circular expanse framed by couches and a wide, empty swath in the middle that had been co-opted by Sai and Rovo for exercises. The two were in the final throes of something that had them pushing off against each other, leveraging their own force to compensate for zero gravity. Rovo hung from the ceiling, his boots pressing off the roof and his hands pushing against an old food container. Sai did the opposite, pressing up from the floor.

"First one to give out loses," Gregor said as Aurora came up beside him. "It is a ridiculous game."

The big man, Sever's primary muscle, watched his squadmates exercise with a predator's hunger. The man's mitts lingered on his giant hammer's haft, sitting next to him on the ground. Aurora didn't have to ask if he'd called next.

"We're landing soon, and Wexer looks busier than we thought," Aurora said. "We'll have to play it light."

"Do we do that?" Gregor said. "Play it light?"

"Why does nobody think we can keep things quiet?"

"Because you're loud brutes, that's why," Anaskya said from the room's other side, where she lounged on the couch and played with Kaia. "Always punching and shooting, fighting each other. The moment you set foot on Wexer, the whole planet's going to know you're there."

DESPITE AURORA'S strong desire to space Anaskya, the scientist had it right: Eponi landed the ship in their designated docking bay, and by the time the ramp had stretched from the ship's side to the docking bay floor, prospective merchants had already crowded in. The motley band ranged from shrouded hagglers with huge packs strapped to their backs to straight-standing sellers with bots pushing carts loaded with fuel and parts. All waiting for Sever to descend with humming desperation as they sliced the air with insults about one another's goods.

"What're they doing here?" Rovo asked, cleaned up from his exercise and standing with Aurora and the others at the ramp's head. "Do we look like marks?"

"We're the only ship that's not a freighter landing so far," Eponi said. "Cargo runners don't tend to buy all that much."

Aurora kept Sever back and told Kashmal and Kaia to get off the ship first. Kashmal, with his young daughter and similarly small bank accounts, would hopefully cool interest enough for Sever to slip off the ship unnoticed.

"Why do we care?" Gregor asked. "We can say no."

"It's not us buying things that I'm worried about," Aurora said. "It's what they'll be able to sell once they've seen us."

DefenseCorp offered standard rewards for information leading to wanted individuals, and turning over a whole squad could make someone a healthy amount of cash. If Anaskya hadn't emphasized getting Sever off her ship so she could return to doing. . . whatever it was she wanted to do, Aurora wouldn't even bother leaving the craft today. Let the merchants see Kashmal and think this whole ship was his alone.

"What a problem," Anaskya said, still on the couch, "but you're all so competent, I'm sure you'll be fine."

"She cannot remove us," Gregor said. "Why are we taking orders from her, again?"

"We're *choosing* to leave," Aurora replied, "because I can't stand this ship, I can't stand her, and because she's as wanted as we are. Helix and their investors are going to be wondering where their lead researcher ran off to, and I don't want that heat on us."

"Yes, leave me to survive on my own," Anaskya said. "So noble of you."

"We offered, you didn't want to pay," Aurora said. "Your call."

Anaskya, being a runaway who'd lost her most valuable asset—copies of the virus Helix had been planning to sell—during their escape, had little cash to offer Sever, and the squad felt zero motivation to provide charity protection to someone who'd tried to infect Sai with her deadly disease. Besides, Anaskya could always sell the ship for the cash when she really needed it.

In short, Aurora didn't give a damn about Anaskya and wasn't going to waste more time with the woman. The scientist was lucky enough to still have her life.

When they left the ship, Kashmal and Kaia's appearance had the desired affect. Kashmal's hangdog look and his daughter's grubby outfit served to scare off anyone hoping for a big cash payday, and the merchants took their robots and their packs away as Kashmal asked for deep discounts and deals.

"I'll say this about the scumbag," Rovo said. "He knows how to pull a desperate look."

"It's not a look," Aurora said, taking the first step down the ramp. "Kashmal doesn't even have a ship to sell."

The man, though, was a scientist like Anaskya. Kashmal could find a job anywhere, probably even here on Wexer. They'd be fine.

Sever, though, needed a contract. Needed cash.

Aurora hit the docking bay floor, took a deep breath of Wexer's mineral air, its metallic scent lingering on her tongue. Above, a translucent sky shimmered with the white-glow reflection as the river light folded back off the atmosphere. Spacecraft engines thrummed continuously as traffic flowed in and out. It'd been a long time since Aurora had set foot on a world without being ordered to kill something already there, and she lingered in the peace for a long second.

But only for a second.

"You all have your afternoons to yourselves, but be back by dark," Aurora said, speaking into her wristlet. The computer broadcast her words on the narrow band Sever used, a frequency likely, hopefully, unique to them on Wexer. "I'll send out a notice as soon as I find something."

Sever Squad needed a job, and on Wexer, Aurora knew where to find one.

TWO

Street Cash

No guns on the streets. Aurora laid the command on Sever before vanishing to find them some work. Apparently the captain knew some haunts on the world that she didn't feel like sharing with Sever. Sai would've taken offense at the secrecy, except he had other objectives and getting a bit of off-ship free time fit right in with what he wanted.

Sai had left his wife and children years ago to take up with DefenseCorp. The cash provided had given his family a better life than any possible if Sai had stuck around, dithering away on routine security gigs. With long space travel diluting time, taking the contract meant breaking ties, meant Sai might never see his family again. Even assuming he didn't take a laser to the back.

None of that, though, meant Sai couldn't send messages back home. Before, he could just walk to the *Nautilus*'s communications bay and rip off a sentimental note, or an action-filled, suitably redacted update. Since Dynas and their journey through dead space, Sai hadn't been able to say a word. His family might be sending one message after another to the *Nautilus* and getting nothing in reply.

Fixing that meant finding Wexer's comm station, likely a sprawling mess beneath a large dish busy beaming out data by the petabyte to the intergalactic airwaves.

"You're taking that, really?" Eponi asked Sai as they waited for their turn to leave the ship. Rovo took second after Aurora, and the captain's orders called for a few minutes between disembarking to avoid attention. "Isn't that, like, completely against our goals right now?"

Sai reached over his shoulder, patted the katana's hilt. The long sword rested in a sheath going down Sai's back, something he'd cobbled together during the journey. Normally the blade would slot right in Sai's power armor, but that'd been lost on Dynas.

"I lost the sword once," Sai said. "I'm not losing it again."

"Nobody said anything about losing it."

Sai gave Eponi a level stare. The pilot had set Sai up on Dynas, and no matter how much Eponi claimed Sai would've died without her help, her actions had caused him to lose his power armor, to lose that katana in the first place. No matter the logic, Eponi's trick still burned.

"Take care of yourself," Sai said. "I'll be fine."

Sai's wrist chimed, the timer dinging his turn to ditch the ship, and he took the ramp in long strides.

"It's not you I'm worried about," Eponi said, her words carrying down the exit.

Sai ignored the comment and let Wexer's bright afternoon whisk him away from the docking bay, through the shallow wall ringing the ship, and into the open city. From what Sai had read, Wexer held itself as a stable world, terraformed just enough to kill the volcanic action that'd lead to the blasted landscape. Other than the creamy rivers, Wexer had become one boring rock.

Stability didn't mean beauty: what buildings Sai could see, sculpted from that gray-blackrock coating Wexer's surface, were wide and short. Supports buttressed the sides, most painted over with colors, graffiti claiming this or that. Dusty logos showcased corporate outposts mingling with residential huts, everything mish-mashed together.

Wexer rose organically, a desperate rush for the planet's precious metals bringing fortune-chasers and those who profited from them together. Sai saw both in the hawking merchants—they might've left Anaskya's ship, but they were still hunting marks here—and the shadow-eyed humans drifting around.

Aliens mingled here too, more than Sai had seen in a long time. DefenseCorp held a human preference. Mainly, so the company said, because it was more profitable to make weapons, ships, and armor for one species than a thousand. Because of that, Sai still tended to take a longer look at anything with more than two arms, translucent skin, or with a nose that went from face to feet.

As he walked, Sai felt eyes on him too, most trailing from his face to his tied black hair that he'd let grow, and then to the sword on his back. The Sever Squad demolitions expert picked out arms aplenty in the crowds around him, mostly cheap rifles and pocket pistols holstered on waists, but nobody else had a sword like his. That said, with Wexer offering approximately zero security, having your own protection was, more or less, required.

And Aurora had said no guns. Either her memories of Wexer were outdated, or she had a lot of confidence in Sever's looks. Maybe Gregor could stalk a place like this without getting roughed up, but the rest of them?

"Nice blade," growled a man, hooded and hunched over on a big pack. He leaned back against a building's side, a teal-shaded spot advertising mining insurance, and cast a gap-toothed grin Sai's way. "Shame you brought it here."

Sai would've kept walking. The comm station ought to be right around the next block, but the man's words stuck him.

"Shame?" Sai said. "Why's that?"

"Because now I gotta fight you for it."

The man stood, shrugged his shoulders with a sigh that seemed to place the burden for this situation wholly on Sai. The crowd burbling around them noticed something was in the offing, the flow leaving a berth between Sai and the man, a few lookers taking drinks or a snack and posting up around the swordsman and his challenger.

Well, they'd have to be disappointed.

"Sorry," Sai said. "Not tangling with anyone today."

Even if Aurora hadn't said they should keep quiet, Sai had left his random scuffle days behind. His ego didn't need salving by slicing up stupid people on the streets. So he turned, took a step further, and hoped the man would drop it.

Hoped he would, knew he wouldn't.

Sai caught the motion from one of the bystanders: a lanky dude who looked like he'd been scarred by a blast furnace, but nonetheless blew his eyes wide and his mouth open as he watched something over Sai's shoulder.

The gravel ground behind Sai crunched in time with the look, and Sai ducked. The punch, a clumsy one, flew clean over Sai's head. The gap-toothed man took back his blow, gave Sai room to stand up straight, then threw the mercenary an apologetic grin, spreading his hands as if asking forgiveness.

"Don't mean nothing by it," the man said. "It's just there's not many ways to earn a living on this world. Fightin' happens to be mine."

Sai breathed deep to push back the desire to draw his sword and skewer the man right then and there. The wild punch had tripled the number watching them, and a ring had formed around Sai and the man, a classic dueler's court. All the attention on Sai and his katana. Everything Aurora hadn't wanted.

Well. Sai had tried.

"You earn a living by attacking people on the streets?" Sai asked.

"Look around," the man replied. "There's cash to be had. For both of us."

Cries went up around them, calls for bets to be made. Hard cash, with several people shifting through the crowd, announcing odds and, through some application on their wristlets, taking people's bets and moving on to the next.

"Whomever wins, we split our cut," the man said. "Promise not to scrape you up bad."

"So this isn't about the sword."

"Oh no," the man wagged a finger at the katana. "I win, I get that blade."

"And if you lose?" Sai folded his arms.

"If you win?" the man flounced, his dirty jacket and hood somehow staying in place, over to his junk pile. He reached down, picked up a long pole with a single curved edge coming off the top. "I'll let you take this."

The scythe wouldn't be worth it. Sai wasn't a farmer with wheat to cut, and he sure as hell wouldn't be bringing a weapon that large into the packed corridors so many of his fights seemed to require. A scythe wouldn't be much good in a fight like this one either, where the katana's focused point should have an edge.

But, Sever did need cash. With DefenseCorp controlling their accounts, none of them had much for money. Anaskya had floated the food and fuel to get them this far, but now?

"Fine," Sai said. "You want to lose your weapon, let's go."

"There's some spirit," the man said, taking his scythe in his hands. "Figured you wouldn't leave me wanting."

"You might regret that." Sai reached over his shoulder, drew the katana. The blade, polished to gleaming levels, caught Wexer's light.

The crowd around them kept growing, and more than a few called out support Sai's way. More still shouted for the man with the scythe. Now engaged, Sai looked at the man closer, trying to suss out if his adversary was really just a hustler or someone more dangerous. The hooded cloak shaded most of the view, the man's eyes barely peaking out, little sparks that flashed as he made the first move.

A low sweep with the scythe, cutting in at Sai's knees and with enough reach that the crowd drew back a step. Sai, though, went forward, flicking his wrists to the right and sending the katana's blade down to block the scythe. The force of the swing coupled with the katana's sharpness should've sheared the pole in half. Instead, the scythe banged off the sword, throwing sparks and, with its force, knocking Sai off-balance.

The man laughed, set the scythe going in an overhead chop towards Sai's head. Again Sai raised the katana, sidestepped the scythe's sharp hook. This time, when blade met pole, Sai pushed back, shoved the scythe up hard. The big weapon took the man's arms up with it, exposing his chest for a match-ending stab.

Sai sank the katana and went for it, rushing forward

from his block to put an end to the fight. The man, far from panicking, kept up his gap-tooth grin. The scythe was back over his shoulder, nowhere near able to block the attack, but the man twisted his right hand, near the pole's base. With a click, the scythe's pole split in two, the bottom half breaking away. From the lower half, a second bright blade stuck straight out as the man brought the new weapon back across his body.

Didn't matter. The half-scythe blade was still too small, still not in position to block Sai's stab. A fancy trick that was just a trick.

Sai thrust, planning to stop the katana's point above the man's heart. The man flicked his wrist again, and the small blade fanned out, thinning itself into a steel half-circle in an instant, just in time to bounce away Sai's attack. The blow still forced the man back a step, but with the space, and with Sai's confusion, the man brought back the original scythe.

"A hook and a shield?" Sai said, stepping back. "Interesting choice."

"I like to think so," the man replied, then cast his eyes around the circle. "Keep those bets coming, folks! You're seeing a show here, take the chance to make some cash!"

Sai took the man's salesmanship and used it to gauge him more. With the scythe split, Sai had reach. The katana ought to be more stable than either of the man's weapons too, winning out in a smashing contest.

But, more important, who the hell was this guy?

Sai couldn't picture just anyone hanging out on a planet like Wexer waiting for fighters to come along. Much less anyone able to hang in there with a weapon like that scythe. Which made the man a mystery.

Which made him even more dangerous.

"C'mon then," the man said, clacking the scythe hook against his shield and sending sparks into the rocks. His wild grin belied his steady stance, his set shoulders. "When I make you bleed, they'll really cheer."

THREE

Fixed Bet

AURORA ORDERED Gregor to stay for the first shift. Anaskya ordered him to leave as soon as Eponi hit the ramp's bottom and vanished into Wexer's streets, leaving Gregor with a dilemma.

"Don't think about it," Anaskya said, standing up to Gregor near the ramp's top. "This is my ship, not yours. Get off it and go."

The willowy scientist didn't stand a chance of moving Gregor's physical mountain self, but she did have a point. This was her ship. Sever had commandeered it after Dynas, but now?

"What will you do?" Gregor said. "Our things are still here."

"How is that my problem?"

"I can give you your privacy," Gregor replied. "I cannot let you depart with our gear."

"Do you know what it's like for me to deal with soldiers like you for so long?" Anaskya said. "Quite frankly, it's awful. You're all such violent people."

Gregor looked at the scientist. Aurora, Rovo, or Eponi

could have come up with a snarky reply, something clever and cutting. They had those talents. Gregor had his own. He reached out, gripped Anaskya's shoulders with his big hands and lifted her off the ship's floor. She squirmed, squealed, and shot Gregor a furious glare as he held her level with his eyes.

"Violent people can be very dangerous," Gregor said. "I would watch what you say around such people. You could get hurt."

"Put. Me. Down."

Some could learn lessons, others could not. Gregor set Anaskya on the floor and she back-pedaled away from him. He glanced down the ramp, ignoring the scientist while wanting very much to leave her and the ship behind. If he could guarantee Anaskya wouldn't try flying away with their armor, their weapons while Gregor took a walk?

"What are you doing?" Anaskya said as Gregor went past her, towards the ship's cockpit.

"Protecting you from yourself," Gregor said.

The cockpit's controls and screens splayed out before him, most of it indecipherable. A few pieces, though, matched what Gregor was looking for: the ship's battery capacity. Most spacecraft relied on solar panels to catch starlight and recharge themselves mid-flight, but getting the energy to launch from a planet's surface took time.

Gregor tapped a button, one little used and yet invaluable in the right circumstances: the toggle flipped the ship's power draw so its batteries sent their energy back to Wexer's grid, or to anything else plugged into the craft. Gregor had used drop shuttle batteries for the same thing, and all those switches looked alike.

Before long, Anaskya would find her ship unable to move a meter, much less launch off-world.

"What'd you do?" Anaskya asked, standing in the bridge's entry. "Don't you dare break anything."

"I looked up where I want to go," Gregor replied, backing away from the console. "Enjoy your ship, doctor."

On the way out, Gregor took a look towards his hammer, resting against the couches. Sai had taken his sword, but the blade fit into a nice sheath along the man's back. Gregor's hammer, without its power armor slot, would stick out and likely send the populace fleeing for help. Not subtle.

"Next time," Gregor said to his weapon, and he went down the ramp.

Wexer's natural light felt good as Gregor stepped into it. He drew in a full breath: real air, not recycled and stale. His ribs tingled, his back sent a pained ripple through his nerves. Dynas had left scars in him, and Gregor didn't know how long they would take to heal, if ever.

Mechanical motors coughed to life behind him, whirring and whooshing away as Anaskya pulled up the ramp. Gregor tossed the doctor a wave and a big smile. She responded with a very particular gesture.

A firecracker, that one.

Outside the ship, Gregor didn't really have anywhere to go. A pick list of personal priorities started and ended with food and fighting, and without the latter, defaulting to his stomach seemed like a decent start. What would Wexer have to eat?

"That, at least, is a mystery I can solve," Gregor muttered, leaving the draining ship in the dust and heading out to the docking bay concourse.

There were crowds, and then there were *crowds*. Gregor had patrolled the first often enough on other worlds, the people moving about their day to day lives that just happened to find themselves mashed together in their journey. This crowd wasn't so innocent.

The shouting, the cries for cash and the occasional massed surprised gasp put the crowd to Gregor's right firmly in the second camp: one that formed for an event. Given the cracking sounds, the very *metal* cracking sounds coming in between the cheers, that event fell right in with Gregor's other priority.

Food took second place this time.

Pushing through people and aliens largely dressed in loose shrouds, light coats, and hoods meant to block blowing dust from launching spacecraft, Gregor made his way near enough to the crowd's ring to see a familiar sword flashing in the bright light. Sai had been off the ship for a few minutes and he'd already found a fight?

Maybe Wexer wouldn't be so boring after all.

Sai's opponent caught Gregor's eye too. Not every day you would see a split weapon like that. Gregor preferred his hammer because the damn thing was simple: a big mallet and a handle to wield it. Anything fancy, like this guy's bladed shield and his splitting pole made more chances for something to break, something you couldn't afford in a fight.

Though this didn't quite seem to be a normal fight. Sai kept his distance from his opponent, parrying the occasional swings with the katana's longer blade. The demolitionist never attacked, though, settling for a defensive stance as the crowd grew larger, louder, and more bets laid down around Gregor.

"You wanna place one?" someone nudged him, and Gregor looked to see a gruff woman, nearly his height, holding her forearm and its attached computer, complete with betting screen and coin card reader ready to go. "Fight's not over yet. Nobody's been hurt."

"Just watching," Gregor replied.

"Watching? Would think a man like you would be in the ring," the woman laughed. "Maybe round two."

"Maybe." Gregor started to turn back to the fight as the woman went after another client, but the way she moved drew his eyes back.

She didn't push her way through the crowd like a bookie, like someone rushing to collect as much cash as possible. Rather, in a light scarlet shroud that hung over what looked like an outfit meant for rough work, she sliced her way through the pack, found tiny gaps between people and slithered on. Impressive, especially considering the weapon belt she wore.

Gregor heard more calls for bets and followed them as Sai parried another half-hearted attack attempt. Two other bookies roamed the crowd, each one moving with practiced ease, and each one looking like they belonged, as the woman said, in the ring instead of around it. The crowd didn't notice, kept their eyes on the fight.

What had Sai pulled himself into?

Gregor turned back to the action in time to see Sai change his mind. Flipping his wrists, Sai moved in for a thrust, quick-stepping towards the other man. His opponent shifted his blade shield to block, when Sai revealed the feint and snapped the katana in a curving rightward swing to strike the man's sword. The blow knocked the man's weapon away into the dirt, with Sai moving with his swing to stand over the weapon as the man shook out his hand.

The crowd cheered, and Gregor joined in, clapping his big mitts over his head.

Sai had the reach now, the fight would be over in a moment.

"Surrender?" Sai called. "It's been a good round."

"Don't you see I've still got a weapon?" The man replied. "Take this one from me and we'll talk."

The crowd cheered louder at the retort, and Gregor would've cheered with them, except he noticed a familiar figure moving behind Sai, sliding through people without a hitch. The woman, that bookie, only now that Gregor paid attention, he didn't hear any more calls for bets. Gregor swept a look around and couldn't find the other two, hiding without their betting screens held high.

Did they think the fight decided?

"If that's what you want," Sai said, readying his katana.

Now his opponent played defensive, getting distance from Sai, but, Gregor noticed, not shifting from side to side. Sai, content to take a straight line at the man, advanced slow. The katana had half its length on the blade shield, more than enough space to poke at the man without risking a counter.

A scarlet flash drew Gregor's eye again. The woman, now at the crowd's front, slipping in front of another man who noticed, who heard the woman say something to his face, and who blanched and dropped back.

The woman stood taller than the man she'd displaced. Would've had a clean view from all over the ring, but she'd chosen to go behind Sai rather than watch the fight straight on. Chose to get to the front when she didn't need to.

Unless she had another reason for being there.

Gregor moved. Worked his arms and shoved people aside, swimming through the packed bodies around the ring. He kept one eye on the fight, Sai calling again for the man to forfeit as he tested the shield with the katana. A quick strike series that the man almost parried. Almost.

"Blood!" shouted someone in the crowd, as if he'd found pure gold on the ground. "Blood's drawn!"

The shouts reached higher, with some calling for the bookies, for the bets they'd placed. Gregor tuned out the noise, focused on the woman. He caught her in snaps as he moved through the crowd, her arms crossed by her waist, her hooded face watching the fight as if there was nothing else in the universe that mattered.

Gregor caught a few curses as he pushed through, but nobody cared enough to come after him, not when Sai, receiving another rejected surrender from his opponent, set his feet for what everyone could see would be the finale.

The woman saw something. She shifted, right hand reaching beneath the scarlet to pull out a tiny pistol. Too small to shoot anything more than a light stunning shot, but she aimed it at Sai, keeping her hand tucked in, away from casual eyes.

She raised the weapon as Sai moved in, whirling the katana into a low swing, and Gregor slapped the pistol from her hand. Grabbed her neck with his other hand, holding tight.

"Keep the fight fair," Gregor said.

"Making a mistake, buddy," the woman replied, her voice deep and angry.

Sai caught the blade shield in his swing, twisting the katana so his sword caught the nick between where the circular shield connected to the pole. With a hard yank, Sai sent the weapon flying up and over, landing it in the dirt beside its better half.

Cheers, jeers, and shouts for cash broke out as Sai's opponent stuck up his hands.

"Not going to press it further?" Sai said, sheathing the katana. "I thought you were going to make me kill you."

"Already lost enough today, friend," the man replied. "No need to die too."

Gregor released the woman's neck, stepped back as she bent down to retrieve the pistol. He expected her to turn the gun on him next, and was very ready to deliver a snap kick to relieve her of the opportunity. Instead, she holstered the weapon, flipped on her wristlet and held it aloft, shouting for anyone who had bets to come collect their winnings.

As the winners flocked and the losers left, the woman shook off her hood, her platinum hair shining, and matched Gregor's look for a long moment. In that face, Gregor saw barely covered scars, saw a black slit tattoo crossing the woman's left eye, and that she wouldn't be forgetting or forgiving Gregor any time soon.

Well. She'd said he belonged in the ring. Looked like he might get the chance.

FOUR

About A Job

As PLANETS WENT, Wexer fell somewhere short of fun. Eponi could leave the blackrock, the white rivers, and the scrap fabric fashion behind and never regret it. Aurora gave them the afternoon to do what they needed to do before an evening regroup back at Anaskya's ship, and Eponi planned to burn it finding a way out.

She'd fought with her loyalties over Dynas, alone in an adrift subspace shuttle with zero options. Up there, with her own conscience and nothing else, Eponi had found returning to Sever's band the only thing that made sense.

Then they'd ditched DefenseCorp and struck out on their own, sacrificing all the benefits, the job security, all because Aurora and Sai were a little bent because big daddy company wasn't quite so perfect?

Please. Like they were any better.

Still, Eponi had gone along with it because she could read a damn room. If she'd said no in there, Gregor would've dumped her out an airlock, or maybe Anaskya would have hired Eponi on, but if there was one thing worse than working for DefenseCorp, it'd be working for someone who wouldn't hesitate to prick you with a disease just to see what would happen.

Wexer's fresh air helped sooth thoughts that'd been burbling in the ship's close confines for the last few weeks. The ships landing in the docking bays around Sever's helped even more, each one a possibility for a way out, for a new life.

Eponi went along the bays, heading towards nowhere and taking in the big and small ships. Freighters, mostly, but many built for specialty tasks: miners, refiners, and vacuum sealers designed to take material up and expose it to cold space without bleeding all the ship's air in the process. The things looked like massive metal funnels, their tiny cockpits blowing into big aft compartments.

She could fly any of these things, could walk right up to one of the captains watching over their craft and ask about a job.

Except flying rocks back and forth across Wexer had to be the most boring gig of 'em all.

Shouts and laughter drew Eponi's eyes away from the vacuum sealer and over to a pop-up bar meant to serve captains and crew who didn't want to walk too far from their ships to find satisfaction.

The circular bar, tended by a fast-dealing black-speckled robot, sported a few screens relaying sporting highlights from around the galaxy. Three spacers lounged the afternoon away at its counter, downing beverages and watching, as Eponi saw when she approached, karts blitz around the icy track at Colune Seven.

The planet had an hour-long day-night cycle, and flash froze and melted as it whipped around its star. A kart racer there would start on water, have to make the hard switch to ice, and flip back to water by the race's end. A tricky one because you never quite knew what condition the track would be in when you hit any point.

Eponi had loved the course. So unpredictable, so dangerous, so fun.

"The leader's going to miss it," Eponi said, taking a seat next to the other three captains. "He's pulling too fast into the transition."

The other three, a man, a willowy white Casparian, and, next to Eponi, a colorful woman looked over her way.

"Watch," Eponi continued, nodding towards the screen.

The lead kart, a yellow and green number, blitzed across the dark ice. Lights from following cameras and course beacons hinted at the path, but those lights soon drowned in Colune Seven's coming dawn. Like a flickering lamp, the night faded around the kart, the ice beneath it quickly getting that melting sheen.

The course curved hard at an icy bank, one that formed every race thanks to metal frames put there by the course runners. Colune Seven's track changed often, but there were enough constants to keep all the racers from dying in unpredictable conditions.

This guy, though, had too much confidence in his kart's speed. He raced the melting ice, slowing slightly as he went into the bank, hoping the ice slope would help him keep his speed through the turn. Instead, the bank's top melted away as the kart flew up, causing the vehicle to flip over a shorter-than-expected edge and nosedive into the icy sea on the other side.

Not a fatal mistake, but enough to cost the leader his position.

"Okay, good call," the woman said, her dyed ruby hair pulled into a single long braid meshing with her similarly ruby-shaded eyes and a faux leather swamp-green ensemble that looked like it'd seen its share of scrapes . "You know Colune Seven, then?"

"Raced it," Eponi replied. "Several times."

"So you're a racer?" the woman asked, and flipped two fingers to the bar bot.

The bot complied, slapping down two small glasses with an amber liquid, its very top frothing with the same white caste of Wexer's rivers.

"I was." Eponi eyed the drink. "What's this?"

"Cold Spice," the woman replied, handing Eponi a glass. "Unique to Wexer. Fermented with waters coming right from the planet's core."

There were countless reasons to refuse a stranger's drink. Countless reasons, too, to accept it. Mid-afternoon in a crowded docking bay, with a drink served by a non-human machine, seemed about as safe as Eponi could get.

She downed the stuff.

The froth hit Eponi's tongue with space's silver kiss, numbing where it touched as the liquid raced through her mouth and down her throat. The spice followed, a warm, sweet glow like molten honey. The two sensations mingled, popping Eponi's taste buds with tingling happiness.

"Wow," Eponi said, looking at the glass after she put it down. "Wouldn't have expected something like that here."

"Most don't know it exists," the woman replied, her voice like smoked sandpaper. "Local delicacy."

"Thanks for the showcase," Eponi said.

"You want to pay me back, bring a kart circuit this way."

Eponi let a half-smile wilt on her face, "I said I was a kart racer. Not in the game anymore."

"You're not that old?"

"Old enough for there to be someone newer to sign."

"I know that tone," the woman held another two

fingers up to the bar bot. "Name's Tarla, and if you're looking for bitter regrets, you've come to the right place."

"Eponi," the Sever pilot replied. "And I'm not looking for regrets. Not really."

Tarla gave Eponi a coy look, and Eponi caught a slight shift in Tarla's eyes, the red and green irises rotating a little, as if focusing in on Eponi. Getting, or taking, a perfect picture. The sudden chill climbing Eponi's back took the edge off the second Cold Spice, but she knew how it felt to get her picture taken, knew what it was like to have cameras on her.

But in the eyes?

"Hey," Tarla said after they'd gulped down the second drink. "I know what you're thinking. What sort of freak puts these things in her eyes?"

"Maybe."

"It's for my work," Tarla said. "Helps keep me outta trouble."

Eponi couldn't resist, turned Tarla's way again and leaned her elbow on the bar, planted her palm against the side of her head. Those Cold Spices packed heat, and Wexer's crisp air wasn't doing enough to keep the fuzz away.

"What's your work?" Eponi said.

"Wouldn't you like to know." Tarla returned to that slick smile. "How about I get us a third round and you tell me why you came to Wexer?"

"Moving fast for the middle of the afternoon?"

"I use the time I have," Tarla said. "Better than complaining about the time I haven't got."

Eponi wasn't sure that quite made sense when the situation involved drinks before dinner, but she'd shared so many meals with Gregor and Rovo lately that she wasn't going to kill this conversation over quips.

"We're here for work," Eponi said, feeling around the backstory Aurora had drilled into them a couple days ago, when they came closer. "Hired muscle, mainly. Ex-DefenseCorp."

That last had been a risky inclusion, but Sai fought for the designation. Otherwise Sever would trip up whenever people inevitably asked where they earned their experience. Better to be clear, deflect any suspicion right away.

"The big boys? Heard getting away from them isn't easy," Tarla said. "What'd you do? Just disappear?"

"Asked'em real politely to let us leave."

Tarla laughed. The bar bot delivered a third round. From far behind them, down the concourse and away, Eponi heard a loud cheer rise over the departing ships, the nearby screen, and the quiet conversation between the Casparian and the other captain.

"Sounds like something fun's going on," Tarla said, sharing Eponi's look that way. "You said you were here looking for work? Normally I'd say Wexer's a poor choice for people like you, but it might be you made a good choice coming this way."

"Mmm?" Eponi sipped at the Cold Spice this time, let the frosty froth linger.

"Think your group could play nice with others?" Tarla didn't match Eponi's pace—she downed hers just like the last two.

"For the right price," Eponi said. DefenseCorp had relegated Sever to solo missions for most of Eponi's time with the team, a result, so Aurora said, of wanting more cash faster. Big operations took more time, had to spread the reward across more bodies. "And the right job."

Tarla nodded, "Isn't that always the case?" She reached out, tapped Eponi's knee with her right hand.

"We're all just drifting through, looking for the perfect fit. I've never found it, but this one comes close."

Eponi looked at the spot that Tarla had touched, covered the glance with a sip. Another loud cheer came over on the wind.

"What's the job?" Eponi asked.

"There's a big mine that a client would like to start using," Tarla said. "Thing is, it's been overrun by some vagrants that don't want to give it up. We're going to clear'em out, but I could use some extra cover."

"And the price?"

Tarla gave a number that had Eponi fighting to keep her eyes straight, her shoulders from twitching. Apparently a failed attempt, as Tarla started laughing again.

"Haven't worked private before?" Tarla said. "The pay's better, but nobody's coming to help if things go south."

Eponi finished the drink, let the warm end bring her composure back, "Half the missions we did for Defense-Corp didn't give us any help either."

"Then this ought to be easy for you." Tarla's arm buzzed, she glanced at her wristlet, its screen lighting up with a message. Eponi straightened, tried to see what splashed on Tarla's screen, but didn't get a look at it before Tarla wiped the words away. "Apparently my group's getting itself into some trouble. How about you talk it over with yours, let me know what you think tonight?"

Tarla stood up off the bar stool, seeming entirely fine despite the triple shot. Eponi did the same, hoping Tarla didn't notice her right arm keeping the slightest, steadying hold on the bar counter.

"Sure," Eponi said, the word sounding, feeling chalky. "I'll let you know."

"Do that," Tarla replied. "Glad I found you, Eponi."

Tarla reached out, gave Eponi a single pat on her shoulder, then swept away into the continually churning crowd. Eponi followed Tarla's walk until she couldn't see the ruby braid anymore.

"Would you like another?" the bar bot said, behind her. "Your friend covered everything."

"No," Eponi said. "Please no."

Suddenly a boring evening had too much possibility to drown.

FIVE

Sending A Message

ROVO CAUGHT up to Kashmal and Kaia before they'd gone all that far from the ship. With Aurora giving them essentially free time, Rovo figured he'd wrap up a bit of business before finding some way to get a message from Wexer to his family. DefenseCorp might declare Sever dead, and the last thing Rovo wanted was his mother, father, and sisters thinking their brother's body floated face down in some far away swamp.

Kashmal and Kaia had spent the flight time from Dynas to Wexer engaging in what Rovo could only call a sort of space therapy, mediated by himself. Sever's communication specialist kept an eye on Kashmal, who'd previously kept his daughter locked in a bedroom because of the valuable virus lodged in her genes, as Kashmal attempted to reclaim the right to be the girl's father. The two had reconnected over play time, watching the few child-friendly movies in Anaskya's stored, and very horror-heavy, collection, and working through a long apology series from father to daughter that, by its end, had Kaia giving Kashmal a tight enough hug that Rovo almost, *almost*, shed a happy tear.

Perhaps Rovo felt the responsibility because he'd adopted the role, and saved Kaia's life, on Dynas when Helix agents chased after them. Giving the girl back to a father that'd neglected her so thoroughly felt wrong, but Kashmal at least had the training for a career that didn't involve throwing himself into enemy fire on a regular basis. And without Helix hovering over them, Kashmal wouldn't have a reason to keep Kaia locked up.

"You're still following us?" Kashmal said when Rovo caught up to them. Kashmal, with Kaia pointing to every little thing and asking what it was, had his eyes on a big circular screen displaying passenger ship departures and destinations. "Don't you have other jobs?"

"At the moment?" Rovo replied. "Nope. Figured I'd make sure you were off to a good start."

"I'm at least twice your age."

"And half as kind," Rovo shot back. "Kaia, are you okay?"

The girl announced that she was, and also that Wexer was the coolest place she'd ever seen. Coming from a closet to a starship, Rovo couldn't argue with her. Here, in the docking bay area, the crowds shuffling around mixed aliens, humans, and bots together in a cash-chasing mishmash. Everyone had somewhere to be, orders to give, or jobs to do.

"There," Kashmal said, pointing to a long-named freighter. "That one's going core-ward. Four spots left. Kaia, let's go."

"You have the cash for that thing?" Rovo said.

"I never had to pay DefenseCorp for the full rescue, due to your desertion," Kashmal grinned. "So thank you for that."

"You could pay us instead. We did rescue you."

"No, Anaskya took me off-world. You simply happened to come along."

"You abandoned your daughter," Rovo said. "I saved her."

"Incorrect," Kashmal said, as if explaining an equation. "Without our timely return, you both would have died. Thus, as much as you saved Kaia from the closet, we saved you from your own enemies."

Rovo would've countered, would've kept going until, as he'd wanted to do so many times, he laid Kashmal out with a slugging strike in the street. Kaia, though, killed the fight, as she so often did, by asking what was wrong.

Deep breath, Rovo. Deep breath.

"Your father and I just remember things different," Rovo said, kneeling down to Kaia and reaching into the pouch on his belt. The skinsuits didn't have much storage. so Rovo had taken the belt'n'pouch from the mechanical closet on Anaskya's ship. "Here, take this. It's real simple, but it'll let you send a message to me no matter where you are."

In reality, the device was designed to help DefenseCorp give turncoats and spies a chance to communicate in secret. Fixing the device into a wearable necklace had been Rovo's pet project during their post-Dynas jaunt. A golden locket on a chain, Rovo slipped it over Kaia's neck, then popped the locket open to show the girl how to use it.

"Press the little heart here and talk," Rovo said. "It might take a while, but I'll hear what you say and I'll know where you are."

Depending on where Kashmal and Kaia flew, sending the tight message from one satellite to the next could run years upon years. Rovo knew he'd probably never see Kaia again, but maybe, just maybe, she'd remember him this way. A far off guardian that might, that would if he ever heard the message, try to come to her rescue.

Kaia wrapped him in one last, tight hug, and then Kashmal pulled her away, giving Rovo a curt goodbye.

Guess that's what saints earned in this life.

After the pair walked away, Rovo looked around, feeling a little like a leaf blowing in some long summer breeze. Getting to the comm center and sending off a long message to his family seemed like an objective, but a hazy one. Not burning for immediate action.

Still, nothing else presented itself among the passing crowds. Out of idle curiosity, Rovo wandered over to a random building's wall—a storage spot for batteries—and pulled up his wristlet, tapped into the Bug he'd put back in his ear, as Rovo always did when he went into the field.

The little device could scan and decrypt messages beaming through the airwaves, and while Wexer seemed to be an unimportant rock in the galaxy's various power struggles, there might be something interesting floating through the air. Rovo flipped through the frequencies, listening.

Radio chatter sprang through his ears. Calls to air traffic control about launch orders, delivery requests for late lunches or early dinners, standard business chatter from one worker to another. Wexer earned its blandness.

He did catch a straight-up local news broadcast, a static daily update fed into a bot that read the words aloud on repeat. Normally Rovo would skip away from these without a second thought, except Sever needed a job, and when a story started with illegal seizure, that usually meant opportunity.

A large mine network had been overtaken by the very creatures tasked to dig through the rock and develop the ore veins. According to the bot, who read the news of threatened bosses and contract disputes with a dead duck's emotion, the mine's owners were planning on kicking out the diggers and changing things over to a mechanical crew.

Because that's where the galaxy was headed: all machines, all the time.

Rovo shook his head, sped on to the next band.

"There's some fight going on near the docking bays."

The words came in with surprised interest, and Rovo glanced at the radio band. One reserved for local law enforcement.

"Need to intervene?" A bland reply came through. "We can send a drone."

"Nah. Looks like they're taking bets. It's controlled."

"We don't need more blood on the streets."

"One's got a big sword," the original sender laughed. "Don't think the streets'll be clean for long."

Someone cursed, and Rovo cut the channel, looking to the left, back along the docking bay's long berth stretch. He couldn't see the fight they were chatting about, but he only knew one person with a big sword.

Sai would know not to attract attention, but sometimes attention found you whether you wanted it or not.

Rovo took off, walking fast, towards where the fight was supposed to be. He didn't have a weapon, something a few minutes on Wexer had already made him regret, but Rovo had two fists and two feet. Sometimes that was enough.

The departing crowd gave Rovo better directions than the radio ever could. People grumbling loudly over losses, crowing over their wins all pointed Rovo in the right direction, one that eventually brought him to Gregor and Sai, the latter wiping off his katana.

"Here," Gregor said, spying Rovo. He held out two things Rovo took for batons, then noticed the bladed edges. "A prize for you."

"For me?" Rovo said. "What happened?"

"Some idiot tried to win my sword," Sai replied. "It didn't work out for them."

"You killed someone already?"

Gregor laughed, slapped Sai's shoulder, "See? The rookie thinks you're a cold killer."

Sai shrugged off Gregor's arm, whipped the katana up and into its sheath along his back, "I didn't need to kill him. The man's alive, along with his friends."

Rovo glanced around, didn't see any friends. The crowd had returned to its normal flow, though they gave Sai and Gregor space aplenty. Apparently holding a katana convinced people it wasn't worth getting close to you.

Trading words, Gregor and Sai filled Rovo in on the story, and the attempted trick to swing the match towards the end.

"So a random person challenging you on the street turned out to be a cheater?" Rovo said. "I'm shocked. Real shocked."

"Careful, rookie, or I'll test my sword's sharpness on you next," Sai said.

Rovo held up the two bladed batons, "Yeah, well, I've apparently got these now. So watch out."

Gregor laughed, because that's what Gregor did.

"Aren't you supposed to be watching the ship?" Rovo asked the big man, who waved off the question.

"I drained its batteries," Gregor replied. "Anaskya won't be going anywhere."

"She doesn't know how to fly anyway," Sai added.

Anaskya might be a brilliant scientist, but Rovo hadn't seen her step near the cockpit. Some people were only cut out to be passengers.

Left to themselves, Gregor, Rovo, and Sai went on to the comm station. Taking turns, Rovo and Sai sent off their messages to space, while Gregor fiddled with the newly-won batons, managing to get them back together into the singular scythe. Now, with Sai's katana and Gregor's hammer, Sever had three weapons that made subtlety impossible.

Still, for all that, Rovo managed to tell his family that he lived. He wished his sisters happy birthday for all the birthdays he missed, told his parents that he loved them, and, in general, not to trust anything they heard from DefenseCorp for a while.

Together, they picked up pastries and several supposed Wexer delicacies from some street shops as daylight began its slow, slow descent into Wexer's silvery night. Returning to Anaskya's ship, Rovo felt like he'd made something of the hours.

Kaia had even sent a message, a simple one saying that she already missed him, that they were about to head for the stars on a big new ship.

Not a bad way to end the day.

As they entered the docking bay, Anaskya's ship had its ramp down. Standing at its bottom were Aurora and Eponi, with the scientist nowhere to be seen. From Aurora's stock-straight stance, Rovo felt a particular mood, one that had bad news written all over it.

"Morons," Aurora said as they approached. "Where'd you go?"

"Comm center," Sai replied.

"Mmhmm," Aurora said. "And what did you do there?"

"Sent messages home," Rovo replied.

"Encrypted?"

"Of course," Rovo said, and Sai nodded. "We're not stupid."

That DefenseCorp could pick up and scan any standard message blasted through space was common knowledge. That they'd be interested in any soldiers thought dead broadcasting their survival, well, that was also common knowledge.

"So I guess I only have to be pissed," Aurora paused, took a big breath, "because you started a fight in the middle of the street?"

"A duel," Sai replied. "And I didn't start it."

"Doesn't matter," Aurora said. "You lost. We all did. Whomever you fought? They know who we are, and unless we do what they say, they'll send DefenseCorp down on our asses."

Rovo folded his hands behind his head. Good days only lasted so long.

SIX

Armed Democracy

Tarla had been waiting when Aurora came back to the docking bays, leaning against an advertisement for cheap mining gear taken from those no longer alive to use it. The mercenary waved Aurora's way, her predator's grin only growing as she picked up Aurora's mood.

The bar had been a bust. Its dim confines, lit up in geothermal orange, had given Aurora plenty of chances to chat with potential clients, from gun runners to rum runners to, well, just runners who needed protection from what they were running from. Problem was, every conversation eventually came to Aurora and her squad.

Aurora was a crap liar, and nobody wanted to tangle with DefenseCorp deserters.

"Not worth paying for life and then dying later," said one, laughing once he figured it out. "You get blacklisted by DefenseCorp and if you're not dead that night, you won't make it through the following day."

Blacklisted, in DefenseCorp's eyes, meant more than being barred from deals. It meant a price on your head, one plenty would be happy to collect. Aurora and Sever had done some of that work themselves for big-name buyers that'd thought DefenseCorp's services could be cheated. They'd died in visible ways, with big explosions or open-air obliterations. Nobody doubted what'd happened, and DefenseCorp's clientele stayed loyal.

Tarla, though, didn't look scared. Looked pretty damn arrogant in that green outfit. She smoked a stim-stick, meant to lace the lungs with adrenaline and caffeine. Not as good as other ways to wake a person up, but the things were cheap and everywhere.

"Aurora," Tarla said when Sever's leader made her way over. "I didn't hear about any DefenseCorp contracts on Wexer."

"There's always work cleaning up your messes," Aurora countered.

"It's not so easy when you abandon the mothership," Tarla replied, keeping up that grin, as if Aurora's words hadn't cut anything at all. "Bet it'll be even harder to survive when you're supposed to be dead."

"Are you getting at something, Tarla?"

"One of my friends happened to have a fight this afternoon," Tarla replied. "Not even an hour ago. With someone running around wielding a katana. One of your squaddies has one, right?"

Dammit, Sai.

"Tarla, I'm not playing the game. What do you want?"

Tarla stepped off from the wall, matched right up with Aurora. She stood taller than the Sever commander, but Aurora's steel spine made up for a lot. Tarla breathed the stim stick's lemony flavor right into Aurora's face, making her blink, but Aurora suppressed any cough, any flinch.

"Look," Tarla said, relenting ever so slightly. "You don't have to tell me what you're doing here, but if the bulletins are right and DefenseCorp's declaring you and your squad dead, then your miraculous survival might not be what they want to hear."

Aurora stayed silent. Didn't say no, didn't say yes. Tarla was leading to something, and Aurora would wait for the woman to get there.

"We're on Wexer for a job," Tarla said between puffs. "We were hired along with another crew, but they didn't work out. Now there's an opening. If you're looking for work."

"Didn't work out?"

"Things happen," Tarla smiled. "They couldn't cope."

Sure. Couldn't cope.

But as much as Aurora might hate working with Tarla, the former DefenseCorp squad leader appeared to be offering something Sever needed: a job, with cash waiting on the other end.

"So what's this job about?" Aurora said.

"Kicking out some interlopers for a company that wants to mine on this rock," Tarla said. "Shouldn't be difficult, but the boss wants enough people so the targets will just leave without a fight. Aggressive negotiations, you get the idea."

Like a thousand other contracts DefenseCorp had sent Sever on throughout the years.

"I do get the idea. When does it start?" Aurora said.

"We're striking out tomorrow," Tarla said. "Dawn, west side. Shouldn't take all that long to get to the mine. Boss is supplying transport, we supply the muscle. If you want in, I can get you the details."

"Maybe," Aurora said. "We're taking a different approach. The squad decides to go, not just me."

Tarla laughed, "Democracy might work for governments. It doesn't work for this. Take it or leave it, Aurora."

"Tell me again why you left DefenseCorp, Tarla?"

Aurora replied, getting heated in spite of herself. Tarla's constant sly grin deserved to be punched off. "I forget."

"Did you, Aurora?" Tarla said. "I thought I made a pretty big impression." She blew some more smoke, turned away from Aurora and started walking into the city, away from the docking bays. "Let me know tonight!"

"I don't even have your band," Aurora said to Tarla's retreating form.

"You'll find it," Tarla called back.

"SO NOW," Aurora said to Sever's members as they stood in Anaskya's ship's central room, its owner glowering from the couches. Apparently she'd tried to hire a pilot and leave, but the ship's batteries had drained too far for liftoff. A coincidence Aurora decided she wasn't going to investigate. "I'm looking at all of you and wondering what you think."

"Personally," Rovo said, "as much as I like Sai showing up that ass-hat in the streets, I feel we should abandon Wexer as soon as possible. DefenseCorp's going to come looking for us and we need to stay off their radar as long as we can."

"Scared?" Gregor asked the rookie. "Even with your new toy?"

Aurora looked at the scythe, now split into two bladed batons, looped into Rovo's belt. An interesting weapon, one that Rovo likely had no idea how to use. Deadlier to himself than his enemies, but Aurora had to check herself. This wasn't DefenseCorp. She didn't have the authority anymore to order Rovo to sell the weapon before he stabbed himself with it.

"Definitely," Rovo said. "I've read the reports. I know

what happens when DefenseCorp catches deserters. It's not pretty."

"But it's what we signed up for," Sai said. "Over Dynas. We chose to go this way. You did too, Rovo, because you wanted to help that kid." Sai held up a hand Rovo's way before the rookie could get mouthy. "A good reason. Don't get mad." Sai turned back to the group, and Aurora caught the fatherhood in his face. "It sounds like we have a job offer here, and if we're going to start making a name for ourselves, start earning cash, then we should take it."

"Definitely agree," Eponi said. "It doesn't sound hard. We go in there, do what we do, cash out and leave this rock forever."

Rovo didn't look convinced. Aurora turned to Gregor, "What's your opinion, hammer man? You want in on this one or not?"

"I don't run from a fight." Gregor shrugged. "Let's do it."

Aurora nodded, "Sorry Rovo, you've been outvoted. We'll risk DefenseCorp—"

"Captain," Rovo interrupted. "What would you do? You didn't say?"

Aurora pressed her lips together, took a big breath. The standard moves to buy time when forming a response from a ragged wreck into polished prose. Or something.

"I think it's a risk. Not just because of DefenseCorp, but because Tarla's not someone I trust," Aurora said. "I don't think she's setting us up, but her people don't play by any rules. It's cash first, last, and all the time. That said, we need cash, so maybe taking a page from her book isn't a bad call."

Nobody disagreed with that, and with the decision made, Sever broke to spend the night prepping for the early morning. Aurora and Gregor were the only ones left with power armor after the assault on Dynas, so Sai and Rovo went out shopping for gear. Gregor went to work on his hammer, while Aurora went to go find some way to find Tarla.

"Hey," Eponi said, catching up to Aurora as the captain went down the ramp. "Can we chat quick?"

Wexer's long evenings—it's days were more than twice standard length—made for stellar pictures. The sky, with the bright white rivers clashing against black space, turned a shimmering purple. A breeze picked up, the slow temperature change swinging air from one part of the planet to another. Ship launches and landings continued to crackle, engines lighting up the night like shooting stars.

Aurora wouldn't call herself a sap, but she'd found every world had its beautiful moments.

"So you can tell me why you're not hunting down armor with Rovo and Sai?" Aurora said. "Or do you have a spare suit back in the ship?"

Eponi's power armor had been folded up and packed in with Rovo's back on Dynas. One of the DefenseCorp agents had it, and had lost it, in the cataclysmic crash shortly before Sever, Anaskya, and the others had fled the planet. Given Eponi's preference for piloting, Aurora wasn't as concerned: if this guy had any vehicles, Eponi could hide in them. If not, she'd get a weapon and stay well away from any fighting.

"I don't, but I'll catch up to those two," Eponi said. "I wanted to say that I met Tarla earlier. Today."

"Today?"

Eponi dished the details, saying she'd met Tarla walking through the docking bay. That Tarla had recognized her from DefenseCorp materials and asked what she was doing on Wexer. That, when Eponi had mentioned looking for work, Tarla had tossed Eponi her contact info.

"She did all this while you stood in the street talking?" Aurora asked.

Eponi's face tightened, but she didn't flinch away. A good sign.

"It wasn't a long conversation," Eponi said. "You want her info or not?"

"Since you already have it, Eponi, why don't you send the message?" Aurora said. "I trust you."

Trusted or no, Eponi didn't follow Aurora when she resumed her walk. Sai and Rovo were off looking for gear, Aurora was going for a different sort of weapon: information. Someone on Wexer would know who'd taken over these mines, who wanted them, and why. After Dynas, where Sever had been thrown to their near-deaths without a clue, Aurora wouldn't be going in blind.

As she crunched along the blackrock, sparse overhead streetlights giving way to a sparse collection looking for food, fun, or on silent ventures best left to secrets, Aurora played back Eponi's expressions, her tones, and her reactions.

The pilot had lied. The question was, about what?

Was it the alcohol on Eponi's breath that the pilot didn't want to talk about, or had Tarla said something else? Promised something more that had Eponi getting excited?

Aurora had hoped Wexer would offer an easy way forward, a small step into a post-DefenseCorp life. Instead, it packed the same problems as everywhere else.

At least, unlike Dynas, it wasn't a swamp.

SEVEN

Departure Conditions

NOT A SINGLE SEVER member waved goodbye to Anaskya's ship when they set out in the morning. Aurora rented several storage lockers in Wexer's docking bay complex and Sever stuffed them with the few things they weren't carrying on their backs. Sai, Rovo, and Eponi, without any power armor, nonetheless had padded vests and energy-dampening fatigues that would, at least, cull some power from a laser's burn. Sai had found some aftermarket rifles too, modified weapons the shopkeeper said didn't have owners anymore.

When Sai asked why that was, the shopkeeper had shrugged and replied, "Does it really matter?"

Wexer's dawn crept in slow, giving time for the five members to make their way through nearly-deserted streets as the white-purple night gave way to silvery morning. Even the constant spacecraft churn slowed as pilots caught sleep before making their landings and departures. Anyone on the streets catching a look at Sever ducked their heads into their shrouds and kept on walking.

The usual reaction to Gregor and Aurora hulking in their armor.

Rovo's new scythe hung from a rigged-up sheathe, hanging at a slight angle from his back. Sai's katana set nearly the same, while Gregor's hammer rose like a beacon from the slot in his armor. Grenades abounded on belts, and Sai had spent the night putting together a few improvised explosives in case heavier duty called.

Stim sticks were everywhere on Wexer, and Sai puffed on one now to get himself awake, the jittery spike making him slightly ill, but chasing sleep's remnants far, far away.

Eponi had made contact with Tarla, who'd dropped an address near the edge of town. A hike that prompted Eponi to ask for a transport, for Aurora to shut it down.

"I want to see what we're walking into before we get there," Aurora said.

Well, now Sever saw it, and it was a mess.

Sai hadn't seen any part of Wexer's city that he'd call pretty, but getting near the outskirts shifted the tone from hardscrabble shipping and survival to industrial engines at work. Massive machines loomed above squat offices for their owners, waiting to be sent out to extraction sites to dig, destroy, and develop.

Wexer was a resource-rich world, designated to be drained and, when not an ounce of valuable material remained, turned into a featureless dump for those who couldn't afford to live anywhere else.

Not that Sai was cynical about the whole thing: the galaxy had more planets than anyone could possibly ruin. Some just made better targets for rock-chopping companies than others.

Tarla's meeting coordinates put Sever inside a vast, wire-fenced yard where heavy skiffs sat in rows waiting to haul equipment from one spot to another. The big craft rested on the gravel ground, their metal slats digging furrows and rising up around Sever until it felt like they were in a silent metal graveyard.

"Spooky," Eponi said as they moved around the craft, following the directions on her wristlet. "Normally I like hanging around ships, but it's too quiet."

"Keep it that way," Aurora said, looking around in her armor. "Eyes and ears open, Sever."

So suspicious. Sai reached up and put a hand on his katana's hilt. Ready to draw, though any ambush in here wouldn't give him much time to bring the blade to bear. A blade which, no matter how much Sai liked it, wouldn't compete with the small pistol in his right hand. The clunky rifle remained slung over his shoulder, a last resort.

"If you're thinkin' to use that thing, best try it with nobody and nothing around first," the shopkeeper had said when Sai pointed to the modified weapon, hanging behind the counter. "Don't get me wrong, that weapon carried its owner through Hell and back, and it'll do the same for you. Just might be a bit ornery till you get to know her."

Sai hadn't had an empty field to go shooting in, and with the job starting today, he hadn't spent the time he wanted digging through the rifle's insides. Lasers needed precise chemical and electrical outputs to work, and once you started improvising with the factory settings, your chance to end up dead stood to equal that of your targets.

But huge, overworked weapons were cool, so Sai'd bought the thing.

Rovo, his cash accounts not so sturdy, chose more basic gear. Appropriate for a rookie.

The parked skiffs gave way to a loading space: still gravel, but wider and ringed by the usual things one might need for a skiff trip on a world like Wexer: back-up power supplies, crates with pre-made, powdered meals and water, accessories for digging, measuring, and more. All had signs calling out prices, flush with exclamation points and wild, booming letters.

Venturing forth without gathering all these provisions would be tantamount to suicide, going by the displays.

Sitting on a creaky chair, raising a steaming thermos to greet them, was a decked out woman. Though nothing compared with power armor for intimidation, the woman's puffed up green jacket complemented thick pants absolutely studded with belts, clasps, and tools attached to both. A walking accessory collection.

"Aurora!" the woman said. "Glad you could make it!"

Sai and Sever let Aurora take the lead, stomping ahead in her white-black speckled armor to stand over the woman, who didn't look the least bit intimidated.

"Tarla," Aurora said. "I thought you had a team, or did they finally decide to ditch out on you?"

Tarla grinned, lifted the thermos above her head.

Sai had his katana out and pistol ready as shapes rose around them, standing up from within the heavy skiffs or aiming around them. He wasn't surprised to see the gap-toothed fighter from yesterday among them, the man even tossed Sai a mocking salute from his station on a skiff, long rifle raised and ready.

"My Twilight Rangers are right here," Tarla said. "Looks like we got the jump on you, Aurora."

Sai couldn't argue with that. Sever had marched right to the meeting place without the scouting, the defensive measures they would've adopted if any attack had been suspected. DefenseCorp would've included that likelihood in its briefing, would've had suggested approaches and methods.

Sever didn't get those luxuries anymore. They'd have to

be smarter, savvier, and less willing to take offers from people like Tarla at face value.

If they didn't, no amount of power armor and fancy swords would keep Sever alive.

After the little show, Tarla called in her team, and the five person crew ambled in to greet Sever with cautious nods. Names flew back and forth, and Sai slotted them away for later. Tarla's group had a grifter look about them, a style mishmash coupled with random gear. Like Sever might look after a few more years turning private contracts into cash.

"Are we all supposed to be friends now?" Sai said to the mercenary who'd fought him in the street, the man's big rifle strapped over his back.

"Aww nah," the man replied. "Name's Perro, and I'll be getting my scythe back."

"Sai, and it's not me you'll have to take it from."

"So I see," Perro said, looking past Sai. "Has he cut himself with it?"

"Not yet," Sai said, listening to Sever's other members holding serve with Tarla's team.

A heavily armed icebreaking event. As if this whole thing was leading up to a casual athletic contest and not a lethal eviction of some rock squatters. A surreal feel, too light-hearted for the job. Sai would have to remind himself that the cash was what counted, not the circumstances.

"Oh here he comes," Perro said, turning to look down the skiff row. "Bet you've never seen anything like this before."

With a shuddering whine that said far too much dust had ground into its engines, a heavy skiff broke loose from the long line and rumbled towards the group. Standing at its head, with giant goggles hanging around a neck that sported at least three chains, was the stern-faced muscle that Sai would've expected outside a violent nightclub. Wexer wasn't particularly cold or hot, but this guy had a vest on, puckered jeans, and leather gloves, as if competing in some fashion contest on a rugged island.

"You're right," Sai said to Perro. "This is a first. Hopefully a last."

"Who is that guy?" Rovo asked.

"He's the one cutting your cash," Tarla said. "So give him a clap."

Gregor did his deep chuckle. Sai sheathed the katana, deciding the moment had become too ridiculous for swords. All ten mercenaries looked towards the big boat coming their way, and for better or for worse, Sai felt that anticipation, the burn that came before something big happened.

At least, this time, he knew it wasn't a virus.

The skiff settled on the group's edge, doors on its sides sliding open as it touched the ground.

"Welcome aboard, flunkies!" the man announced, his voice shattering what peace remained at the day's beginning. "The name's Calico Max, and I hope you're ready to get me a mine!"

Go on enough jaunts across the galaxy, visit enough strange planets, and you would meet enough people and other creatures with names as absurd. Rarely, though, did a name mesh with its owner's craziness with such aptitude. Sai hadn't seen anything more perfect.

The skiff itself, as the whole crew clambered into it, failed to match Calico Max's expectations. Rather than gonzo wall art—Sai expected self-portraits everywhere— the skiff had zero personality. Just plain, hard metal coated in a dull reddish brown matching the skiff's outside paint job.

"It's a rental," Aurora said when Sai joined her on the skiff's deck, complaining how boring the whole ride was.

"Right, but it's *his* rental," Sai said, nodding towards Calico Max, conversing with Tarla as the skiff's engines started back up.

Aurora and Gregor had used a lift on the skiff's side to ascend to the main deck, a broad space covered with thick tiles. Two standing slots near the bow and one to the aft had been fitted with heavy-duty lasers, while the skiff's usual pilot house had been papered over with thicker plating. This may have been a rental, may have skipped out on the chance to spice its personality, but Calico Max at least knew he was heading for a fight.

Sever and the Twilight Rangers knew it too, and gathered with their weapons on the skiff's deck. There wasn't much need for a tour—Calico Max said there were four beds for anyone who needed'em, and a small kitchen with food, water, and a table to consume anything that deserved consuming.

"This one should take two days," Calico Max said. "One to get there and show'em the door, the second to kick out anyone that doesn't listen and head back home. The way I see it, we'll have'em running in terror inside the first hour."

The words washed over the mercenaries without a single shout, yell, clap, or thrust-up fist. Sai took that as a good sign: Tarla's crew wasn't green, and knew as well as Sai did that any mission starting with a brief from a guy like Calico Max wasn't going to be smooth.

Sure, they'd get the job done, but Sai double-checked the power-pack loaded into his pistol just in case.

Odds were good he'd be shooting it before long.

EIGHT

Smooth Ride

WEXER'S MORNING kissed the skiff as it sped away from the city, the squat buildings disappearing as they zoomed into blackrock ridges and narrow canyons. Rather than the gnarled windings Gregor would expect from natural causes, the smooth seams had man-made markings: carved out by massive mining work, extracting Wexer's minerals and shipping them away to be turned into, well, ships.

Gregor stayed near the bow, resting his hands on the railing and feeling the cool air whip through his close-cut hair. Aurora hadn't given the order for Sever to separate, but they'd done so anyway. Aurora and Sai had spread across the upper deck, while Eponi and Rovo had dropped back inside the skiff to grab breakfast.

And, of course, to get a read on Sanje, the Twilight Ranger piloting the skiff.

A sudden laugh, almost a yip, drew Gregor's eyes away from the landscape as the skiff banked around a lazy left turn. Calico Max and Tarla were continuing to dig deep into their conversation, which had continued non-stop since the skiff had launched off. The two seemed to be tight, though if Gregor had to read them, he'd say Tarla was playing Calico Max for future contracts.

Perhaps Sever would have to start acting the same. Gregor smiled at the thought of Aurora making small talk, buttering up potential buyers. How many minutes would she last before Aurora slapped someone, or straight up shot them?

"That's a nice hammer," said the white-haired woman from the street, coming up beside Gregor and matching his elbow stance on the rails. "Too bad you didn't bring it yesterday. I would've fought you for it."

"A fair fight, or another trick?" Gregor said.

"The trick gets the cash. Nothing personal," the woman replied. "Name's Briany."

"Gregor."

"Surprised to see me here?"

"No."

Briany waited for Gregor to go on, and when he didn't, she nodded, matched his look forward. The skiff sang into a wide valley, black walls rising high around them. Deep pits littered the valley floor, along with leftover, rusted metal studs where drilling machines had been mounted who knew how long ago. Small critters, little lizard-like things, scrambled away as the skiff zoomed by, vanishing beneath the rocks.

"Tarla says you're all ditching out on DefenseCorp," Briany said after a long minute. "Bold move."

"DefenseCorp nearly killed us," Gregor said. "We decided we could handle our survival better without them."

"Until they come find you."

"Who will tell them where we are?" Gregor looked Briany's way. The woman had two large rifles strapped to her back, both synced up to a green-glowing battery pack. "You?"

Briany laughed, "Why? I'm not their friend. Besides, I want to see that hammer in action."

"For that, we would need a fight," Gregor said.

Up ahead, the valley narrowed as the mining pits gave way to chipped slate ground. The two sides came together, almost forming an arch beneath which the skiff aimed to travel. Along the rock ridges, shapes crossed along the ledges in fast motion, quick enough that Gregor assumed they were more lizards, or larger creatures scurrying away at the skiff's approach.

That idea vanished when the first one stood up to fire.

"Talpa!" Perro cried, the sniper moving from his lounging perch on top of the skiff's pilot house. "Cover!"

Sever and Twilight were already moving, their instincts kicking in as more Talpa poked their heads over the ridges and began loosing low-grade laser fire towards the skiff. The green-white bolts frayed as the Talpa fired from their snub-nosed guns, ending up off-target and everywhere. Gregor ducked behind the skiff's bow railing, Briany doing the same as she scooped her rifles from behind her back. Gregor's power armor registered the threats, slapping his helmet shut over his head, the visor lighting up with bad news from all sides.

"Ask for a fight, and you'll get one," Briany said, grinning. "The gods in the stars must've heard my wish."

Gods in the stars? Gregor hadn't heard that one before, but, when Briany stood up and let loose with both rifles, that battery pack turning their shots into solid, lethal blue streams, he couldn't deny something had a hand in Briany's devastation.

The Twilight Ranger's firepower struck the ridges where the Talpa, earth-toned, furry creatures, hid. Briany's streams hit the stone and broke it apart, melting and exploding the rocks. Chunks rained everywhere as the skiff pressed on, Briany spreading her blast around them like some sort of whirling, cosmic lightning.

Until a thrown rock struck Briany's head and knocked her out. The stone came from above, and Gregor followed its aim through the smoke and ash-blown cliff sides to see more Talpa running alongside the skiff. Some had the energy weapons, most had slings or their own big, clawed, paws launching missiles down their way.

The skiff, trapped in the canyon despite Calico Max's frantic commands to climb, could only go forward. Sever and Twilight started returning fire once Briany's all-consuming light show died, but their angles were bad. The Talpa could shoot, could throw, and then duck behind the rock.

The bow and aft cannons had already been torched by targeted Talpa shots, leaving rifles as the only option against an enemy with better position.

The battlefield had to change.

Up ahead, the canyon narrowed further. Rock slabs bridged the gap, lined with Talpa waiting to deliver easy shots as the skiff ventured beneath. Already, the skiff shuddered as laser fire pounded into it, smoke rising and filling the air with acrid burning smells.

"Throw me!" Gregor shouted to Aurora, who was using her power armor to cover Tarla and Calico. "Now!"

The captain didn't wait, offering a clipped warning to the sheltering pair before breaking into a run towards Gregor. As Aurora bounded along the skiff, Gregor drew his hammer, turned around and put his back towards Aurora. Crouched, ever-so-slightly, and felt his boots ready their charge.

Aurora hit Gregor hard with a flying tackle, carrying

him up and over the skiff's front railing. Talpa bolts crashed around them as Aurora's boost jump brought them several meters high. Gregor, his armor monitoring his velocity, kicked in his own boots as soon as Aurora's flagged. The stored kinetic energy picked up from walking around blew out Gregor's boots and launched him farther.

The double boost jump was a tried and true Defense-Corp technique, one that put Gregor straight on course for a bloody banging with the nearest Talpa overhang.

Perfect.

Gregor lifted the hammer as he flew at the bridge's right side, brought it down as he neared the overhang. The Talpa scattered, as any sane thing should, as Gregor's massive form flew towards them. The hammer struck the rock bridge, releasing its own stored energy. Gregor felt the rock crumple beneath the hammer's strike, stone breaking apart into dust as shockwaves ran along the bridge's length. The bridge's right side, molded with some Talpa construct to the canyon sides, cracked and split, breaking off as Gregor's hammer continued its propulsive blow.

The bridge crumbled, swinging down towards the canyon floor. Gregor fell with it.

There was a price to pay for wielding a hammer like his, for begging after moves like the one he'd just pulled. Bruises and broken bones littered Gregor's life, and he'd suffered more concussions than any one man ought to. His ribs still hurt from the shellacking he'd taken back on Dynas, and as Gregor plummeted to the canyon floor, he knew they'd hurt still worse in a moment.

Talpa, stones, dust, and a few of those scurrying lizards fell alongside him, crashing down.

And then they kept falling, while Gregor jerked backwards with enough force to crack his neck as his head snapped. It took all Gregor's considerable strength to keep his grip on the hammer as he flew back, banged into the skiff's front—leaving a Gregor-shaped dent—and then went up and over that same railing. The pull vanished as Gregor's back hit the skiff deck, leaving him looking up at a sky he didn't expect to see.

Gregor had figured he'd be unconscious by now. Instead, he stared up into a scarred, black-braided face cocking a crooked smile his way.

"A great catch to start the day!" the man cackled. "Javelin's on his game!"

Javelin, though, wasn't ready for the skiff's sudden turn left, the jets throwing the man off his feet. Gregor rolled with the motion, reached out and caught Javelin's foot before he kept on rolling right off the deck. One good rescue deserved another, after all.

The skiff pilot had seen what Gregor had done, and shot the big boat up the collapsed bridge, now a ramp up and out of the canyon, to the surface. Cheers went up around the skiff as Sever and Twilight found their targets without cover, easy pickings on Wexer's rock.

"Give me a hand?" Aurora said, her suit beaming the words through the short-range band to Gregor's ear, and the big man dropped Javelin and leaned over the front.

Aurora clung to the bow, her armor's activated catches digging her into the skiff's hull. Gregor almost winced at the damage: between his dent, Aurora's scrapes, and all the new blast scarring, Calico's skiff would need to spend some serious time in the shop. But, considering Gregor had sent his last skiff on a doomed nosedive into a building, a dent wasn't all that bad.

After tugging Aurora back onboard, Gregor looked to see if he needed to pull out a rifle, or if he should jump from the skiff and commence whacking around with the hammer, but before he could reach for a weapon, Tarla called out the all-clear. Without cover or surprise, the smaller Talpa had fled, ducking into holes or dashing into the canyon to escape a blasting.

"Cowards," Javelin said, the lanky man winding cabling around his shoulders. The man didn't seem to be wearing anything other than various ropes and cables, all looped around his limbs. Each one ended in some sort of grappling claw or a sharp, glinting spearhead. "Figures they'd run right when things get interesting."

"Thank you for the save," Gregor said, glancing towards where Briany had been knocked out, to where she no longer lay. "Do you know where Briany went?"

"Below deck," Javelin said. "Tarla and Calico took her down when you went on your berserk run. Good stuff there, my man. Good stuff."

"We needed a way out."

"Sure did, sure did," Javelin said, then he nodded towards the canyon rim and the now-empty Talpa bridges. "Bet you anything we're hovering right on top of their town right now. We think they're all gone, but if we stay here, they'll get us. Sure will."

Gregor slotted his hammer back into its holster and shrugged, "They may get us, but they will not like it."

Javelin laughed, "Not wrong there, not wrong at all. I like you, big guy."

Whether or not Javelin liked him, Gregor had to check in on his squad. Aurora had clomped off as soon as Gregor had her on the skiff, and he found his captain hanging aft, demanding that the pilot put them down. Sanje initially pushed back, but when Aurora pointed out how many parts of the skiff appeared to be burning from blast damage, the man reconsidered.

"It's amazing how much more people will listen to you

when you tell them they're going to die if they don't," Aurora said as Gregor moved near her.

"Not everyone can see right away," Gregor said. "Thank you for the assist back there."

"Nice idea," Aurora clapped his armored shoulder, sounding a metal clang across the skiff's deck. "Things were going to get ugly in that canyon."

"The Talpa knew we were coming," Gregor said, and Aurora turned so they could see each other straight on through their visors.

The skiff settled onto the rock, kicking up dust. Its lower doors opened, and Gregor heard the cautious steps as everyone began emptying out, surveying the damage and any new potential threats. This wasn't their final destination, but for now, they'd have to secure this patch of dark rock.

"They were very outgunned," Aurora said. "I don't like it when someone fights when they know they're going to lose."

"Why?"

"Because it means they're fighting for something more important than cash," Aurora replied, "and that makes them dangerous."

NINE

Skiff Flying

Eponi caught the glances. The subtle side-eyed looks and half-smiles as the skiff flew down the canyon. Up until the Talpa dropped their ambush on the crew, Eponi felt Tarla reserved something small for her and her alone.

So Eponi took Rovo's offered option to escape the looks and ducked into the skiff proper. Even without power armor, the skiff's insides were cramped in their rust brown metal confines. They vibrated with the skiff's acceleration, the engines pouring a soft churning whine throughout the craft. Rovo wanted a second breakfast, and a chance to pour over rosters.

"We're matched," Rovo said when he and Eponi sat at the cramped table in the kitchen, set at the skiff's front.

Little windows like bullet slits let in Wexer's daylight, the outside moving along fast enough for Eponi to feel queasy for a hot second until, with a long blink, she centered herself. Kept her focus on Rovo and his wristlet, which the rookie had taken off and put on the table to act as his notepad. The skiff's own dead white inset lights added to the natural glow, their glare pocking Rovo's screen as he scribbled away.

"Twilight Rangers," Rovo went on. "Five of 'em. We've got the sniper, Perro. The heavy gunner, Briany. She's a scary one."

"Is she?"

Rovo glanced up at Eponi, "You don't think so?"

"Have you seen Gregor?"

"Ah, guess that's fair," Rovo said, then turned back to his wristlet and continued reeling off names. "There's that guy Javelin. Don't even think he's wearing anything beyond those cables."

"Mmmhmm," Eponi said, getting up and meandering to the skiff's fridge. She wasn't particularly hungry, but she would be. Best secure any good flavors now. "What're you doing all this for?"

"Don't you want to know what we're up against?"

"They're on our side, Rovo."

Rovo drummed his fingers on the table, a dotting sound as Eponi swiped through the screen showing the fridge's inventory. Peanut butter and chocolate protein? That'd work.

"Are they?" Rovo said. "Because I'm getting a weird feeling from this group. They're mercenaries, Eponi."

"Same as us, now."

"Sure, but. . . this guy? The pilot, Sanje? Every other second he's sending messages to somewhere," Rovo said.

"What?" Eponi sat back at the table. "How do you know that?"

Rovo tapped his ear, "My Bug. I've been having it scan around since this morning to see what kind of activity we've got going here. Sanje, at least, has friends somewhere that he's talking to." Rovo rubbed his chin. "He's not stupid though. He's putting strong encryption on every-thing he does."

"Can you break it?"

"Eventually."

Eponi nodded. Whether eventually meant in an hour or a month, she wasn't sure and, frankly, didn't care. Rovo was probably worried Sanje was feeding some Defense-Corp monitor their position, offering up Sever as a bounty to be collected. Possible, sure, but Tarla would have to know if Sanje was making a play like that, wouldn't she?

And if Tarla knew, then why do the whole dance to bring them on this job?

"I wouldn't worry too much about it," Eponi said. "The crew we have, the target? You heard Calico—"

"There's a character."

"We're on the fringe, Rovo. Everyone's a character out here. Look at yourself."

"What're you saying?"

Eponi grinned, prepped a few withering comments about Rovo's fashion choices, personality, and awful predilection towards really fruity, really sweet beverages, but the words died when shouts came from above. When lasers hit the skiff's deck and sides.

They rode out the Talpa attack under cover, occasion-ally popping out to take a shot or two from the skiff's few real windows: no glass, but slats that could be slid open and slammed shut. Without power armor, neither one felt the need to jump up top for heroics, though Eponi did want to shoot the damn skiff pilot.

Who goes straight into an ambush? Who keeps on pressing through into enemy fire for no reason?

"If you hadn't smashed that bridge," Eponi said to Gregor afterward as they stood on the blackrock waste above the canyon, gnawing two protein bars Eponi had snagged. "This skiff would've been blown apart."

"They were just Talpa," Gregor said, though the way both of them kept hands on their rifles suggested the small creatures weren't quite so harmless.

"I've raced against a few," Eponi countered. "They're tricky. Definitely not stupid. People fall for'em because they think they're cute."

"These were not cute."

Gregor kept on looking towards the horizon, where dark mountains rose up towards a glittering silver edge. Wexer did have its beautiful points, though Eponi would trade this planet in a second for one with water and something green. The thought brought her back to Dynas, and she amended it: water, green, on a beach with a cocktail and zero chance of getting shot in the back.

"What're you thinking about, space cadet?" Eponi said.

"Briany," Gregor replied. "She took a hard hit."

"Happens in a firefight."

"We were all surprised," Gregor said. "I should have covered her."

"At least you were in the action. Rovo and I were hiding down below."

Gregor chuckled, "Better there than where the Talpa could get you."

Eponi couldn't argue with that. Gregor fell back into silence and Eponi let him, looking back towards the skiff. Sanje had just announced the touch-ups were almost done and they'd better get moving if they wanted to finish the bloodbath by dinner.

Aurora, Tarla, and Calico had spent the time since the Talpa attack standing away from everyone else. Aurora seemed to be, going by her power armored gestures and occasional loud curse, doing her captain thing. Tarla had a constant smile on her face every time Aurora turned to Calico, wiping it away whenever the Sever leader came back her way.

Calico looked damned scared. As he should be.

Perro and Rovo were practicing with the scythe thing Sai had won off the Ranger yesterday. They danced on the rocks, Rovo stumbling all over himself. Eponi figured he hadn't fought with anything up close . . . ever?

Sai had disappeared in the skiff with Briany and Javelin, the cable guy taking a turn as the group's medic.

"Think we can trust them?" Eponi asked Gregor.

"I've worked with worse," he replied. "I've worked with better."

"That's not an answer."

Gregor eyed her, "Then no, I would not trust them."

That's what Rovo said too. What was Eponi missing? She hadn't done detective work before, hadn't made the grade to join DefenseCorp's agency arm with its clandestine missions and dark secrets, but she wasn't stupid.

"Eponi!" Tarla shouted from near the skiff's bow, and Eponi jerked at the familiar tone in Tarla's voice. "You and your big friend coming? It's time to move."

"Sure," Eponi called back, standing.

She heard Gregor get up behind her, felt his questioning eyes on her back as they went. She flushed, not from embarrassment, but from a familiar angry heat. Of all five Sever Squad members, Eponi was the only one with a career outside the smash'n'burn DefenseCorp life. Aurora had pointed out to her often enough that Eponi was something of an outsider, even though her reasons for joining DefenseCorp were the same as everyone else: desperation.

Just because she had dreams beyond shooting people shouldn't make Eponi suspicious. If Tarla had talked to

Aurora like that, Gregor wouldn't question it, would go on as if—

"You all right?" Tarla asked, waiting up for Eponi near the skiff's entrance. "If you'd had that look on your face yesterday, I might not've said hello."

"It's been a rough morning."

"Has it?" Tarla said. "I think Briany has you beat there."

This time, the flush had less to do with anger.

"Right, yeah," Eponi scrambled for empathy. Found it. "How's she doing?"

"Out of action for today," Tarla said, "but I don't think we'll need her."

Tarla's prediction proved out once Sanje had the skiff rolling along, sprinting over the expanse towards the mines. Why they hadn't taken the overland route initially and opted for the canyon became clear quick: the Talpa weren't going to give up the approach.

Long-range lasers, frayed and wild like the Talpa's smaller arms, shot from those looming mountains. The green-white bolts lanced down around them, scattered and haphazard. Eponi, behind the pilot house where she could watch Sanje's driving, guessed the Talpa had one, maybe two cannons. And old ones at that.

Perro, the sniper, had hooked himself to the pilot house's roof, where he'd set up with his massive rifle looking to catch a pot shot. Everyone else, except Gregor and Aurora, crouching behind the bow armor, had fled inside.

Tarla's pilot hunched over the skiff's four levers, each one controlling a different jet. The outside two were for steering, the inside for speed. Newer models had consolidated things to two, but Wexer was a few light years away from up to date. Sanje ran his hands along the levers like a frantic child, pushing and pulling each one as the skiff's defense systems projected the next shot.

"You don't have to swerve so hard," Eponi said as Sanje veered away from another blast. "You're slowing us down. They're not good shots."

"All it takes is one!" Sanje shouted.

"And all your twisting is giving them more chances," Eponi said. "Keep the skiff straight, make slight moves. You'll keep your speed that way."

Sanje didn't follow her advice, turned hard left to avoid a bolt that blasted apart a rock two meters beyond the skiff. Perro, from above, cursed.

The big floating craft moved like a boat through the air, its jets pushing the skiff through the turn like Eponi might swim through mud. Sanje wanted the skiff to fly like a fighter jet, like a kart.

"Switch with me," Eponi said. "You're going to get us killed!"

"No way," Sanje said, fumbling with the levers to get the skiff pointed back at the mines. "Back off!"

The slow turn back towards the mine gave the Talpa an opening, and the critters took it. The next laser blast scored a broadside hit on the skiff, blowing off some of its plating and littering the ashes in the skiff's wake. Someone shouted from below decks, angry, but Eponi couldn't catch the words.

She did know, though, that Sanje was out of his depth. That he'd get Sever, Twilight, and even Calico Max killed before they hit the mines. Eponi did not want to die out here, in this blasted, lost land on some cheap contract.

Eponi swung into the pilot's house, and when Sanje pulled the skiff through another lazy turn, Eponi pushed him aside and stepped in, taking the levers. Sanje seemed too surprised to contest the move, offering up a yelp. He reached for Eponi, but she yanked the skiff back in the right direction, and Sanje, without his hands holding anything, bounced across the pilot house and rammed into the wall.

"Sit down and watch," Eponi said. "You might learn something."

Sanje did sit, he did watch, and he cursed Eponi out constantly as she settled into the skiff. As she read the machine's heart, its muscles, and its mind. The levers felt loose in her hands as Eponi threw the throttle forward, switched to a tight grip on the levers keeping the skiff straight. In front, dim-light screens showcased previous shots as green streaks, with yellow markings offering up projected incoming strikes.

The middle screen gave Eponi a clear view from a camera embedded in the bow, and with it, she measured her maneuvers.

The Talpa fired from dead on, each shot aiming to split the skiff apart. Each bolt only had a tiny width, each one could be avoided with slight shunts. So Eponi danced around those mint projections, pulling back just enough, but sharply, on each turning lever, the sudden switch in jet direction bouncing the skiff left and right without turning the whole craft around.

The lasers fell alongside them, close but still missing by meters. The blackrock landscape gave way to craggier fare, and the first hints of a slope. Before long, they'd be at the mines. Alive and ready, thanks to Eponi, a damn fine, trustworthy pilot.

"Hey," Sanje said, clinging to the pilot house where Eponi once had. "Don't think I won't remember this."

Eponi laughed, "Don't think I care."

TEN

Enemy or Victim

THE OFFER SHEET TO swap divisions with DefenseCorp had been basic. A rundown of the responsibilities when he changed over from a communications analyst to a frontline member, all of them falling in line with what Rovo expected, what he wanted. Until he reached the end.

Pulled out in bold black lettering sat a paragraph demanding Rovo's acceptance of his orders, no matter what the objective, no matter the politics or any personal feelings around the situation. By putting his name on the line and accepting the cash on offer, Rovo would have to be willing to burn down a village, murder civilians, or anything else DefenseCorp's buyers wanted him to do.

"We're not asking you to change how you feel," said the recruiter in the room with him, watching Rovo review the form. "We're asking you to ignore it."

Amoral. That was the organization's philosophy, though DefenseCorp turned out to be not quite that evil. Individual commanders had latitude in completing their contracts, and most tried to evacuate dissidents before shooting them. Tried to relocate rather than obliterate civilians. But the language was there, the lines were set.

Now, Sever didn't have to follow that language, but Calico Max seemed to expect it.

Rovo, belowdecks on the skiff as it flew towards the mine, listened to the vested man rant to Tarla in the kitchen about the cost to repair the laser-scarred armor. About how the Talpa had no right to this territory, about how—

"He goes on, doesn't he?" Sai said, sitting next to Rovo.

They were at the kitchen's back, near the windows looking where the skiff went, the mines and their mountains edging up huge. Every oncoming laser flash winked through those windows, splashing white-green across the table. Beyond Calico and Tarla, the other Twilight Rangers had scattered throughout the skiff.

Checking on Briany, most likely.

"Not a fan," Rovo replied. "Sounds like one of the far-too-many loud mouthed bosses I've seen before."

"On your messages?"

Rovo nodded, winced as another flash came by. At least Sanje had stopped swerving the skiff so hard now. All the twisting had forced Rovo and everyone else to keep their hands holding on to something or get bashed around the skiff's insides.

"I'll never understand how the worst people find their way into power," Rovo said.

"I try not to think about it," Sai said. "Easier that way."

"Suppose," Rovo said. Another laser flash. "They're really gunning for us, aren't they?"

"The Talpa?" Sai said. "I would. Their best chance is to break us down out here, strand us in the open. Now that their perimeter's been breached, they know what's coming."

True. The Talpa force that they'd scattered from the canyon ridges was probably dashing back home now, and had no doubt sent a message or seven back to the mines about what was coming.

And messages could be caught.

Rovo reached up to his ear, massaged the little circle device lodged in between his lobe and actual canal. The Bug responded to the motion, running through frequencies where it found traffic. In Wexer proper, Rovo had it listening in to air traffic and local news, trying to catch any hints about whether someone had recognized a deserting DefenseCorp squad.

Out here?

"They're panicking," Rovo said as the Bug found a signal, found the tight and quick growls and grunts, coupled with clacking claws, that the Talpas used for a language. "They think they've already lost."

"What?" Sai said. "You can hear what they're saying?"

"It's not encrypted," Rovo replied. "These aren't sophisticated transmissions, but wild messages. They're telling the vulnerable ones, the kids and the sick to head deeper into the mines and dig further."

The clacks came constant, a back and forth as the ambushers described Sever and Twilight, the skiff and the coming doom. The advance Talpa and their snub-nosed guns represented, apparently, most of the defense and they were not going to beat the skiff back to base. The little creatures had staked everything on the ambush.

"They have nothing else," Rovo said. "If their one gun shooting now doesn't hit us, it'll be just like Calico said. A total bloodbath."

"Then why are they even staying?" Sai said. "Who holds a position they can't defend?"

Rovo shook his head, "I don't know. Nobody's talking about a retreat. Not a single one of them."

Sai put his hands on the kitchen table, clasped them together and issued the heaviest sigh Rovo had heard the man make. During the weeks spent floating from Dynas to Wexer, the rookie had burned hours hanging with the other Sever members, and over long nights lubricated by Anaskya's generous wine stocks, he'd gleaned a little more about what kept all of them in the game.

Sai had a family, sure, but he'd come from a planet where the weak had been smashed by the strong. What'd been a push for democracy had been crushed by Defense-Corp lasers, by troops that delivered contractual justice without compromise. Sai had seen those conquering mercenaries as heroes.

Now?

"This job just became a lot less fun," Sai said. He reached back, tapped the katana's hilt. "Don't think I'll be taking this out today."

"Why?"

"My mother wouldn't want it slicing up innocents," Sai replied. "I don't either."

Rovo didn't have a family relic on his back, but he felt the same about his own rifles. The Bug kept chattering away in his ear, and nothing he heard pushed his fingers towards the trigger.

"That's the whole contract!" Calico shouted, his voice rising up enough to make Tarla frown. "Every last one of these things has to go, and I don't care how long it takes to clear every tunnel, but that's what I'm paying you for."

"You want an extermination, you'll have to pay extra,"

Tarla countered as Rovo and Sai fell silent, listened in. "You said this would be an intimidation job, that they'd run away when we came close. Now one of mine's hurt, and we're flying through fire. Not the terms."

"What terms?" Calico said, folding his arms and setting his face in stoney frustration. "I hired you and that other squad for two days to get me my mine back, and the mine isn't mine until all those damn things are gone. Those are the only terms you need to worry about."

"Then consider this a renegotiation," Tarla replied. "We'll handle the laser. Any others that shoot at us. Anything else, I want more."

Calico balled a hand into a fist, but before he could make a move, Tarla had a pistol drawn and pointed right at his chest. Calico froze. Rovo's eyes bugged out. This was, without a doubt, the craziest negotiation he'd ever seen.

"We have the weapons, we call the shots," Tarla said. "Think real careful before you run that sweet mouth of yours Calico. Pay us today, and that mine's yours for long after tomorrow."

Calico let his fingers uncurl as another Talpa shot blasted by outside, the skiff shunting slightly to avoid the laser.

"You're not like the others I've hired before," Calico said, almost disbelieving.

"You'll never find another like me," Tarla said, not moving the pistol. "Do we have a deal?"

"The cash is yours," Calico gave her the slightest nod. "Now can you get this gun out of my face?"

Tarla slipped the pistol back into its holster, gave Calico a pat on the cheek, then turned towards Rovo and Sai. Calico rubbed the spot where Tarla had touched, then shook his head and ducked away from the kitchen.

"That, my Sever friends, is how you negotiate," Tarla said. "Now, I don't think I've met either of you before?"

Sai stood up, crumpling the protein bar's wrapper and dropping it in the waste compactor slot by his knee, "Let's keep it that way."

The Sever demolitionist moved past Tarla, not bothering to say another word. If the move offended her, Tarla didn't show it. Instead, she looked towards Rovo, raised her eyebrows in a question and rolled her eyes towards Sai.

"Think he didn't like the bloodbath thing," Rovo said. "He's got a family."

"Oh does he?" Tarla said. "Because so do I. Right here."

"I get it," Rovo said. DefenseCorp played up that bit too, every member in your squad was a part of your family, blah blah blah. The sentiment withered a little when DefenseCorp slapped your face with it every other minute. "He has his principles."

"What about you?" Tarla said.

"I'm still figuring that out," Rovo replied, slipping his eyes past Tarla to look, to hope that someone else would join him in the kitchen. "Can't say I disagree with him, though. I didn't sign up for this to shoot helpless creatures."

"A strange word to use for things that almost killed us back there," Tarla settled in at the table. "Do you have a name, or am I going to have to guess?"

"Rovo."

Tarla tilted her head slightly, reached up and tapped a single finger to her temple, "Rovo. Nice name. I'll remember it."

Rovo didn't know what to say to that, so he said nothing. The skiff, though, seemed to respond with a sharper swing, drawing both of their glances out the window to see the skiff slide behind a huge ridge line, its slope swooping upwards.

They'd reached the mine.

"Look at that," Tarla said. "Here we are. We'll have to continue this conversation later."

"Sure?"

Tarla stood, Rovo moved to follow as Eponi's voice came over the skiff's speakers, announcing their guess had been correct. Time to arm up, and move out.

"Oh, Rovo," Tarla said. "Try not to let your friend's principles get in the way of my family." Her hand went to the pistol on her belt. "Calico has to pay for innocent lives, but I'll take your friend's for free."

Gregor and Aurora took initial watch while Sever and Twilight left the heavy skiff, assembling on the hillside. Calico Max declared that he'd wait back at the skiff, holding it down until their return. Briany, hurt but conscious, would be waiting with him, and nobody had to ask whether she'd also be making sure Calico didn't decide to ditch out and leave his hired squads behind.

Rovo, his scythe put back into a single, long weapon on his back and a rifle in his hands, looked up at the cool white sky. Not a cloud in it. Not that he'd seen a cloud anywhere on this planet. The mountain rock felt soft under his shoes, dry and crumbling. The air gave his nose a crisp kiss.

He focused on all those things rather than on Tarla's words, on her threat. On what he was about to do.

The Bug hadn't stopped playing the Talpa transmissions, and their panic had only grown once the skiff made it inside the heavy laser's range. The little creatures still weren't running. They were afraid, but they were willing to die for the mine.

Rovo didn't know why, but he could admire the

courage. He could hate the idea of slaughtering the Talpa. He looked for Sai, found the swordsman standing by himself, like Rovo, and looking off into the indeterminate distance. Rovo didn't find any answers out there, and he bet Sai wouldn't either.

When Rovo had told his family that he was abandoning his desk job on the space station, routing away intergalactic communications from one system to another, his father had said he was sacrificing the best thing life could give: stability. Rovo had made the trade looking for excitement, looking for a legacy.

Dynas had been a terror, but saving Kaia and stopping a virus had been a choice he could believe in. This?

"Aurora," Rovo said, realizing he'd walked almost up to Gregor and his captain. "We need to talk."

"About?" Aurora said. "It's time to move, Rovo. It's getting late and I'd rather not spend the night in the mine."

"That's just it," Rovo replied. "I'm not going to move. Not against the Talpa, not here."

"Explain."

Rovo did, spilling out what he'd heard on the Bug, the new deal between Calico and Tarla. By the time he finished, by the time he answered Aurora's questions, both squads had formed up below, waiting for Aurora to give the go-ahead.

"Rovo," Aurora said. "I'll promise you this. We'll talk first. See if we can avoid any fighting. But if we have any chance to succeed, I'm going to need you standing with me. Talking with me."

That? That Rovo could do.

"Swear that you won't start shooting them?" Rovo said.

"Calico's paying us to clear the mine," Aurora replied.

"Whatever Tarla's other deal, if the Talpa leave, we get our cash. Nobody needs to die today."

Yet, as Aurora called for the group to move out, Rovo could only see ten heavily armed killers, promising anything but peace.

ELEVEN

Peace Or Purge

THEY TOLD her it would happen fast. Once, twice with the trigger on a rifle and she'd lose the sensation, the gnawing feeling of *wrongness* that came with every body, human, alien, or otherwise that she burned down. But she never really lost it, and Aurora suspected none of them ever really did, you just figured out how to bury it.

Rovo hadn't learned that yet. He'd shot his fair share of Helix guards on Dynas, but who knew how many of those actually died. If any. And taking out an enemy in a running fight wasn't the same as what Sever marched towards now.

DefenseCorp guidelines didn't preach protecting new kids. Once they'd been pushed to active duty, a squad member ought to be treated like any other. A dumb approach, but no doubt pushed by profit: contracts had to be fulfilled, and you couldn't guarantee an easy one for all the newbies.

Swim or die.

Aurora didn't buy that philosophy, especially now that she didn't have a ready stock of new recruits to fill Rovo's shoes should the kid decide his morals were more important than the mission and run. She'd have to protect Rovo from himself, and from everyone else.

Calico's approach meant to put the skiff at the mine's main entrance, at the end of that long jagged canyon through the blackrock desert. The Talpa ambush forced an audible, and while Eponi's slight dodging—Aurora had kept a hidden grin at her pilot's takeover from Tarla's—had saved them from the longe-range laser, it'd veered the skiff off to the side, so that the squads approached the mines from an angle meant for tossing out extra dirt.

The giant blackrock drift they'd docked at stretched upwards for a few hundred meters, building up into Wexer's afternoon sky and blocking anything on the other side, so the climb appeared like a slate ramp to some celestial heaven. Aurora didn't hold with those beliefs: she'd seen too much awfulness through the galaxy to depend on some divine rescue, but she could appreciate the idea.

Even if every step slipped beneath her power armor's weight. Even if her muscles were cramping up at spending the day wearing the metal suit while barely moving in it. Joints protested, tendons twinged, and the weeks spent in null gravity on Anaskya's starship announced their deleterious effects on her muscles.

Just another day on the job.

Rovo, now crunching up the hillside behind her, mentioned the Talpa were going on the defensive. That there'd be little resistance because all the ones with weapons had burned their surprise in the ambush. Aurora kept her rifle out, held one-handed so she could use her other to steady the occasional slip'n'slide on the rock. Ready to fire, though accuracy would be crap during the climb.

If the Talpa had been smart, they'd have saved their strike for now.

"How long's this damn hill?" Javelin shouted. "Can't take a step without losing two!"

"Not much farther," Aurora called back. "Keep at it, and keep quiet."

"Thanks for the tip, but you can shove your orders," Javelin replied. "I don't work for you, lady."

"Her name's Aurora, and you'll treat her like you treat me," Tarla cut in before Aurora decided whether she should shoot Javelin right then and there. "You've got two captains on this one, and both of us know how to keep you alive better than you do, so shut up and listen."

A hard leash. Not surprising for Tarla. The woman bled a rougher, frontier leadership. Aurora preferred the icy, competent version: less time spent on banter, more focus on the mission, but Tarla could direct her crew as she chose.

So long as they didn't get in the way of the objective.

Soaked in sweat despite Wexer's cool air, and with Gregor marching alongside her, Aurora crested the hill and stared into the back end of a debris funnel. Silver, shining mag-lev rails ran from an arched tunnel, one standing four meters high at its top and looking very well kept up, as if it'd been built yesterday instead of, well, Aurora didn't exactly know how long the mine had been here, but given the size, yesterday wasn't it.

The silver rails split as they left the tunnel, switching off into four different ends, three of which held the floating carts that made mag-lev so valuable for this sort of thing. The carts, sloped, ivy containers, hovered centimeters over the rails, which ended each branch in a blocked bar. Aurora could feel the power coursing through those things now, like a tingling running through her suit.

The mine itself buried into the bigger mountain now standing before her, stretching up to Wexer's white, cloudless sky. If the hill had seemed a climb to heaven, the mountain stood as an ominous barrier to it, the sky's brightness making the mountainside's blackrock even darker, as if some fracture in time and space split down from above and expanded before them.

Branching from the mountainside were solar antennae, the arms expanding out in meters-long collections to grab the energy powering the mag-levs and everything else. On some planets, clouds and worse might make the power unreliable. On Wexer?

"Well-built," Gregor said. "I am impressed, on a planet like this, to find something so advanced."

"It's because the Talpa made it," Rovo said, joining them at the hill's crest.

"What?" Aurora asked.

"They're masters at this," Rovo said, pointing to the tunnel, the floating carts, the shining arch. "DefenseCorp gets tons of contracts to guard Talpa groups as they set up these mines, burrow and build out worlds with hostile surfaces."

"So they built this for Calico?" Aurora said.

"Don't know," Rovo said. "But something has the Talpa thinking they deserve this place. What I'm catching over the Bug says they think this is their home."

"Bought and sold without getting them involved," Gregor said, reaching back and drawing out his hammer. "Pawns."

Gregor always had a soft spot for the ones stuck at a deal's bottom. Guess that's what happens when you grow up chopping rocks on a comet. Or was it an asteroid? Aurora could never remember, in part because Gregor tended to keep his mouth shut. The man could wallop, could razz rookies, but when it came to his own opinions, Gregor kept them to himself.

"We don't know everything," Aurora said as the other squaddies hit the top. "Remember that we're working for Calico. Doesn't mean we shoot anything that moves, doesn't mean we ditch the job at the first sign too. The galaxy's not a nice place."

As much as Aurora wanted the cash for completing the gig, she wanted the reputation more. She'd gone in the bar on Wexer hunting for work and didn't have the contacts to walk out with a contract: nobody knew who Sever was. Doing this one right would open other doors, would give them a chance to really start out on this private mercenary venture.

If that meant a bad day for the Talpa, Aurora might be okay with that. If it meant a thousand innocent, dead miners . . .

"What're we waiting for?" Tarla said. "We're not going to drive 'em off sitting out here."

"Right," Aurora said, then took a clomping step ahead of everyone else. Turned around so the heavily armed group could all see her. "The goal is to negotiate and get the Talpa to leave the mine. The goal is not to shoot everything we see. So don't fire unless something shoots at you."

"They've already been shooting at us," Perro, the Twilight sniper said. "Briany's back down at the skiff wearing a new scar, and you want us to go in peaceful?"

"I'm not dying so you can have a chat," Javelin added. "You want the furry little things to negotiate? How about we show 'em what happens if they don't?"

A strong start. Aurora had been leading the expedition for all of an hour and she could see her plans falling apart. In a tight squad, with five or six, one bloodthirsty boy could get his trigger-finger taken away by the others coming together. The bigger the force, though, the more like minds they'd find, the more Aurora would have to persuade.

Looking across these faces, Aurora saw friendly eyes from Gregor, Rovo, Sai, and the Twilight pilot Sanje. The others, including Eponi, standing near Tarla, kept their hands near their weapons. Half and half split between guns blazing and peaceful negotiations. Not enough to play mediator.

"You're not wrong," Aurora said. "So here's how we're going to play it. Rovo and I will go in alone, first, to show we're not a threat. If they negotiate with us, maybe we can keep anyone from dying. If they won't, then we're not risking any of you."

"It's our contract too, Aurora," Tarla said. "I'm coming with."

"Fine, then let's go."

If Tarla wanted to send herself along, better that than one of her other killers. The other squaddies didn't object, and with a ticking clock set to sixty minutes before the others would charge in rifles blazing away, the trio set out into the mine.

Past the archway entrance, the Talpa continued to showcase their prowess. Rather than waste time and energy hanging lamps from the ceiling, the creatures lined the mag-lev rails with diodes, whose silver-white light splashed up and around to illuminate the tunnel around them. A steady grind came through the ground and walls around them, massive rocks being moved.

Aurora had been in plenty of rocky shafts before, targeted to clear out this and that for a DefenseCorp deal, but she hadn't been in a Talpa construct. Hadn't seen walls like this, with each section bearing marks she couldn't parse. Scratches that looped in and around each other, all fitting within flattened meter-wide patches.

"Can't read much of it," Rovo replied when Aurora asked. "But it looks like names. Little details about each one."

"The Talpa?" Tarla asked. "They're signing their work?"

"Looks like it," Rovo replied. "Maybe it's a tradition?"

"Or maybe it's their story," Aurora said. "We write our names in books, in databases that are supposed to go on forever tracking family trees. Maybe they do the same thing on these walls."

Rovo gave Aurora a look that said he didn't quite expect that from her, and Aurora threw him a straight-eyed stare in reply. He shouldn't be surprised Aurora could make insights beyond a tactical approach to a firefight.

"Sentimental," Tarla said. "I like it."

"Do you?" Rovo said. "Sounded like your squadmates would rather shoot everything in here than learn about them."

"Rovo," Aurora warned.

"Oh, it's all right Aurora," Tarla said. "He's upset. He heard me negotiate a bonus if we have to exterminate all the Talpa in the mine when they refuse to leave." Tarla put a hand on Rovo's shoulder, matched his strides. "It's all business. If the Talpa want to go, they can go. If they stay, then we get compensated. Fair is fair."

"Not to the Talpa," Rovo said.

"And not to our cash accounts either," Tarla replied. "This business isn't about being moral, Rovo. It's about earning enough to retire before you die."

"There are different ways to die," Rovo said, Tarla laughed while Aurora winced.

Rovo hadn't felt it. Hadn't found that box to put the bad things away. He'd have to learn, and soon. Aurora couldn't have someone questioning everything on the squad, not when their survival might depend on taking gray contracts.

But that would be a conversation for another time, because the tunnel they marched down opened up into a centralized shaft, and what a space. Below and above them, the blackrock fell away into a broad silo criss-crossed with mag-lev rails. Long welded poles navigated from top to bottom, with platforms humming up and down, some loaded with floating carts that would, as the platforms hit various levels, zip off and on.

Those silver diodes kept up their lighting efforts, matched now by tremendous, mushroom-like domes attached to the shaft's sides between levels. The globes, attached to thick stalks, oriented themselves to track the moving platforms as they came into view, creating a shifting silver lightshow that initially blinded Aurora until she tracked its purpose.

The humming grind that'd bubbled their feet through the tunnel grew into a crackling, snapping chorus in the shaft. Mag-lev's contactless motion left a whir in its wake, but here the actual mining work made itself known, tearing and rending coming from other tunnels above and below them.

All automated, all working to transport harvested minerals from one place to another.

"Aurora, Tarla," Rovo said. "Don't move. The Bug's telling me we're being watched."

"Not watched," Aurora said as her power armor's helmet and visor flipped over her head, its screen lighting up with potential threats all around her. "Targeted."

TWELVE

Tricksters

SIX ARMED AND dangerous mercenaries stood outside the mine tunnel, bathed in the creamy, late afternoon Wexer light. Like a bad joke's beginning, the two sides split along affiliation, with Sever lounging near the mag-lev carts and Twilight adopting the hill crest as their turf. Javelin, Sanje, and Perro. Sai, Gregor, and Eponi.

Looking between the two, Sai found one difference:

Twilight talked. Swapped strategies. Concerns for Briany floated across the air to Sai's ears, while Sever stayed quiet. Eponi kept looking at the ground, as if answers to her questions could be found in the blackrock. Gregor watched the mine entrance, since Dynas, he'd been ever more content to vanish inside his own head. Sai bounced between the lot, waiting for a message to come streaking back from the mine: Aurora asking for rescue, or saying mission accomplished.

Wexer's breeze filled the silence, sending ripples every now and then cascading down the mountain. The air whistled as it struck the mine's tunnel, catching its counterparts from beneath the earth and tangling up in dust-stirring dances. Peaceful, maybe, if there weren't so many weapons standing nearby.

"It feels different, doesn't it?" Sai ventured after Perro cackled at some story Sanje wrapped up. "On the other side?"

"I fought, once, for myself," Gregor replied, holding his hammer haft with both hands while the head rested on the rock, like a massive walking stick. "They claimed we were nothing, workers that could be replaced. Because they had training, were paid to watch us strike the rocks, they were more valuable. I showed them that their cash wouldn't protect them."

"Didn't you get thrown off the comet after that?" Eponi said.

"Yes."

"So didn't they show you?" Eponi replied. "Like, isn't it worse to lose your home and your family over a bar fight than getting a bloody nose?"

"I broke their noses."

"Uh huh," Eponi said. "What feels different, Sai? The weather? The fact that we're not taking orders from some big company?"

Gregor, Eponi came from other backgrounds. They wouldn't see it the same as Sai did, as DefenseCorp putting down the revolt that tore apart his home, killed his father. DefenseCorp had been paid for its actions, no doubt a high sum, but the soldiers that had torn their way up his building to save Sai and his mother hadn't been cruel mercenaries.

At least, not in his memories. They had worked for something greater. They had saved lives.

"I followed orders," Sai said. "From the start, through raising my family and switching to Sever, I followed orders and that made me happy. I assumed DefenseCorp was doing the right thing, and that was enough."

"Naive much?" Eponi said, biting on the word. Sai knew her past as well as anyone, knew she'd been the same with her kart racing ventures. "I never thought Defense-Corp was anything more than money."

"Tell that to my mother, they didn't get a bonus for saving us."

"Like you know that."

Gregor lifted his hammer, stood up in the power armor, "There is a problem."

Another conversation killed before it could reach the real point. Not that Sai was real sure where he and Eponi would've wound up. Persuading Eponi that DefenseCorp wasn't evil? That it wasn't about the money? Sai didn't believe that himself.

Just, perhaps, that doing things for the money sometimes had other benefits too.

"What problem?" Sai asked.

"Aurora's saying they're surrounded," Gregor said. "In the mine's center. I say we go."

Twilight noticed Gregor's move and their trio crossed the mag-lev rails, Perro leading the way. They dropped their casual attitude quick, and all three had weapons ready, faces bearing a predator's expectant look. Sai didn't know if Tarla had told her team about the bloodlust bonus, but given the hunger in those eyes, the Talpa wouldn't be making it through the night.

Gregor relayed what he knew, and Perro jumped on the idea, "Looks like we ought to have been moving yesterday. Let's go."

"Wait," Sai said. "We can see the skiff from here. We abandon this spot, they could circle behind and cut us off."

"You want to play rear guard, you do it," Perro said.

"Tarla didn't give me any orders, didn't hear your captain say nothing either. Your call if you want to stay here and keep counting rocks."

The sniper didn't wait for Sai's reply, but jerked around and stomped off towards the tunnel, Sanje and Javelin in tow. Eponi shot Sai a look that said everything she needed to say, a combination of dismissal, resignation, and just a flavor of worry around the way she carried her rifle. She joined Twilight's group, and Sai didn't try to stop her.

"Go," Sai said to Gregor. "Keep her out of trouble. And, if you can, don't let them slaughter the Talpa."

"You like the little ones?" Gregor said, hanging back. "Why?"

"Because to them, we're the monsters," Sai replied. "And I didn't sign up for that."

"The little ones tried to kill us."

"If someone invaded your home, wouldn't you?"

Gregor hesitated, nodded, "Yes."

With a raised hammer salute, Gregor marched off into the tunnel, the boosters in his power armor giving his strides enough range to catch him up to the other four. Sai watched the kicked up blackrock dust settle back to the ground. Embraced the quiet and took a long breath.

When Tarla and her crew inevitably decided to burn the Talpa to the ground, at least Sai wouldn't be adding another nightmare to his collection.

A clack to Sai's left broke the thought. Sharp and sudden, Sai traced the sound over the hill's edge, back towards the skiff. The breeze whipped on by, perhaps the cause, but Sai had argued to stay and watch the skiff, so watch the damn skiff he would.

Leaving his katana holstered, Sai went with his rifle and stepped over to the hill's edge. Down the slope, marred by the squad's footprints, sat the skiff as they'd left it.

Resting there in the light, no sign of an attack. As Sai looked, though, several more rocks shivered a few meters beneath him, quivering on the hillside before sliding down, their skitters dying out as the slope shallowed nearer the base.

Sai looked at his feet—could his steps be heavy enough to cause the rocks to move? He squatted, and felt heat splash over his head, warming his hair. His eyes caught the vanishing laser flash, and Sai whirled, bringing up his modified rifle.

A Talpa crouched behind one of the mag-lev carts, its snub-nosed weapon almost larger than the dusty, brown-furred creature. Beneath the cart, Sai could see the creature's thick legs leading to large, scooping black feet, though the color may have come from all the Wexer dust coating it. The Talpa's head didn't make it over the cart, so Sai had to decide: take a shot at the rifle end creeping out, or make for a different shot?

By the time he drew the katana or took a dive, the Talpa could get another blast off, so Sai settled for suppressive fire. Raising the rifle, Sai pressed on the trigger. Crackling yellow energy bolted to the cart and over it. Some shots splashed against the cart itself, cratering holes in the thing's sides, starting blue, metal-burning fires.

The weapon itself hummed as Sai held the trigger, as though winding up an engine. Normal rifle barrels grew hot in use, but Sai felt the grip warm up, saw sparks pop out around his hand.

The Talpa target squeaked loud, but didn't move. Didn't try to take a shot. Keeping his hand on the trigger, despite the heat, Sai started forward. As he stepped, the rock beneath his feet shifted, rolling back away from him. As if the hill were starting to collapse.

Sai glanced down, knowing every moment he wasn't

aiming and firing at the cart would give his target a chance to move or squeeze off a counter-shot, and saw not just rocks beneath his feet, but long, wide claws jutting out from the ground. Sai managed a curse before the claws swept his feet away.

The Sever swordsman hit the ground, managing to keep hold of the rifle in his left hand as his view changed from blackrock to white sky. Sai rolled left, trying to get away from those claws. The ground crumbled as Sai moved, letting his shoulder dip in and giving him a good set on his side to take aim. The second Talpa poked its head from the rock, a narrow pointed thing with a deep amber snout, and followed Sai's noise to his rifle point.

"Don't move," Sai said.

The Talpa squeaked, its cheeks vibrating with the sound, and before Sai realized what it was doing, the thing sucked down beneath the rock, disappearing. Sai blinked, then remembered that wasn't the only Talpa he was facing. A quick look back at the cart confirmed his first target had moved.

A strong pressure on his back confirmed exactly where.

The Talpa chittered low, slow, and poked Sai in the back again.

"Okay, okay," Sai said, letting the rifle slip from his hands. "See? No weapons."

The Talpa squeaked, nudged Sai upward. Any number of things that could mean, but Sai decided to bet on the creature wanting him to move.

"I'm going to stand up, all right?" Sai said, speaking slow. "Don't shoot me."

Sai brought his legs beneath him, brushing through the dirt. He barely breathed, feeling the rifle against his back. The first time someone had pointed a weapon at Sai with murderous intent, he'd fallen into a panicked spiral imagining his children, his wife without him in their lives.

Now, Sai knew how to push that away: he wasn't in his family's lives anyway. He'd made that choice, no sense letting it scare him now.

The Talpa backed up a step, its clawed feet scraping on the rock while Sai stood. He wasn't facing the creature, and as much as he wanted to stare his attacker in the face—and maybe find an opening—turning quick would probably get him shot.

As Sai straightened up, the ground near his feet bubbled again and the second Talpa's head rose from the rock, followed by the rest of its plump, furred body. Like a hairy water drop with claws, the Talpa bobbed and watched Sai with its beady eyes. The two creatures chittered at one another, their cheeks popping in and out so fast that Sai wondered at the muscle strain all that talk must take.

Then the rifle pushed him in the back.

"I feel you," Sai said. "What do you want?"

The Talpa in front blinked, a half-second splash of white lid over black eye, then pointed a claw towards the tunnel. The little creature followed its own direction, ambling towards the mine's entrance. The rifle poked Sai's back again.

"Want me to walk?" Sai said. "Fine. I'll walk."

One step, two steps after the leading Talpa. To test the idea, Sai stopped after two, and felt the rifle press his back a heartbeat later. So the Talpa thought they had a hostage, but they didn't know how to treat what they'd caught.

Sai would've kept at least a meter between himself and an unrestrained captive. Sai figured he could whirl and knock the rifle away, or just hit the Talpa and disable the creature right there. So why didn't he?

Why did he keep walking, into that tunnel, surrounding by the Talpa's scratching claws?

Because Sai would be damned if Tarla would get her blood money.

THIRTEEN

Tunnel Run

THE TUNNEL FELT LIKE HOME. Natural rock pressed in close, hollowed by efforts manual rather than natural. Gregor hadn't seen mag-lev on the comet: zero gravity made such things more effort than they were worth, but otherwise the passageway sucked him back to long days, long weeks, and long years softened by time.

His left knuckle ached. A phantom pain tied back to the punch he'd delivered ages ago, the one that'd brought the guards, that'd kicked Gregor off the comet and into the nearest DefenseCorp recruiting station. If Gregor hadn't thrown that strike, he might—

Hah, no.

The punch that kicked him off that comet would've been coming one way or another. Too many people with too little to do packed into a swirling ice ball. Fights, even, were tolerated, except Gregor's tended to risk breaking the station itself apart. Turned out you could get a body moving pretty fast without friction, and there were enough thick skulls on that comet to threaten breaking glass that couldn't be broken.

On Wexer, in the power armor, Gregor went slow. He could've caught up to Eponi and the Twilight trio, whom he could hear chattering as they went down the silver-lit passage, but he'd had enough idle conversation for the day. Between Sai's apparent doubts and Rovo's full-blown crisis over the damn Talpa, Gregor felt like he'd turned into some sort of therapist.

He carried the hammer for a reason, and it wasn't to make people feel better.

Up ahead, the chatter cut off sharp. No shouts, no screams, just human voices one second and then nothing the next. Gregor stopped, twitched his neck left and right. The trigger sent his helmet up and on, the power armor's visor firing up. Red highlights shone towards the top of his vision, but also at the bottom.

Energy signatures. Potential threats both ahead and behind.

Gregor turned, looked back the way he'd come. The silver tunnel didn't give much away, vanishing around a slow curve. Forward, the curve continued, no doubt bending around to the mine's center. Neither offered an indication of what the threats might be. Rovo had said the main Talpa force was scrambling back from their skiff ambush.

Had the little creatures made it?

Gregor had a choice: either go back for Sai, or press on towards Aurora and the rest. Gregor patted the hammer's haft against his left palm, its weight a pendulum between the options. Aurora had Rovo, would have Eponi, and all of Tarla's Rangers helping her, though the sudden silencing ahead felt ominous.

Sai had only himself.

Gregor might not be a DefenseCorp fighter any longer,

but its prescribed habits bound themselves to his spirit. Leave a fellow squad mate alone at their peril.

"Even if Sai is good with that sword," Gregor rumbled as he turned back the way he'd come and took off.

The power armor stored kinetic energy from every footfall and spent it on every other step, pushing Gregor through the tunnel as fast as a sprinting man. He bounced off the tunnel's curves, the armor digging into blackrock. DefenseCorp's construction apparently beat out Wexer's geology, as the natural earth gave way, acting almost like a cushion to Gregor's bull run.

The Talpa did not act like a cushion.

The Talpa flew when Gregor hit it, right back into Sai, who managed to catch the thing only for its Gregor-caused momentum to drive Sai back a few steps. Gregor slowed himself, the power armor boots digging into the ground, in time to see Sai fall backward onto what appeared to be a second Talpa, this one holding one of those snub-nosed rifles.

"Hey," Gregor said, playing out the momentum the last few steps until he loomed above the Talpa-Sai combo with his hammer held up. "Didn't see you all there."

Sai groaned, and the Talpa Gregor had rammed squeaked once before rolling off of Sai's chest and plopping onto the ground, paws splayed out. The other one wriggled from beneath Sai, reached one pointed claw towards its snub-nosed rifle, and Gregor smashed the weapon with his hammer.

"Won't be needing that," Gregor said. "Better you things surrender before I decide to see how well you squish."

The one Talpa standing regarded Gregor with its beady, baleful eyes for a long second, then erupted into a chittering rage, sending so much chirping noise Gregor's way that the big man winced at the sheer energy. He'd never seen a Talpa before today, and the thing stood less than half his height, but Gregor couldn't deny they had spirit.

Which would make it harder to crush'em all if Aurora went that way.

"They surprised me," Sai said, sitting up and looking at the downed Talpa. "Damn things can come right out of the ground."

"Shouldn't have left you alone," Gregor said. "My fault. Getting so caught up in the switch to private side profiteering that I am losing my instincts."

The awake Talpa hadn't ceased its squeaking, turning its head from Sai to Gregor and back. Abruptly, it seemed to realize its companion wasn't moving, and the Talpa scurried across Sai, catching the Sever member with an inadvertent—or was it?—claw to the jaw to inspect its friend.

"You're not the one that got captured," Sai rubbed his chin where the Talpa hit. "I think they were taking me to join you in the center. What's happening there?"

"Didn't make it," Gregor nodded towards the two Talpa. "That one's still alive, isn't it?"

Picking himself up, Sai crouched with the Talpa over its friend, "Looks stunned to me. You did crush him pretty good."

"Guess that's what happens when you run through mines," Gregor said. "Maybe that's why they didn't allow it back on the comet."

"Plausible," Sai said. "You have anything helpful in that armor?"

Every DefenseCorp power armor suit had a substantial backpack meant to be loaded up with essentials, like extra power packs for energy weapons, food and water for longer excursions, and, what Sai was looking for, something that could keep you from dying.

Eponi had carried Sever's primary medic kit, but each of them had the bare minimums. A shock-jock for kicking someone back from the unconscious, adrenaline, a small amount of universal blood, and a scattered collection of stitches, bandages, and pills meant to numb any injury away until you won or succumbed to it.

Not that Gregor knew how any of it worked with a Talpa.

"Might hurt it as much as help," Gregor said. "Maybe we bring it to its own people?"

"Not a bad idea," Sai said, then reached out and tapped the awake Talpa. The creature jumped at Sai's touch, its chittering sprinting up the octaves as it pressed back against the wall. "Hey, we're going to take your buddy to find help, all right?"

The Talpa's squeaking went low and ended in an upward swing, as if the thing had asked a question.

"We won't hurt it," Gregor guessed at a response while Sai shrugged. "I'll be real gentle. Promise."

"For Gregor, that's a big thing to say," Sai replied, standing up and away from the downed Talpa. "He's not a very gentle man."

"No," Gregor agreed, and moved, slowly, to pick up the downed Talpa. Its friend didn't make a sound, didn't twitch or try and stop Gregor, but watched. "See? Nice and slow."

Back on Dynas, when Gregor had snagged Kaia off the roof, he'd curled the girl up in his armored arms as softly as he could manage. He did the same thing here, slipping his hands beneath the furry creature and lifting it up to his chest, careful to move the unconscious Talpa as little as possible. He knew, as did anyone doing Defense-

Corp missions, how dangling limbs could lead to bad things for a beaten body.

"Could almost see you as a dad," Sai said as Gregor straightened with the Talpa. "Nice pick-up."

"I am a soldier, not a monster."

"Sure are."

The standing Talpa watched Gregor hold its friend for a long moment while Gregor stared back at the small creature. Gaining trust with anyone, anything involved being calm, being slow and clear. Gregor had learned that much on his first assignments, running security on worlds DefenseCorp policed for hefty fees. For as much violence as DefenseCorp advocated everywhere else, on its peacekeeping contracts, less drama meant more bonuses, so every form of conflict avoidance was hammered into its officers.

Gregor had suppressed all that with Sever, but the habits still lingered, ready for deployment when necessary. And now, stuck in a hostile mine potentially surrounded by enemies that wouldn't look kindly on Gregor crushing their friend?

He could use some de-escalating.

"Are you ready?" Gregor asked the Talpa. "We're going to walk now. Towards your friends."

The Talpa squeaked, high but not as frantic as before. Gregor took a tentative step down the tunnel, keeping the injured Talpa level in his arms. He heard the other Talpa scrabble along the rock after him.

"Look at that," Sai said from behind. "The Hammer becomes a diplomat. I'd never have guessed."

"You are not helping."

"Sorry, not sorry," Sai replied. "After you get taken hostage by these things, life gets weird."

Gregor couldn't argue with that. Instead, he picked up

the pace. The power armor adjusted to his stance, guiding Gregor's feet so every move maximized distance without sacrificing balance. The suit was so good at it that Gregor often had trouble walking after he removed the armor, tilting this way and that as if he'd had a few too many rounds at the ship's commissary.

The Talpa kept up with the pace, occasionally zipping ahead to look back at Gregor, presumably to make sure its friend was still there. The injured Talpa didn't move, but Gregor caught muscle tremors and twitches as they walked. The little thing had to be alive. Had to be.

There were many things Gregor wouldn't mind mashing to bits, but the Talpa fell so far short of menacing, dangerous, or evil that, well, here he was, trying to help one.

Light grew as the tunnel reached its end, what Gregor assumed was the mine's core. Aurora and the others should have been here, should be waiting. The power armor's helmet flared red all over, potential threats surrounding Gregor's position, but no fire came. When Gregor rounded the last curve, saw the tunnel break into a wide shaft, he saw why those threats coated his visor.

Heard, too, the rookie talking fast. Not in Common, but in short, clipped noises. Like someone with a stutter and no sense of tone or pitch.

"What?" Sai started as they left the tunnel, the Talpa running with them dashing ahead.

Gregor could only agree: Rovo, Aurora, Eponi and Tarla's Twilight Rangers stood on what looked like a square lift, one locked into place and even with the tunnel's exit. They stood in a circle, weapons raised and pointed in every direction. At first, Gregor tried to see what other ledges the Talpa, presumably, were using for cover, until he realized the shaft's walls were brown. That they looked furry, and had claws.

Rovo had said the Talpa had most of their rifles at the ambush, had said the only ones left here wouldn't have much. Gregor saw that the rookie had it half right: the Talpa didn't have many guns, but they had rocks. Lots, from small to large, all black and ready to be thrown at the mercenaries.

As Gregor walked onto the tunnel's exit, those silver rails linking to the stalled lift, the Talpa around the shaft noticed what was in his arms. Squeaks and chitters rose up and down, until the whole shaft filled with the noise.

"Good timing," Rovo said, looking Gregor's way. "I think they were about to kill us all, but now you're making them think."

"About letting us go?"

"Mostly, they're trying to figure out whether they can take us out without hurting that one," Rovo replied, and at his words, the other mercenaries took closer aim, moved fingers to triggers. The rookie noticed. "No! No you idiots, don't do that. We can still get out of here alive."

The rookie had confidence, Gregor would give Rovo that. But Rovo was an idealist, figuring the Talpa wouldn't kill them all.

For once, Gregor hoped the rookie had it right.

FOURTEEN

Hard Truth

BEFORE THE TALPA surrounded them in the tunnel, Eponi had been walking with the three Twilight Rangers, who'd been asking her questions about Sever, about working for DefenseCorp. When Eponi exhausted her both sides recounting on her former employer—good job security, poor life expectancy—she dug in a little on her own interests.

"How'd you find Tarla?" Eponi asked.

"We didn't," Perro replied. "She found us."

Javelin and Sanje echoed the sentiment, the details crawling out in a twisty story centering on a transitory space station not too different from Wexer, one known for being a waypoint for those seeking to change their futures and forget their pasts. Perro, Javelin, and Sanje plugged their names and skillsets into the station's central database and within a day, they'd found each other.

"You know, Tarla had her specs, we matched," Sanje finished. "Like, the way you flew the skiff back there. Your skills, the moment, they matched. Mine, maybe not."

Eponi remembered Sanje's bitterness, that flash saying

he'd never forget her move, but the pilot must have swept it away. Buried to dig up again later, or permanently gone, Eponi didn't know.

She didn't get much chance to learn: after Sanje spoke, claws broke through the rock above, below, and around them. Eponi managed a single curse, stepping back and tripping over the damn mag-lev rails. She hit the ground, tried to roll, then felt the air blow out from her lungs as one of the furry things landed on her. With Eponi's left arm pinned on the rock, gasping for breath, she pushed at the Talpa, tried to get it away, then froze.

The claw nestled against her throat, smooth and dry and almost comfortable, except for the point pressed into her. Eponi looked down, and while every Talpa she'd seen —not many, admittedly—had been brown, this one's fur had gone a shaggy white, all the way up to its black eyes, looking straight back into hers.

Behind the Talpa, Eponi saw Javelin's legs sweep away. Two Talpa dropped onto Perro, bearing him to the ground. She couldn't see Sanje, but the way his mouth shot off words that would've made just about anyone blush, Eponi assumed he wasn't doing much better.

So she stayed still.

For a kart racer, not moving, not acting was about the hardest thing she could do. Literally every moment of her adult life had primed Eponi for decisive action, but instead she felt that claw against her throat and she waited.

Everyone wanted something. Eponi knew that too, and while the Talpa wasn't exactly making its demands clear, it was waiting. The thing could've torn her apart by now, but instead, the furry monster kept its claw steady, its eyes focused, and, like Eponi, waited.

A loud chittering came down the tunnel, the echoes making it difficult to tell how many Talpa were making the high-pitched noise. As it bounced around Eponi, the Talpa holding her down twitched, its claw cutting Eponi's skin ever-so-slightly, and the creature jumped away. The Talpa hit the tunnel's wall and dug, its front claws flying while its rear ones scooped rock and flung it back at Eponi.

She threw her arms in front of her face to deflect the stones, heard the Twilight Rangers doing the same as their Talpa made similar escapes. Only Javelin managed to get a shot off, a laser fired blindly that missed everything. By the time Eponi finished cursing him out for even trying something that stupid—shooting without aiming in a packed tunnel? Who was this guy?—the Talpa had vanished, the blackrock packed in where they'd dug, as if nothing had happened.

"Well, that was weird," Perro said. "Don't know about you all, but I wasn't expecting to get jumped by mole monsters today."

"Me either." Sanje brushed at the dirt on his outfit, grimaced when it didn't come off. "They don't play fair."

Javelin laughed, "Didja see them? Coming from the top of the tunnel like that? Wish I could dig like they do."

"So you could, what, live in the dirt?" Perro replied.

"Gentlemen," Eponi interrupted, rifle in her hands, nerves steadied. "If we could focus?"

That focus, plus a few more minutes walking, led them to the central shaft. To the others, already pinned down by the Talpa force coating the walls. Rovo waved them on to the lift, an order Aurora and Tarla seconded.

No way they were going to beat all the Talpa without power armor, no way Eponi cared to get her brain smashed in with one of those rocks, so they'd joined in and waited.

"They're bringing Sai and Gregor too," Rovo said.

Eponi listened to the rookie play the translation game

with a Talpa, one that looked a little larger than the others, one that sat on another lift one level higher, peering over and squeaking down at Rovo. The rookie and the creature seemed like a match for each other, making the noises with Rovo doing an occasional translation for the rest.

"Not quite what I expected," Tarla whispered and Eponi almost jumped. The Twilight Ranger captain must have made her way through the tight bunch to Eponi's side. "Do you think your man has what it takes to get us out of here?"

"My man?"

"He's about your age, isn't he?" Tarla said. "I can't imagine Aurora with anybody, ever. Sai has a family, and you don't seem so into hammers."

"I'm not *with* anybody," Eponi hissed as quietly as she could, mind blown that Tarla was even saying these words, that Eponi was replying to them. "How are you asking this now? When we're about to die?"

"That's exactly why I'm asking," Tarla said. "If not now, then it might be never."

Unable to resist, Eponi threw a confused, stunned look Tarla's way only to see the Twilight Ranger captain had shifted back to Aurora's side. While Rovo continued his apparent mission as ambassador to the Talpa people, Tarla and Aurora whispered to each other, their syllables getting more and more heated with every back and forth.

Around her, Eponi saw some sweat on foreheads, heard the tight breathing, saw fingers resting on the triggers. The tension was increasing, and if something didn't happen soon to relieve the pressure, the whole thing would snap. Eponi had seen it before, at the start of kart races, when all the craft hovered near each other, pilots trying to time the starting gun, careers and maybe lives on the line.

"Rovo," Eponi said, loud and breaking the squeaking

chatter. She felt a million eyes on her, but the attention didn't faze Eponi: she'd had more, billions back in her kart racing days. "Get us out of here, now, or we're all going to die."

"Trying, Eponi," Rovo replied. "They're not feeling like letting us go."

The biggest wins came from the most daring gambits, the twist through a narrow gap that would leave you dead or in the decisive lead. Hesitate, doubt, and you'd wind up losing. Wind up watching as better, braver pilots passed you by.

Eponi didn't want to get shot, Eponi didn't want to shoot the Talpa, so she had to thread the gap.

"Then tell them if they don't, others will come looking for us with bigger, better guns," Eponi said. "Calico will burn this mine from space if he has to. There's no way out for them that doesn't have us leaving this place."

"Eponi," Aurora warned. "You don't—"

"No, it's a good play. They have families here. They don't want them hurt," Rovo replied. "Let me try it."

Except, before Rovo could revert back to his squeaking and chittering entreaties, Gregor and Sai walked in from the tunnel. Eponi had to look twice to see that Gregor carried a Talpa in his arms, the creature limp and possibly dead. Gregor and Sai, for their parts, seemed just fine, as did a madly squeaking Talpa walking by at their feet.

"What is it saying?" Aurora asked Rovo.

"Um," Rovo said softly, clearly trying to listen to the squeaking Talpa. "It's, uh, saying that we're not as bad as we look."

"That's something?"

The squeaking Talpa finished its speech with a low, hooting finale, leaving the shaft quiet for all of a short breath before all the other Talpa erupted in a brutal cacophony that had Eponi putting her hands over her ears. The others on the lift with her weren't doing any better, holding hands to heads in vain attempts to quell the shattering noise.

Aurora, at least, tried to take some action. With her power armor helmet blunting the volume, she aimed her rifle straight up and squeezed the trigger. Bright yellow laser fire burst upward and struck blackrock, melting it save a few chunks that clanked their way down the shaft, a ping-pong noise Eponi could hear as the Talpas went silent.

"Tell them we're leaving," Aurora said to Rovo. "They can let us walk out of here, or they can fight us, and die trying."

Bold. Eponi felt pretty sure Sever and Twilight would bite it if all these Talpa decided to go on the offensive. Rovo felt the same way, because he started to protest, claiming he was making progress with the creatures.

"That's an order, Rovo," Aurora said. "Let's go."

The rookie swallowed the command, turned back to the watching Talpa, and spoke the words. Or squeaked them. When he finished, the Talpa kept the same look they'd had this whole time, curious and ready. Then the one that'd been talking with Rovo before, a fat one that nonetheless looked to be missing chunks of its fur, leaned over its platform's side and issued a low series of chirps.

"That's it," Rovo said, turning back to the group with a grin. "They're letting us leave. So long as we don't come back."

"Well," Tarla said. "Let's not give them a chance to change their minds, shall we?"

The Twilight Ranger stepped off the platform, went between Gregor and Sai, and headed back down the tunnel. Her Rangers followed, and at Aurora's order, so did Eponi and the rest. Several Talpa climbed down to take the wounded one from Gregor's hands, and suddenly what had looked like the prelude to a particularly grim fight went the peaceful way.

Eponi felt happy to be alive, but as soon as they left the central shaft behind, the contract particulars nuzzled in. Calico wasn't paying them to make peace with the Talpa. He expected the creatures to be gone.

"We're not getting paid for this one, are we?" Eponi asked Aurora as they clomped through the silver-lit tunnel.

"Better than being killed for it," Aurora replied. "We were outplayed."

"Can't we just turn around now?" Eponi said. "Take them by surprise?"

"You want to slaughter the Talpa, Eponi?" Rovo said, walking near them. "Because that's what'd happen. That's what Tarla wants too."

"I'm not saying kill them," Eponi replied. "Can't we drive them away? Scare them like we did the ones that attacked us on the way here?"

"They're not animals," Rovo said. "They won't just run from their home."

No, Eponi didn't want mindless death. The less shooting, the better. But without cash, she wouldn't be getting any closer to the karts. Without cash, she wouldn't be free.

Sever had voted to leave DefenseCorp and go private. Become mercenaries.

Apparently, Eponi was the only one who knew what that meant.

Making The Case

Rovo HELD Aurora back as the others left the tunnel. Tarla's Twilight Rangers kept right on going, heading down the hill towards the skiff. Some debrief would no doubt happen with Calico there, followed by a decision whether to head back lasers blasting or return to town and, Rovo figured, find even more gunmen to annihilate the Talpa.

Calico wasn't going to give up on the mine just because the Talpa said it was their home. Just because, as the Talpa told Rovo, they'd built the mine in the first place. Calico bought a contract, a bad one, that the Talpa had signed but didn't like, that they wanted destroyed. Build the mine, give it up, so the contract said.

Circumstances had changed.

"They didn't think Wexer would fit them well," Rovo said to Aurora. The rest of Sever dawdled on the hilltop, giving them space but not following Twilight down. "It's a perfect place for them. Everything they need, including minerals they can sell. No more planet-hopping to do dirty work for mining companies."

Aurora listened to the whole thing with a straight face. No emotion. So little to read beyond that red hair and steel eyes that Rovo started tripping over his own words, talking himself in circles, trying to say that no contract was worth wiping out what seemed like the best possible result for the Talpa.

"Stop," Aurora said. "I get it. The Talpa like what they have. The problem is, they don't really have it. Not legally, anyway. Can't they make another mine like this somewhere else?"

"Maybe?" Rovo said. "We didn't have time to get into all that, but what I heard was that they're willing to die for this place. They won't leave, no matter what."

"That's unfortunate," Aurora said, "but it's also their choice."

Rovo stepped back as if Aurora had slapped him, "Really? You're saying that? The one who led us all through Dynas talking about how awful the virus was. How the whole operation should be destroyed from orbit? You can't act like you have no conscience."

Aurora grabbed Rovo's vest. With the power armor boosting her strength, Aurora had no problem picking Rovo up from the ground and holding him, feet dangling, over the blackrock.

"Don't tell me who I am," Aurora said. "I make the choices based on what's best for the squad. Always have, always will. Right now, we need cash, and we need a reputation. Ditching on this contract gets us neither."

Rovo could say, honestly, that he'd never been picked up like this. He'd been the older brother, never subjected to physical torment from a stronger sibling. And his limited time with Sever, the creature in Dynas's swamp notwithstanding, hadn't included strongman moves like this one.

But the Talpa could help him out.

"I told the Talpa that," Rovo said, his voice stretching as the vest pulled at his arms, his chest. "They said they could pay us more, much more than Calico."

"What? When did they say that?"

"We kept talking while we were all huddled on the lift," Rovo said. "I figured we could negotiate. When I said someone would burn the Talpa down, even if it wasn't us, they made a different offer: help protect them until Calico gave up the contract, and they'll pay us. Raw precious stones."

Aurora set Rovo down, he took a long breath.

"Say that again," Aurora replied. "But clear. I want to know amounts, and I want to understand the offer."

Rovo did, explained exactly what the chittering Talpa had told him. More than triple Calico's price, and potentially more beyond if Sever helped the Talpa secure their claim to the mine. No need to kill anyone, provided Calico annulled the contract.

By now, Sai, Gregor, and Eponi paid closer attention. They'd set up far away enough to be polite, muttering to each other, but steady looks Rovo's way spoiled the illusion. Rovo caught whispers, dismissed them. If he convinced Aurora the rest would fall in line.

His commander didn't reject Rovo's argument right away. Instead, her eyes took a far-off look, a silent brooding that Rovo linked to Aurora's deep thoughts.

"It's the right choice," Rovo said, softer this time. "The Talpa don't deserve to die just because they made a bad deal."

"Would they pay Calico to leave it?" Aurora said. "He's going to need something to walk away."

"They would," Rovo said. "They'd negotiate with Calico. Find something that works."

Aurora nodded, "That's the tactic, then. Calico's not a fighter. We pitch the agreement, collect our payment, and everybody lives."

"Think the others will go for it?" Rovo said.

"If you can persuade me, you can persuade them."

Wexer's evening had set in, that glistening white bouncing onto a steadily vanishing sky. Deep blues and purples splashed overhead, while the mine and its mountaintop shone as Wexer's light and life-giving star dipped behind its mass. The air's chill deepened and the wind picked up with it, racing through Rovo's hair as he delivered his arguments to Sai, Gregor, and Eponi.

At first the trio narrowed their eyes, and Rovo wondered if he was making some unknown insult before realizing, when Eponi shaded her eyes, that the light was the problem, not his pitch.

"So we let the furrballs live," Sai said, "and get our cash?"

"Right, if Calico goes along."

"Means I don't get to use my hammer," Gregor said, the big weapon sticking up from behind his head like the galaxy's worst fashion accessory. "Yet, knowing us, I will find a way."

Eponi, though, didn't look so confident. She didn't even speak up until Rovo asked her directly what she thought.

"Stones, right? That's what they're offering?" Eponi said. "I don't know about any of you, but I'm not sure how to turn that into cash. I *do* know that Tarla's not going to let this job walk away from her. You're talking like we only have to convince Calico, but she's going to be there. Her squad wants cash too."

"They'll find another job," Aurora said. "Not our problem."

"It might be, if they don't like our terms."

"Then Gregor might get to use his hammer after all."

Not the response Rovo expected. Definitely not the ice in Aurora's voice. The captain hadn't said anything about a past with Tarla, but if Rovo had to guess, the two weren't exactly best friends.

"So are you in or out?" Rovo asked Eponi. "I'm sure we can find someone to help turn the Talpa's gems into cash. Wexer's a mining planet, right?"

Eponi took a long look around the group, then shrugged, "Doesn't look like I have a choice."

"Wrong," Aurora said. "Now, more than ever, you do. I'm not DefenseCorp. I can't force you to be here. Or, at least, I will not. But when we go to that skiff, we'll be doing it united. If you can't, then you'll leave now."

As to where Eponi would go if she left now, Rovo didn't ask. Didn't bother to push. For all Aurora's words, he didn't see that Eponi really did have a choice. She'd deserted her previous employer, had no ship and little cash on a backwater world. Walking away from Sever would mean ditching the only friends she had.

"Okay," Eponi said, shoulders straight, head high. "You win. I'm in. Let's go save some critters."

Getting the win over Sever was, as all too many posters and slogans and speeches had drilled into Rovo, only half the battle. Really, only a third. The group sloughed their way down the hill towards the skiff, with Rovo hanging back near Aurora and running line after line by her. One argument after another, pitch and riposte, tossed back and forth.

Aurora countered everything with a single word: cash.

"We don't know what Tarla and her Rangers need," Aurora said after Rovo's latest appeal, offering a potential Talpa stone split. "This contract covered two days, Rovo.

By tomorrow night, we're supposed to have the Talpa gone and cash in our accounts. These stones, we're talking more days, if not weeks. Then you have to find a buyer. If we didn't have cash from DefenseCorp sitting in our accounts, I'd be saying no too."

"What about covering them?" Rovo suggested. "We buy their contract, then get repaid by the Talpa?"

"If you have that much cash on hand, you're welcome to," Aurora replied. "I'm not placing that bet."

Rovo, safe to say, did not have enough cash to buy off a five-person mercenary crew. Which meant, once they reached the skiff, Rovo had to ask Tarla and Calico to meet him up on the top deck without a plan other than *please*.

Aurora and Gregor, still in their power armor, joined Rovo up top with Tarla and Calico. The latter hadn't changed his outfit at all, despite Wexer's growing chill: Calico's vest and tattoo ensemble continued to look both ridiculous and badass at the same time, though Rovo couldn't unsee Tarla's hands pulling the man's strings. She'd held Calico up earlier, forced the deal down his throat, and Rovo figured she was the real target. Get her to give up on the assault, and Calico would follow.

"So that's the situation," Rovo said as he wrapped up the pitch, which Calico and Tarla had received without much reaction. "The Talpa see the mine as their home, they're willing to pay to keep it. I'm hoping we can find some common ground here."

"Common ground, man? Common ground?" Calico said, his voice ratcheting up as he spoke, like a wind-up toy getting to its taut limits. "There is no common ground here. We, I, my company paid those things to dig out the mine and get it ready. We've got a whole bot fleet ready to move in and start extraction. I can't throw up my hands and walk away."

Not a promising start, that.

Tarla sighed, shook her head and leapt on Calico's closing words, "Rovo, you're the new one. You don't know how this works. The galaxy runs on contracts, my friend. The Talpa aren't animals: you saw, they're intelligent. They know what they agreed to. You yourself admitted to it. They have to keep their word. If they don't, there will be consequences. That's how the galaxy works."

That, at least, Rovo could counter, "Tarla, you know as well as I do that contracts get torn up and changed over for cash all the time. There's no reason we can't do the same for this one."

Tarla rolled her eyes, reached for the bottle of something-or-other that she'd brought up here. Calico, though, overcame his initial shock, his face settling into what might pass for thought in that man's head.

"They'd have to pay me the cost of the bots," Calico said. "And the mine. Not just the land, but what I expected to earn. With interest, for the inconvenience."

"I can ask," Rovo said, jumping for the opening.

"No," Tarla said. "You won't. Calico, the Talpa don't have cash. They can't pay you in anything other than promises. Which means you can't pay us, and if you can't pay us, then we'll take what's owed from what you have."

"Tarla," Aurora warned.

"What, Aurora?" Tarla replied. "Your little rookie here is meddling in adult business. We made a deal, and unless Calico is going to pay us the fee plus our bonus, we're not walking away."

"Plus the bonus?" Calico started. "But you didn't kill a single one—"

"Plus the bonus," Tarla cut him off. "For my inconvenience, and Briany's injury. You want to change the terms, then let's change the terms."

Rovo felt the conversation teetering on a balance he couldn't affect. The Talpa weren't here, they couldn't counter Tarla's points. Calico's eyes, the ones that'd glittered for a moment at conflict-free profit from leaving the mine in Talpa hands, withered as Tarla poked him in the chest with a single extended finger.

"Your choice, Calico," Tarla said, "but choose now. Because if we need to get to work, then I don't want to waste any time."

Calico did what all weak people in positions of power do, no matter their outfits, no matter their bravado. Rovo had seen countless missives for surrender, pleas for mercy come through the DefenseCorp network as the company's forces advanced on lesser foes.

Spines were in short supply, and it looked like Calico didn't have one.

"We made a deal," Calico sputtered, finally. "Sorry, Rovo. They've got to go."

SIXTEEN

Cash Or Conscience

ROOKIES. Always getting Aurora into trouble.

Rovo looked Aurora's way when Calico delivered the no go, and a story split through her mind. She could go with Calico, say that's what Sever agreed to, and march back up that hill in the morning to demand the Talpa leave the mine. That'd be the easier choice, the one defended by the deal Sever had taken when they boarded the skiff out here.

Aurora might be making that walk on her own. Eponi seemed hesitant to ditch out, but Rovo, Gregor, and Sai had made their opinions clear up above. And if Aurora lost her squad, then she'd have to find another.

Tarla followed Rovo's look to Aurora, and that challenge in Tarla's face, in her stance, in the way the woman let her hand slide into her jacket towards the pistol she no doubt wore on her belt affirmed what Aurora thought: ending Sever would make Tarla Aurora's next best option.

And to hell with that.

"Might want to rethink that decision, Calico," Aurora said. "You're risking more here than cash."

Calico frowned, his mouth opening slightly in an expression that Aurora both expected and was disappointed by in equal measure. That disappointment extended to Calico's turn towards Tarla, looking to his hired mercenary for help.

"Aurora, don't threaten the man," Tarla said. "He just wants what's his. Can't you see that?"

"Change in circumstances," Aurora replied, and she let her left hand down behind her leg, the power armor's bulk serving to block the two fingers she flashed. Gregor ought to be watching, ought to be ready. "I know your moral compass is shattered, Tarla, but I prefer sleeping at night. Calico, you move against the Talpa, you'll be doing it without Sever."

"Uh," Calico dredged and came up empty. "What?"

"Aurora's saying she's dumping you, honey," Tarla said. "But don't worry, we'll still take care of your problem. Why don't you head back downstairs, get yourself a drink while we finish chatting?"

"Hey," Calico said, finding, somewhere, what remained of his confidence. "I'm not a child. I don't want to go downstairs."

"Nobody's calling you one," Tarla replied, venomous sweetness lurking in the words. "It's for your own protection."

That, at least, made it through Calico's fogged mind, and the man paled, skittered out a laugh, and made a break for the steps leading belowdecks.

"Now we can talk," Tarla said, bringing her hands into the open sans weapons and folding them. "What're you doing blowing my deal, Aurora? Don't tell me you've found a soft spot after all these years?"

"You heard my terms." Aurora ignored Tarla's jabs: if she gave the woman a chance, they'd bounce back and forth all night hurling insults at each other. "Get Calico to leave."

"And you heard mine," Tarla said. "We need the cash. We're staying and doing the job."

Aurora caught Rovo's look, saw his set stance. The rookie didn't have power armor, didn't have an army behind him, but there was no mistaking the choice he'd made. Somehow, the damn Talpa had convinced Rovo to take a stand for their furry little lives.

Now she'd have to take a stand for his.

"You're not staying," Aurora said.

A whistling breeze kicked up, sprinkling those on the deck with blackrock flecks. Daylight nearly gone, the skiff's lights flickered on, matching Calico's eccentric sensibilities with their purple and white color scheme.

"Aren't you sweet, to think you can order me around," Tarla said, nothing sweet about her tone. "I would tell you to change your mind, Aurora, but we both know that won't happen."

"You're right."

Behind her, Aurora felt Gregor move on the deck, his armor causing the metal to vibrate as the hammer man put Tarla square in his sights. Rovo had the sense to back up and to the side, the skiff's railing to his back, creating space.

"Three on one?" Tarla said, sweeping a look across them all. "I'm flattered, but I'm not stupid. Settle your trigger fingers, boys." Tarla came back Aurora's way. "I'll tell Calico you're ditching the deal. I'm sure he'll be disappointed."

"Somehow, I'll survive."

"But for how long?" Tarla spun on her heel as she spoke, flipped up a nice gesture with her left hand, and went into the skiff.

For a minute, Aurora stood there. Listened to the breeze. Felt it blow across her face and whip her cropped hair. She'd spent so much time on space stations, space ships, space everything that nature had a way, still, of surprising her. Taking her away from all this.

"Aurora, thank you," Rovo broke the silence. "I didn't think—"

"Don't," Aurora said. "You're not that stupid. You knew, I knew exactly where this was likely going to end up."

"All right, yeah, I guess so."

"Then stop acting like it isn't what you wanted," Aurora said. "We just made some enemies, and Eponi and Sai don't know it, and who knows what Calico's going to do."

Turned out that Calico wanted Sever off his skiff. Right then and there. Sever had a few packs with overnight clothes resting on the rocks at their feet as the skiff turned and blasted back towards Wexer's city. Now that night had taken hold, Aurora could see the bright flares, like shooting stars moving in both directions, as ship traffic landed and left from the spaceport in the far distance.

Around her, Aurora caught her squad member's morale and placed it higher than expected. For being thrown out into the middle of a desert without any obvious way back home, they seemed almost happy. Rovo and Sai were busy replaying the exchange with Tarla, while Gregor provided the occasional one-word commentary. Eponi sat on a rock, looking at her wristlet and browsing satellite-synced kart circuit stats.

And Aurora tried to figure out where they'd go from here.

There was the obvious answer: back to the tunnel, the mine, the Talpa and their offered payment. The other option involved using the power armor's communications to beam a request for pick-up to the city. It'd be expensive this late at night, but doable.

Running would be safer, easier, and wrong.

"C'mon," Aurora announced. "Everyone grabs a bag. We're going back up."

"To the Talpa?" Sai said.

"To the Talpa," Aurora confirmed. "We all know what's going to happen. Tarla isn't going to sit on the contract, and Calico's not going to forget with her pushing him along. They'll be back."

"Wait," Eponi twisted away from her wristlet. "You're sounding like we'll be fighting them. The Rangers, I mean. Tarla."

"It's Tarla's choice," Aurora said. "We made ours."

"So we leave DefenseCorp and now we're stuck in another suicide mission?" Eponi said.

Gregor laughed, "Suicide? We are as many as them, and better."

"You think Tarla's going to come back with just her squad?" Eponi bounced off her rock, picked up her pack. "Laugh it up, Gregor, because you're gonna have a lot of people to smash with that hammer. I hope they don't shoot you first."

Wexer's creamy river light gave Sever all the vision they needed to climb up the hill and back to the mine's entrance. The silver mag-lev lights still glowed, but Aurora didn't get much over the hill's crest before two Talpa left the tunnel to greet them, snub-rifles in their hands. Rovo took over from there, and the resulting conversation reminded Aurora of the epically bad body raps of Devos Three, a planet whose dominant species lacked aural hearing and made do on vibrations.

Turned out slapping everything to make sentences was an awful way to communicate.

"Think they pop out from the ground and kill us all, just out of spite?" Sai said to Aurora.

"Pop out from the ground?"

"They do that." Sai pointed to his feet. "Like magic. Right through the rock."

"You know this how?"

"They tried to sneak up on me," Sai said. "After you all went in the tunnel. Almost got me too. Almost."

"Mmmhmm."

Rovo, though, did not get them attacked by a swarm of digging, deadly Talpa. Instead, the furry sentries invited Sever inside, and one guided the squad all the way back to that central shaft.

Before, the mine's core had seemed threatening. Its rock walls had been covered by desperate Talpa, and Aurora had been expecting a fight or worse. Now, without its owners coating its every surface, the Wexer mine showed itself off. While Aurora had thought the silver lighting on the mag-lev rails was just a random choice, the central core proved her wrong:

Up and down the lift pillars, the silver lights twinkled. The rock, scratched by all those Talpa claws, caught the light and bent it, creating a shadow mosaic all around them, one that swirled as the lifts moved up and down, carrying Talpa and mag-lev carts loaded with raw black ore. A fine drum beat carried from down below, mingling with the shoveling sound of moving earth.

"Guess the lucky ones get to have fun," Eponi said as they reached the ledge's end and waited for the lift. "While everyone else has to work."

"It's constant," Rovo said between chirps with their

guide. "The celebration. That way every shift has something to enjoy at the end."

"A constant party?" Aurora said. "Sounds like a nightmare."

"Or a great time," Eponi replied.

As they loaded on the lift, a flat gray platform far more welcoming now that it wasn't being used for an ambush, Rovo continued to interrogate and relay Talpa society's finer points.

Aurora tuned most of it out, instead keeping a watch for any sign the Talpa weren't going to follow through on their promise. If the creatures had changed their minds, then they'd just succeeded in splitting up the crew coming after them. Sever would be alone in any fight, without anywhere to run or reinforcements to call.

She'd kept the power armor's helmet and its all-knowing visor down too, to keep things cordial. Without its scanning popping threats up to her eyes, Aurora felt naked. Vulnerable. You wanted a list of the most important things a squad captain could do? Keep her squad alive.

That's it.

And she'd taken a rookie's word that they weren't going to die in here.

Breathe, Aurora.

She'd been in worse. So many worse situations. Dynas had been one, fighting through the tower in the city, hunting for Sai. There'd been missions where friends had really been enemies, where Sever had lost members to shots in the back. This didn't feel like those.

The Talpa weren't some corrupt government or backstabbing cartel. They weren't mercenaries or outlaws. Not even a company intent on their bottom line to the exclusion of all else. Aurora looked around her, caught Talpa climbing the walls, riding the lifts, carrying what looked like food, like lights, like normal things.

A normal people, who needed help to survive.

Without DefenseCorp playing mission director, Sever needed to plot its own course. Aurora figured taking a stand on behalf of those who couldn't fight for themselves would be a good way to start, risks to life and limb be damned.

"Captain?" Gregor said, and Aurora realized the lift had come to a stop. "I think we're here."

SEVENTEEN

Cave Days

How DID you go from an invading force to someone your would-be victims wanted to celebrate? Have Rovo along, apparently. The rookie barked and squawked his way through the Talpa, bringing Sever right to a vast, hollowed-out nexus near the shaft's bottom filled with music, food, and more furry creatures than Sai had ever seen.

Parties, for Sai, had been transactional affairs. Events built around achieving an end, starting with his father's more corporate gatherings where formal-dressed executives stood in a building's uppermost floor and discussed how best to exploit everyone else living below. Sai had been trotted around at those, asked to smile and curry favor through cuteness.

Later, parties had evolved into adventures for his children. A chance to earn some smiles, some laughs, some memories. But never, never had Sai found himself in the middle of an unbridled revel.

The Talpa streamed around them, running over and around each other, clinging and climbing the walls, such that some hung onto the ceiling and carried out their chittering conversations. Others swept around Sever, pausing for a second or two to offer a squeaked question before realizing neither Sai nor anyone except Rovo spoke their language.

The mine air, stuffy and cool in the tunnels, took on a wild scent combination down here, ranging from wet fur to burning candles to, and Sai's eyes widened when he found the culprit, a massive pile of something that looked like mashed grains. Yellow, mottled, and thick, the slop sat on a blackrock dais standing a few centimeters off the floor. As they ran, the Talpa swept their claws through the pile, snagging bits off of it and licking the food from their claws.

"Think I'll be passing on that," Eponi said.

"Good call," Sai replied. Upon Calico's order to depart, Sai and Eponi had snagged some nutrient containers from the skiff's kitchen and stuffed'em in their packs, so Sever wouldn't starve. "I admire the spirit, but not the hygiene."

Sai also found he could admire the diamond liquor Rovo delivered to them after vanishing into the Talpa sea: made by fermenting some of that grain, grown in Talpa-nurtured underground fields, and compressing it in sealed rock chambers, the stuff had an earthy sharpness that helped wash down the bland protein bars and yogurts.

During the meal, held sitting on the floor off to one side in the raucous chamber, Aurora made clear Sever had to get its rest overnight because she expected Tarla, Calico, and others to come back. Possibly as early as that morning.

The Talpa issued Sever a small cave network off the central shaft to use as a base, though the bedrooms, big enough for a Talpa and its meager possessions, forced Sever to curl up and leave everything they owned, power armor included, in a pile near the central shaft. Gregor, too large even in his skin suit, slept in the network's central corridor.

With a stiff back and a dry throat, Sai woke along with Sever to find an imminent invasion wasn't happening. Rovo scanned the frequencies and didn't find any reports announcing an incoming assault, or any massive departure from Wexer's city, so Aurora stationed a continual watch at the mine's top.

"We know they're going to come eventually," Aurora said, "and we're committed now. So that means we make this place as hard to break as possible."

Fortify a mine?

Captain's orders.

Sai hadn't done much defensive work—Sever wasn't built for protecting—but, with his life on the line, turning the mine from a big mountain with many entrances and exits into a deadly bastion was a challenge he went at with the same determined focus Sai put towards anything.

As his mother hammered into him from his youth: the only thing keeping Sai from any success he chased, was effort.

"Doubt you meant this," Sai muttered to himself, later on the third day, as he strung proximity mines around an old tunnel no longer used but easily accessed on a lower level. "But then, maybe you did."

Three Talpa worked along with him, with each Sever member, actually. Sai couldn't speak their squeaks, but hand and claw gestures worked well enough. Sai couldn't pronounce their real names either, so he referred to them by their looks: Patches, an amber Talpa with several white splotches on his fur, Ruby, a white-furred Talpa with red eyes, and Tar, an inky Talpa that tended to disappear against Wexer's blackrock.

The Talpa proved almost as adept with explosives as

Sai, and they'd dissected the couple mines Sai had brought to build dozens more over the last 48 hours. As they laid down this strand, Sai looked towards Wexer's city, though this vantage only saw the end of the canyon Calico's skiff had been rushing down.

Why was Tarla taking so long? Had her crew turned against her?

She had to know every extra hour gave Sever a greater advantage. The time let Sever lay down more defenses, helped Sever know the Talpa a little more. If Tarla returned with just her Twilight Rangers now, Sai figured they'd be dead or defeated without a single Talpa casualty.

"That's why you're going back," Aurora said that evening. "You, Eponi, and Gregor. The Talpa have freight skiffs, and they're going to run a shipment to the city tomorrow, so Rovo says."

"Wait," Sai replied as they munched on some of the grain. Their protein bars had run out after the first day, and it turned out the Talpa, while possibly disgusting, made fair cooks. "You're saying the three of us have to get into the city unnoticed and try to figure out what's going on?"

"Exactly," Aurora said. "Either Tarla's planning something big that we need to be ready for, or she's given up and moved on."

"And we're wasting time sitting here."

"Right." Aurora waved at the Talpa celebration going on around them. "I'm not sure how much longer I can stand this, so the sooner we either start this fight or find it unnecessary, the better."

"Why me?"

"What?"

"You're asking Gregor, Eponi, and I. Why us?"

Aurora stared at Sai, "I need Rovo to interpret the

Talpa for me. Gregor, good as he is in a fight, has all the covert talents of, well, a large man with a larger hammer, so I'm hoping he'll cover you. I'd send Eponi alone, but I'm not convinced she'd come back."

Sai glanced across the chamber, where Eponi and Rovo seemed to be having a good time learning a ridiculous tumbling dance with a Talpa quartet.

"You don't trust her?"

"With my life, yes," Aurora said. "With her own? Eponi has conflicts."

"Like?"

"Ask her," Aurora said. "Maybe she'll tell you. But I don't want you to just find out what Tarla's doing."

"Because that's not enough?" Sai didn't mean to sound so sarcastic, but this mission kept on getting worse as Aurora described it. "What else?"

"I need you to secure a ship. Anaskya's, if it's still there, or another. I don't care," Aurora said. "Get that ship back here. Rovo's going to have the Talpa clear a landing pad behind the mine. We need a way out, Sai. I won't be trapped here."

"So that's really why Eponi's coming along."

Aurora didn't deny it, "Those are the orders, Sai. Can you do it?"

Could he do it? Sai had no damn idea, but as the skiff shot through the early dawn light, he figured he could try. He, Gregor, and Eponi were all up top, exactly none of them in power armor. With help from the Talpa, all three wore shrouds over their street clothes, dirty things that nonetheless did a nice job keeping dirt off their faces. Sai didn't have his katana, Gregor didn't have his hammer, but Eponi did have her enthusiasm.

"So, so happy to be out of there," Eponi said for what

must have been the third time already that morning. "It's so dark and damp and dark."

"You said dark twice." Gregor didn't bother looking her way, the big man leaned over the skiff's bow looking towards the city's lights like they all were.

"That's my point. Also, I realize it's not polite, but Talpa smell."

"You realize," Sai said, "that they're the ones flying us right now?"

"They can't understand me anyway."

Sai wasn't so sure on that count, but the Talpa didn't throw them off the skiff before they parked the mechanical boat on the city's outskirts. Wexer's mining economy meant a large loading lot sat outside the city, cordoned off by signs declaring this way for buyers, this way for sellers. The Talpa joined three other skiffs already there, all offering up loads of precious metals, raw ores, and other finds beneath Wexer's special soil.

A pop-up market of sorts greeted them, from stands shilling coffee and breakfast foods to others hawking gear and personnel for hire to move the rocks from the skiffs to the ships or refining shops. Most, as was the way on Wexer, wore shrouds and robes meant to keep the black dust from filtering into their eyes, ears, or drinks. None gave the Sever trio a second glance as they left the skiff and filtered into the crowd.

"Ship or Tarla first?" Eponi asked as they went through the marketplace.

"Tarla," Sai said. "If she's abandoned the job, then we don't need to worry about the ship. And if she hasn't, then we'll fly the ship back to the mine."

"You sound confident," Gregor said.

"Compared to Dynas, everything's easier," Sai said. "At

least here, some scientist isn't going to inject me with a virus."

They hit Wexer's central street, the docking bays situated in the city's center. Always humming with activity, the spacecraft engines proved a more satisfying sound than the constant thunks in the mine. With a coffee he'd snagged in his hand—the first one Sai had found since leaving the city three days ago—Sai lingered for a long minute just embracing the sounds of civilization.

"Don't know how much you miss it till it's gone," Sai muttered.

"And you were all like hey, how can you go argue for Tarla?" Eponi said. "Bet you she hasn't spent the last three nights sleeping on a rock."

"Three nights, or a lifetime?" Gregor asked. "You will sleep better knowing you made the right choice."

"Says the guy who just wants to smash things with a hammer," Eponi shot back.

Gregor didn't disagree.

"Okay," Sai finished the coffee, stared at the empty cup for a moment hoping it would magically refill. "Gregor, we can't all go hunting for Tarla. Check on Anaskya, see if her ship's still here. Eponi and I will see if we can't find out what's going on."

"Use the squad band if you need me," Gregor said. "Good luck."

The big man loped off down the street towards the docking bays, a huge silhouette in the blue-silver morning.

"So Aurora sent you to babysit me, huh?" Eponi asked as soon as Gregor left earshot.

"She sent me to figure out what's going on, same as you."

"Sure," Eponi leaned against a nearby building, tossed

a smoldering look Sai's way. "Because who wouldn't send the bomber on a spy mission."

"I can be quiet when I need to be."

"Hope so," Eponi said. "Because if Tarla's where I think she is, we're going to need a lot of luck to learn anything and get out alive."

Sai tilted his head, "Where do you think she is?"

Eponi pointed. Not towards the docking bays, or back towards the skiff lot where they'd first met Calico, but at a taller structure, a squat tower looming over much of the squat city and one that Sai had paid little attention to after they landed. No sign blazed out from its roof, suggesting it was less a store than an office for a company that didn't need to advertise.

"I don't get it?" Sai said.

"Not the building, man, but what's on top."

Oh. The squat tower's roof had a landing pad, and on it, lit up by lights, was a drop shuttle. One Sai recognized, because he'd ridden in dozens over the years.

DefenseCorp had come to Wexer, and Sai could only think of one reason why.

EIGHTEEN

Ship Hunting

GONE. The blocky cargo freighter, low blue lights on and splashing across the bay, was not Anaskya's sleek craft. Any crew inside would doubtless not be Anaskya with her virus and uptight attitudes. The rogue scientist had fled.

Not that Gregor could be all that surprised. It'd been three days since Sever had left, more than long enough to recharge the batteries Gregor had drained, find a pilot, a destination, and blow off a rocky dump like Wexer in search of her next evil scheme.

Evil?

Was that too strong a word?

Gregor had seen morality's band. The heroes on too many worlds that threw themselves into danger and were, for their troubles, immolated on pyres real and political. He'd seen the villains climb the ladders through corruption and murder and intrigue only to find themselves the victims of the person climbing up after them. And he'd seen himself and most of the galaxy, the ones clinging to the middle, doing good where they could and surviving when they couldn't in an attempt to make it from one day to the next.

So he couldn't fault Anaskya for leaving, but he could be disappointed.

Now he had to find another ship, and Gregor had never, in his long history of smashing and bashing things, commandeered a ship.

His fingers itched to hold his hammer, not that the weapon would do him any good in the docking bay, but it would be comforting. Knowing that he could, at least, dent something. There was power in that. Useless power, but power nonetheless.

Around him, Wexer's morning captured a docking bay arising to action, the noises Gregor heard came from cargo being loaded and unloaded by bots while various crews left their ships to find some sort of breakfast beneath the brightening crystal sky. Wexer's wind thrashed awake, whipping up dust and dirt in sporadic devils ignored by everyone walking around them.

Shrouded people already crowded the concourse, shuffling to and from shifts and ships. Gregor pegged the time as that early start for office workers, if such a thing existed on a planet like this one. Turning away from the freighter, Gregor could see a squat skyline lit up with flickering signs declaring this and that, their auras mingling together with the occasional spacecraft engine backwash as ships lifted off to the stars.

One tower stood out above the rest, with a ship docking on top of the damn thing. A piloting trick Gregor would never want to try. Not that he wanted to try any piloting at all: too much finesse required.

But Sai and Eponi wanted a ship, and he'd find them one.

Gregor set off walk along the docking bays. Unlike Rovo, Gregor didn't have the savvy to hack into a locked ship and open up its guts without an invitation. He didn't have a hammer to bash his way in, nor did he have Sai's explosives to blow apart any blocks. Getting onto a spaceship here would require that most difficult of tasks and tools: conversation.

While most people he passed kept their heads down or murmured to each other, words crept into the air as he walked, deals and plans in the making, a joke about last night's adventures.

The little bar sat just off some bays, right in the middle of the main walkway along the landing and leaving ships. A ring with twenty seats splattered with screens and a whirling bot in the middle of it all. No walls, no glitzy signs, just a single white-lit board proclaiming it the *Spacer's Rest*, and nothing more.

If Gregor wasn't on a mission, he'd spend the whole day here. Listen to stories from the star surfers that'd found their ways to Wexer, snagging beverages far better than the preserved stuff that inevitably clogged the messes of the ships Gregor rode on, and for a little while lose himself in lives that were different than his own.

Now he approached the *Spacer's Rest* like a predator, counting the empty seats and looking at their neighbors, the ones that seemed chattier with their coffees and their pre-made sandwiches, spun up in microwaves and delivered piping hot. One seat, next to a man and woman who seemed to be in escalating boasts about some pirate encounter, looked to be the ideal, and Gregor took it.

"It wasn't the third wasp," the woman said, describing a tiny fighter meant to be used in groups, "but the fifth one. You kept saying there'd be more, but I hit the cluster bomb anyway."

"Right, right," her partner said, sloshing a frothy, bright blue mixture around in a clear, plastic cup. "A good move, I'll give you that, but then, guess what, there were MORE!"

The woman slapped the bar, spilled a bit of coffee. "But way behind! They were never gonna catch us. We got away, didn't we?"

"We coulda done more damage," the man sighed, sounding truly sorry about that fact. "If we'd waited another ten minutes, we could've caught their whole batch. Then they wouldn't be able to get the next freighter coming through."

Gregor had to time his entry, make it innocent and impeccable and perfect. Introduce himself with a crafty phrase to make himself a friend and a confidant in a single stroke.

"I like smashing pirates too," Gregor said.

The two turned his way, the man leaning in over his drink to catch a look at Gregor, "Who're you now?"

"A pirate smasher, apparently," the woman said, "and an eavesdropper."

"You talk loudly," Gregor said, then, realizing this was not going exactly to plan, changed tone. "Which is a good thing! Too few people enjoy their lives."

Two skeptical looks greeted Gregor's remarks, and the big mercenary damned Aurora, Sai, and Eponi for sending him on this stupid mission. He wasn't a conversation artist, wasn't a hijacker, was a beat-em-up bully who needed a target.

"You having anything, friend?" the man said, lofting his creamy caffeine. "Or is a man who wants people to enjoy their lives going clean this morning?"

To say that the offer kicked off an hour of successful co-mingling would be, in Gregor's eyes, a massive understatement. While holding the mission in his mind, Gregor rattled through several mugs, always ordering dark, straight and hot. His newfound friends flowed through their outer fringe freighting adventures with increasing abandon, as if having Gregor as an audience upped their story-telling game. The spice the two had been throwing at each other when Gregor walked up shot to an almost worrying level until, after she'd finished her latest latte, the woman set her hands down, declared she was heading out.

"Back to the ship?" the man asked with a laugh.

"Hell no," the woman replied. "Someone has to find our next job. Don't enjoy yourself too much, Apton, cause, unless it's a terrible day, we're leaving tomorrow."

"Quick gigs," Apton said to Gregor as his captain left. "She never wants long contracts that could tie us down, which is why we're still out here, huntin' deals in dumps like this."

"Is being flexible so bad?" Gregor said.

"Naw, it's fine, just fine," Apton shook his head, gazed at his empty sandwich wrapper as if more eggs might magically appear. "Just sometimes I get tired of the race. I cleaned the ship yesterday. I know it'll get ruined soon, but is keeping her pristine for a day too much to ask?"

"A clean ship?" Gregor said. "That is truly rare."

"Oh, she's grand now," Apton said, then tilted his head. "What about yours? Where's she at?"

Gregor tried to find a thread that would get Apton away from this bar and to the man's freighter, and he couldn't find a better one than saying Gregor's supposed ship wasn't all that far away.

"Well, duh, man, no ship's far away on Wexer," Apton said. "This place is so tiny. Love that about it, really, means I can stumble home any time I want." Apton pointed to a bay three slots down, not more than a five minute walk away. "Whenever we're here, we always try to get one close. Captain knows what I like."

"Can I see it?" Gregor said. "I'm making more runs out this way, and if it is as dangerous as you say, perhaps I can take some pointers on what I should put on my own ship."

"More weapons, more cargo," Apton said. "That's all you need to know. But sure, I'll show you what we're rocking, then we can swing by yours and see how we can make it ready to play."

Abusing Apton's trust didn't exactly sit well with Gregor, but when he felt a vibration along his wrist and looked at the screen, saw a stream of urgent messages from Sai and Eponi that boiled down to coordinates and an ask for an evac, Gregor brushed aside any qualms. Too much was at stake.

Apton's claim about his ship's cleanliness wasn't a lie: the craft gleamed in the pearl morning light. More wide than long, the ship's cargo hold ran along the lower half while the upper bristled with turrets, engines, and polarized metals meant to deflect blazing laser energy. For fringe flyers, this wasn't the garbage pile Gregor expected.

"That's the reaction I'm looking for," Apton said. "She's beautiful, I know. Captain and I sank a lot of cash and time into making her what she is. Fast, deadly, and—"

"Why?" Gregor had to ask. Couldn't help it. "All for running cargo?"

"Oh, buddy," Apton said. "This one? We don't run rocks. Food. All that crap. We deliver the rarities, the ones people don't want others to get ahold of. That's why we're dealing with pirates all the damn time, because they want what we got."

Gregor went closer to the ship, marveled at it. He'd never cared overmuch about spacecraft—so long as it brought Gregor where he needed to go, who cared—but he could respect competence, power, speed. Like his hammer, this was a tool developed precisely for its purpose.

Apton followed Gregor as he made the slow walk around the ship, pointing out this and that about the craft. Gregor ignored most of it, instead looking for the entry while trying to block out the steady buzzing on his wristlet. Sai and Eponi needed help, but Gregor wouldn't be helping them any if he blew his cover now.

"What's its name?" Gregor asked as they came back around to the pointed, central spike that had to be its bridge.

"*Prisa*," Apton replied. "Captain named it, never told me what it meant."

Gregor nodded, "And how do you get in?"

"There's a ramp you can use when cargo's not attached," Apton said, waving towards the block on *Prisa*'s lower half. "But that's the boring way. Watch this."

The man tapped something on his wristlet, and from the *Prisa*'s central neck, a hissing pop sent steam rushing out into the dawn as a platform shot down, the bars holding it in place uncoiling as the platform dropped into the dirt.

"Fast evac, fast boarding," Apton said. "Get on, I'll show you. It's awesome."

The pilot ushered Gregor onto the platform, barely large enough to hold the two of them. They held onto a small bar in the center, coated with rubber grip to make holding on easy. With another tap on his wristlet, Apton sent the platform rocketing up into the *Prisa*, a fast entrance that had Gregor's previous drinks sloshing their way back into his throat.

Apton laughed as Gregor coughed, "See, pretty great, right?"

"Pretty great," Gregor said, straightening up, his wristlet buzzing. "Thank you for the tour."

He looked into Apton's smiling face, and dropped the *Prisa*'s pilot with a single punch.

NINETEEN

Stealth Job

TAKE a look at any planet in the galaxy and you'd find it matched so many others. Eponi and Sai walked Wexer's lightening streets, heading towards the tower with shuffling dawn bots and a crowd that dwindled as they left behind the eternal docking bay business for more traditional trades. Eponi found her memories slipping back to the worlds she'd sloughed through preparing for kart races: all those mornings after a race party, spent seeing a brand new sky through yesterday's haze on the way to whatever ship would take her to the next system, the next race.

Sai didn't fall into a similar revery. His hands kept falling beneath his shroud to where his pistols sat, or falling overhead towards where his katana ought to be, only to wind up scratching at his neck or his overgrown hair. Anaskya didn't have shears on her ship, so everyone was a little outside their preferred grooming range.

"You going to be okay," Eponi said, "or will you have to shoot something to keep yourself under control?"

"Not used to civilian work," Sai replied, his face

twitching as he apparently tried to keep eyes on anyone passing by.

"It's not hard," Eponi shrugged. "You went out and around when we landed, right? Just do that, but with a direction."

"That wasn't a mission."

"Then do whatever you have to do to hit that same headspace, dude, because you're making me edgy over here."

Places like Wexer, you didn't draw attention unless you looked for it. The way Sai was spinning up as they moved, he'd catch a guard's eyes hunting for something to distract them through their shift.

Eponi kept her attention on the tower, the ship on top of it, and how best to get there. Wexer didn't have much of a layout plan, and its blackrock paths tended to cut and swerve at strange angles as they ran into buildings or equipment lots seemingly set about at random. The result meant that though the tower wasn't all that far away, it took time getting there.

"Are you thinking about what to do when we reach it?" Sai asked. "Because all I can think of is that DefenseCorp is here for us."

"That's the idea," Eponi said. "We get close enough to find out for sure whether we have to worry about the big guns or not."

"But, how do we get that close?"

Sai's question took on new urgency when they finally closed with the tower, seeing its squat self sealed off by a three meter blackrock wall. A sealed, laser-banded gate marked the only gap, and not one Eponi felt they could use. Two guards stood near that laser gate, looking as bored as guards usually do. They carried standard-issue rifles, wore standard-issue suits, sipped something from DefenseCorp-issued thermoses.

"Well, DefenseCorp's definitely here," Eponi said as she and Sai pulled off to the side half a block away, standing as if in conversation while other people streamed past. "Which sucks."

"We should've taken Rovo's Bug," Sai said, scratching at his ear. "At least then we could listen in."

"Right, because Tarla's definitely broadcasting all her conversations over radio bands."

"Hey, it's a suggestion."

Eponi shook her head. Take the soldier outta the fight and he gets clueless. She snuck another look at the tower. All they needed was visual confirmation that Tarla or one of her rangers was here. That'd be enough to confirm to Aurora that Sever needed to get off Wexer fast, Talpa or no.

Five squaddies with two power armor suits wouldn't hold up against DefenseCorp's vengeance.

"So here's the plan," Eponi said, nodding past Sai. "You're going to boost me on top of that building there. Then you're going to distract the guards, and I'm going to jump from the roof over the wall."

"And once you're on the other side, then what?"

"I get the proof, and then I get out."

Sai tilted his head, "Eponi, don't mean to criticize your plan, but how are you going to get out of the tower once you're inside?"

"I'll walk out," Eponi said. "Just go up to the gate. It'll automatically open from the inside, or I'll ask the guards to let me leave. They won't suspect anyone that's already past."

"Staking a lot on that idea."

Eponi knew she was, but short of trying to blow open

the gate, there weren't many other options. Besides, even if Tarla and the Rangers had been spewing Sever's details to DefenseCorp over the past couple days, they'd still assume Sever had themselves holed up in the Talpa mine. No way they'd suspect a covert strike.

"It's my choice," Eponi said. "C'mon, we're losing time."

"Okay, but I still think this is a bad idea."

"You're welcome to your opinion, and I'm welcome to not give a damn about it."

They crossed the street as they spoke, crowding now with people and aliens, all shrouded up. At first, Eponi didn't understand why all the damn avenues were so bustling, but she'd realized that Wexer lacked the vehicular transit most developed places offered. Without skiffs zipping people from point to point, or taxis, tramways, or even moving walkways, people had to hoof it everywhere.

"Hostile, much?" Sai said.

"I'm just getting myself psyched up," Eponi replied. "Finding the zone."

"Which entails being rude to me?"

"Today, yeah, it does. Now would you lift me up?"

They'd reached the alleyway alongside Eponi's target building, a two-story block blaring its daytime occupation as a Wexer real estate dealer. Because who wouldn't want a prime piece of blackrock land on this desolate waste?

The buildings, too, didn't inspire confidence: Wexer's occasional windstorms seemed about the only geological event on the planet, yet as Eponi looked for potential hand-holds, she saw plenty climbing up the building's side. Pitted divots and pocked patches showed that wear and tear was both allowed and ignored.

The alley dipped away into shadows as Wexer's sparse street lighting and the low morning light embraced hidden activities. For a planet and a city with a minimal governing structure, where cash meant both police protection and civic support, Eponi couldn't say she was surprised by the patchy, anything-goes environment.

Not that she was complaining: you couldn't scale a building and hop the rooftops anywhere.

"Ready?" Sai asked, cupping his hands, back to the main street.

"So ready," Eponi replied, stepping into the cupped offering with her left foot.

Sai bounced her up and right, and Eponi found her first grips along the pitted surface, her fingers digging into the tiny holds, her boots doing their best to dig into their own options. Wexer's cool, desert air kept things dry, so Eponi caught hold a little over two meters up from the ground.

"Good?" Sai asked from below while Eponi plotted her next move.

"Just be ready to catch me."

Eponi wasn't so wrapped up in her own ego that she thought she couldn't fall. More kart racers died because they tried to do what their abilities couldn't handle. Eponi had already made that mistake, and while it hadn't cost her life, it . . . had cost her the life she wanted to live.

Above and to her right, a downward slit looked just wide enough for her fingers. Tensing, Eponi kicked up with her feet and lunged with her right hand, keeping her left where it was. Her fingers fell into the slit, sliding along its length until they fell into the groove, pinching in along the rock. Not much support, but enough to buy Eponi another kick, another divot for her left hand to get a solid grip.

Her feet pulled up to where her hands had been, and Eponi was on the move.

"If I have to catch you now, you'll break my back," Sai said.

"You calling me fat?"

"I'm calling you high."

A better riposte than Eponi expected, but the two lunges had put the first floor's gap in game, a textured line shielding what was probably a later addition to plop the second story on the first. The diamond pattern offered opportunity, and another heave-and-kick brought Eponi's hands up. From that stable spot, Eponi planned out the route to the top, and, before Sai could offer another complaint about his role as landing pad, Eponi shimmied to the roof.

After climbing over the lip, Eponi looked back down and gave Sai the go-ahead signal. He'd watch for her to get into position, then start his dance. Eponi felt a little sad she couldn't just enjoy Sai playing the shiny object: he'd always been the so-called mature man with a family and a box full of bombs, about time he had to be the clown.

But duty called, or something like that.

The building's roof had little on it save accumulated dust, a single vent, and a free shot towards the target tower. Eponi, keeping low, quick-walked across the gravel spread over the roof, crossing to its opposite end. From up here, she could see over the wall to the desolate grounds leading to the tower—no fancy gardens here, just blackrock everywhere.

The laser gate and its guards lay to her left, the guards themselves out of Eponi's sight as she crouched at the roof's edge. The wall sat an alleyway's width away from her, an easy clear in power armor boots, harder in normal footwear.

Nobody stalked the courtyard, leaving an open space ripe for Eponi's jump'n'roll. Looking at the tower showed a shinier construct than most of Wexer offered, apparently someone took the time to spray off these walls. Defense-Corp doing the absolute minimum to keep their buildings presentable.

Few windows graced the outside, a common Wexer fixture, and Eponi wondered if the dust and occasional blowing rock had anything to do with that. Or maybe blackrock just didn't play nice with glass. Either way, Eponi would take the solid structure and the cover it'd give her. That, plus the early hour, hopefully meant nobody would be watching.

"Hey!" Sai shouted loud from the street, and it took all she had for Eponi not to look over. "Don't I know you?"

Who didn't Sai know? Eponi couldn't tell, didn't wait to see. Instead, she backed up along the roof to give herself room to run.

"I swear," Sai continued his booming talk, "you look just like my sister's old boyfriend!"

And that was it. If Sai followed through with his second line, Eponi's game was a go. Eponi kicked forward, sliding a bit on the gravel and wincing at the noise as rock sprayed around her. One step, two steps, arms pumping, and then the first lunge and plant right on the rooftop's edge. Light splashed around her as Eponi went from her cover into the open, and she hoped, prayed, wished, and begged that nobody saw her split second crossing.

The jump felt like an eternity, the landing came in a flash. Eponi fell and rolled, striking the rock with enough force to feel an instant bruise judder through, a sting rattle her ankle, and her breath shunt away from her lungs. But, despite the rocks tearing at her clothes, the dirt in her hair, Eponi had made the leap.

The courtyard spread around her as Eponi stood, a little wobbly, and brushed herself off. With the big walls blocking the sound, she couldn't hear Sai's continued conversation, if it continued, or much of anything else. A little oasis in Wexer's sorta-urban desert.

Eponi straightened, put on the most confident look she could muster, and headed towards the front door. Rather than trying to sneak into a place that looked like it had all of one door, Eponi figured the confidence play would be the better one, dishing up a no-nonsense stare and going right on to the entrance.

The front door wasn't locked, didn't even have anyone watching it. Eponi swung it open, stepped inside to a wide room splayed over with screens, chairs, and makeshift office gear that all looked years out of date. Stock art showing prime DefenseCorp-managed worlds hung on walls, showcasing planets everybody here would rather be. Definitely par for a fringe DefenseCorp outpost.

A single breath caught in Eponi's throat. Filtered air, cool and slightly stale and not, for once, packing the scratchy dust Eponi had felt everywhere else on Wexer to this point. A minor miracle, and for a split second Eponi thought about folding right then and there, giving up to go to some place that wasn't the mine and its grime.

As quick as it came, the notion died under what would actually happen: a quick trial for desertion and a summary execution by airlock ejection, no matter how much Eponi lied that Sever and Aurora had forced her along.

Sorry, no escapist fantasy today.

Eponi didn't see anyone, not exactly a surprise given the early hour, but voices came from above, and a squat beige tile stair opposite Eponi gave the way to get up there. Closed doors offered hints at other rooms off the main entry, but most looked like they had black badge scanners. Eponi had neither a badge nor the time to find one.

She had to get proof, and get out of there. Which

meant finding something obvious. The first floor didn't offer anything, so Eponi walked towards the stair. As with the courtyard, now that she was inside the DefenseCorp building, confidence would play better than stealth. There weren't any good hiding places, and odds were the average DefenseCorp flunky wouldn't know who she was.

Eponi hit the steps at a measured pace, scanning around as she climbed. Her wristlet buzzed and she glanced at it. Sai, asking if she needed the escape opportunity yet. Good news, that. Meant his initial disruption hadn't wound up with him shot or thrown in some rocky cell. Eponi tapped out a quick no as she reached the second story.

If DefenseCorp offered up the first floor for desk work, the second story held meeting rooms. Stilted spaces with glass windows bearing the dark outline to drop shade should the need arise. Chairs sat around long projection tables, and the outer wall bordering each room had a screen covering every meter. Eponi didn't think it likely DefenseCorp cared enough about Wexer to run any significant operations here, but the place could operate as a base for off-world mining and security contracts.

Eponi's muddling through DefenseCorp business came to an abrupt halt when she tracked the voices. In a room opposite the stair, with the door open and windows tinted dark, Eponi heard talking. Heard clear sentences, and a voice she'd marked ever since its owner bought her that first drink.

Tarla. No doubt. Talking about the only thing she could be.

"What I'm trying to tell you," Tarla was saying, "is that you've already waited too long. I came to you two days ago with Sever's location, and you've done nothing."

Eponi wanted to freeze, but instead she backed down

the stair, trying to stay both within earshot but also out of sight, ready to run.

"Hardly nothing," some bored commander replied. "Our superiors requested us to observe and hold for further reinforcement. We're not a combat station, Tarla. My workers handle contract negotiations, not firefights. And we definitely don't do it this early in the morning."

"Then you are useless."

"If you want to go after them yourself and try to earn the reward, you are welcome to it. Just don't expect support."

The conversation seemed to be winding to a close, and Eponi had heard all she needed. Time to leave. She tapped out a quick thumbs-up to Sai to get things going, two-stepped down the stairs and fast-walked towards the entrance. Pushed the door open, stepped back into that dusty night.

And felt a barrel's business end press against her temple.

"Sometimes you have to catch the fish, sometimes it hops right in the boat," Perro said, grinning as he stood near the wall. "These DC jokers might not know who they're dealing with, but we do. Guess who's getting the bonus for bringing you in?"

Five.

"You?" Eponi said, ticking down seconds in her head, trying to keep her heart steady.

Four.

"Who'd have thought the pilot was the smart one of your bunch?" Perro laughed. "Now, I'm gonna have you unclip those pistols from your belt so you don't get any fancy ideas."

Three.

"You sure you want me moving, Perro?" Eponi replied. "Might get hurt."

Two.

"What?" Perro said. "I'm the one that—"

The wall to Eponi's left, right in the alleyway next to the building she'd used as a launch pad, blew in with a roaring, ripping bang. The force threw Perro towards Eponi who, expecting it, curled back in the front entrance and let Perro fly on by. Rock, rubble, and smoke followed the explosion's heat.

Ears ringing, throat once again burning as Eponi breathed in all that dust Sai just kicked up, Sever's pilot broke towards the hole in the wall. Shouts, panicked from the street and more orderly from the building behind her, rang out as order made its first advances against chaos.

Not fast enough.

"I've been messaging Gregor about a ship," Sai said as Eponi broke into the alleyway. "He hasn't replied."

"Then we gotta keep moving until he does." Eponi coughed, kept up her stride. "Pick somewhere outside the city for him to meet us. Tarla's in there, Perro saw me."

Sai marked a spot back near where the Talpa skiff had dropped them and the two broke into the street, running with the fleeing crowd. Glances back showed a sea of dark, shrouded faces, but Eponi wouldn't be surprised if Twilight had a couple people in the bunch.

But they either didn't want to start a fight in the city streets, or missed Eponi and Sai, because no shots came at the Sever squad duo while they went through Wexer. No punches came in, no calls to stand down.

"Still no reply?" Eponi asked as they reached the ad hoc trading market on the city's outskirts, then went beyond it to the desert's edge.

"Nothing," Sai replied. "It's like Gregor's gone dark."

"Ambushed by Twilight?"

Sai was about to reply, when new shouts called out behind them. Not the panicked cries of people fearing for their lives, but angry, jeering calls. Eponi turned to see a craft, a sleek and fancy one, flying in low towards the market. Its wings wobbled, a sure sign the ship's flight computer was fighting with its pilot, and it clearly wasn't on any planned trajectory.

"What the—" Sai started, and, as the ship careened their way, Eponi began laughing.

"It's him," Eponi said as the ship buzzed the market, jets whining as it skidded down towards the desert.

The craft's struts dropped early and scrapped against the rocky ground, throwing up dirt and dust and an awful wrenching noise as the ship itself spun against its own momentum. It did, though, come to a stop, having rotated entirely around so its shiny nose pointed back towards the docking bays it'd no doubt left without any kind of clearance.

"Guess you're not the only pilot in Sever," Sai said as a little platform dropped from the ship's center, Gregor standing on it, waving.

"Oh no, I definitely still am," Eponi said. "He's not touching the flight stick again."

TWENTY

First Strike

THERE CAME a point when one had to reflect on the choices in his life, and for Rovo, that thought came when he finished boarding up another tunnel exit with the Talpa trio he'd been working with all afternoon. Ever since Eponi, Gregor, and Sai had returned with their hijacked ship, things had gone a little crazy.

Aurora's first instinct upon hearing that Tarla had engaged with DefenseCorp to chase after Sever was to flee. Rovo would've gone right along with it, as would every other Sever member, except for the Talpa that came into the room at that very moment, bearing hot beverages and some strangely good pastries that Rovo had refused to learn anything about—fluffy and chocolate-like, though neither ingredient seemed to be anywhere on Wexer.

The Talpa asked Rovo, as the Sever members resolved to ditch off world on the *Prisa* as soon as possible, whether the furry creatures were going to survive after all.

The question had him freeze, had Aurora notice.

"What's the Talpa asking you, Rovo?" Aurora said.

"It's asking whether they're going to make it."

Not even Aurora had a ready answer for that one. Rovo hadn't known Aurora long, but she could be brutal when necessary. Make those hard choices. But condemning a few thousand Talpa to death or eviction at Calico and Tarla's hands apparently crossed a line.

"They will," Aurora said to Rovo. "We'll make sure of it."

The squad had spent their hot drinks and their pastries trying to figure out how.

As a defense, barricading as much of the mine as they possibly could seemed like a good place to start. Eponi's intel suggested DefenseCorp wasn't ready to move quite yet, but they would be soon, so Sever split up into groups with the Talpa and went about sealing almost every entrance to the mine. The Talpa still wanted to be able to make some deliveries, earn some cash—cash that would, if they survived, go to Sever too—so the mine couldn't be sealed off entirely, but restricting the assault to two frontal gates helped focus.

Gregor and Sai took one Talpa crew out to the canyons to set up another ambush, while Eponi worked with another to hollow out a good landing zone for the *Prisa* behind the mine. Aurora was all in on helping the Talpa, but she also wanted an escape hatch. There was a chance, however small, that Sever could cause enough damage and flee, causing pursuit to follow them in their ship and letting the Talpa recover. Maybe even evacuate.

So now Rovo had to figure out what he was doing beneath all this rock, following a silver rail back to the central shaft. His father's warning about leaving a good, stable job had haunted Rovo every night on Wexer, and now, in the mine, seemingly every minute. Morally, Rovo had no doubts, just like he hadn't with Kaia, that he was making the right choice.

Just, why was the right choice wandering beneath the earth with Talpa, waiting for lasers to shoot his way?

"Rovo, status check?" Aurora's voice crackled from his wristlet, the squad's narrow band bouncing around the mine to find him.

"Another tunnel closed," Rovo said. "What's next?"

"Head up top. Think our time's run out, and I'm going to need your help coordinating these furballs."

"On my way."

Rovo chittered to his Talpa escort, sending them on to the next breach to continue their barricading work. Talking with the Talpa felt like doing a workout with his mouth, twisting and squeezing his lips and tongues into different shapes to produce noises that would've earned him weird looks from any other corner in the galaxy except right here in this damn dark mine.

Maybe that's why he'd wound up down here: because Rovo's talents would have him locked away in a padded room just about anywhere else.

The 'Top' Aurora referred to sat, well, at the mine's apex. Not the mountain's actual peak, but the central shaft's highest level. The ride up from Rovo's work site—the mine's openings were all on the lowest sections—took minutes to scale the several thousand meters to the top.

The mine's scale hadn't been all that apparent when Sever had first arrived with Calico, Tarla, and her squad of bloodthirsty buffoons, but as Rovo had spent the last few days here, he began to understand the scale of what the Talpa had put together. why they wouldn't want to leave. The mine and its potential spread for thousands of square kilometers. The Talpa had enough space under the ground here to create a huge city for themselves, especially given the critters were half the size of an average human.

For the furry things, this place was about as close to paradise as they could find.

Rovo would fight to the end to defend his family's home on their watery world. That's all these Talpa were doing.

The question now: Would he die for their home?

"It's a strong force," Aurora said as Rovo entered the mine's upper command center, a new place put together over the last 72 hours on stern orders from Aurora.

Built into the mountain's edge and a straight shot—no silver rails, but silver lights instead—from the lift's top level, the command center had a too-polished look to it, the rapid construction from Talpa claws and their devices sheering out enough rock for thirty people to stand near each other along with a big open air window looking towards Wexer's city.

Aurora stood at that window, and that's where Rovo joined her. The canyon they'd initially flown down with Calico's skiff shot away from the mountain far below, like a gash in Wexer's surface. The cut extended almost all the way to the city, and around it Wexer's blackrock desert blurred as blown dust scattered across. A clear day, a windy day.

"A perfect day," Rovo said, following Aurora's eyes towards that desert, "for an attack."

"Not quite," Aurora said. "That dust is going to keep them going slow. It'll hamper their scanners, and I bet Tarla's told them about the ambush, so they'll be on the look out."

"Didn't we send Gregor with an ambush force? Isn't it bad if he's expected?"

Next to him, the big Talpa, the co-chief of the whole place, a gray-and-amber mottled mess calling himself Belte —the chief had once tried to explain how Talpa arrived at their names to Rovo, but Rovo had checked out after the details crossed into their fifth minute—squeaked up a minor storm affirming that the Talpa most definitely had.

"Doesn't matter," Aurora said. "We need to buy time for the other initiatives. Gregor has orders to fire two rounds and withdraw. The goal isn't casualties, it's to cause them to go slow or even wait for more reinforcements."

The other initiatives. Rovo looked at the small rock table that'd been carved in while the command center had been hollowed out. Directly on its surface and tracked by an obedient Talpa with sharp claws, diagrams and check marks indicated progress on things like the barricades, but also two other special projects that might, maybe, mean the difference between survival and absolute destruction.

"You really think we'll be able to pull those off?" Rovo asked. "I thought those were pipe dreams."

"Before Tarla gave us three extra days, they were," Aurora replied. "But the Talpa work hard."

"If your home was at risk, wouldn't you?"

Aurora shrugged, "When mine was at risk, I joined with the people that took it."

Oh.

Below, Rovo could make out the attacking force forming up in the desert. Ten skiffs shooting across the desert rock in a straight line. They hadn't yet pulled into range of the Talpa's single heavy laser, a device initially meant to help with the mine that the Talpa, with their usual ingenuity, had repurposed into long-range artillery.

Ten skiffs big enough to hold ten to twenty people apiece. That many DefenseCorp fighters, plus Tarla's force and whatever other mercenaries they'd found, could raze a Talpa community with only half that many weapons between them.

Sever would have to make up the difference.

"Sai has the front line," Aurora said. "Eponi's flexible. I'd normally stay up here, but we don't have power armor for everyone, so I'm going down too. I need you to be our eyes, Rovo. Call out what's going on, tell us where to be."

"Can't say I've done that before."

Aurora put a hand on his shoulder, a warmth belied by the absolute ice in her crystal blue eyes, "You will do it today. And tomorrow. As long as it takes to kick these assholes out of here."

"Yes, captain."

What else was there to say?

Aurora ran through some further deployments that Rovo translated to Belte, and then she headed off towards the lift, to her power armor, and the fight. Rovo set his hands on the window's edge, felt the chill window blow through his hair, and watched those skiffs get closer.

The skiffs avoided the canyon, streaking over the clear surface. Almost there.

"Belte, cue up the laser," Rovo said. "Try to swing them towards the canyon. Don't worry about direct hits."

The Talpa chittered an affirmative, then squeaked the message towards the command center's back, where several Talpa stood ready to relay commands. The creatures didn't have many devices—turned out Rovo's intercepts on Sever's initial approach to the mine caught the only two comms the Talpa had—so they used a pretty awesome manual method. Belte's orders went out and one of the Talpa vanished to the mine's central shaft.

It would squeak and squawk, the sound carrying down the central shaft to listeners posted every few hundred meters that would echo the orders until the whole mine heard them, knew what they needed to do.

Seconds later, the first white-green bolt streaked out from the mountain, blitzing towards the skiffs. The shot hit where it needed to, targeting the leftmost skiff and causing the whole line to slide right, towards the canyon.

"Gregor," Rovo said, using his wristlet to beam out the signal on the squad's band. "Two minutes to engage. We're pulling them closer to the canyon for you."

"Ready."

Rovo's fingers itched for a rifle he didn't have. A single pistol sat on his waist. His main rifle had been donated to Gregor's ambush squad, and Rovo hoped the weapon would make it back. Though if the ambush failed, if the defenses fell and Rovo, up here, was pushed into direct combat, they'd already have lost.

The long range laser kept up its barrage, kept pushing the skiffs towards the canyon until the nearest couple had to close together to keep from sliding into the craggy gash.

"In three," Rovo said, his voice dropping to a whisper. "Two. One."

A breath. A look at the black dust clouds kicked up by the skiff jets. The long-range laser kicking off another shot, this one a glancing hit on the leftmost skiff with nowhere else to go. The enemy had clustered.

Perfect.

"Go."

Rovo leaned forward as puffs burst from the blackrock ahead of the skiffs. From this distance, Rovo couldn't make out the figures, could only make out the flashes as those snub-nosed shotguns went to work, spitting green fire. One skiff, the rightmost target, veered hard towards the canyon, as if someone had grabbed its nose and swung it.

Or, perhaps, if someone had bashed it with a huge, kinetic hammer.

The other skiffs scattered, wheeling around or even arcing up into the sky, pushing the jets harder than designed to buy some space before swinging back down.

Some blue and red flashes began streaming back towards the Talpa, lighting up the ground with fiery marks.

"Time to evac," Rovo said. "Get out of there!"

The ambush had done its work, disorganized the assault. The long-range laser took some strong shots at skiffs paying more attention to the attacking Talpa than the distant artillery, and one skiff broke open as its aft took a direct hit. The engines superheated, and Rovo saw the dust clouds as fighters dove away from the craft as it spun away from the fight.

"We're backing," Gregor said. "Two skiffs downed."

Gregor and the ambushing Talpa fled to the canyon, where a hauling skiff the Talpa used for ore sat waiting. Rovo saw the craft pop up and, using the canyon walls for cover, sprint back towards the mine. The attacking force, disrupted, swirled around.

"C'mon, stop," Rovo whispered. "Call it off. Go back home."

Apparently their enemies had more spine than sense. Struggling to evade the long range laser, the enemy skiffs swung by their evacuated friends and picked them up from the ground before turning back towards the mine and speeding on.

"No delay," Rovo said as the eight remaining skiffs formed up, this time spreading out to keep the long-range laser from finding its mark. "They didn't get scared."

The band crackled as various Sever members clicked to acknowledge Rovo's report.

"Stick to the plan," Aurora's voice came in. "Remember, we've faced worse odds for less reason. They want to come in close? Let's make 'em pay."

Give his former employer a bloody nose?

As a cause, it'd have to do.

TWENTY-ONE

A Stand

THE POWER ARMOR shone with more polish than it'd seen in weeks. Not since Aurora had put it on before leaving the *Nautilus* had the suit gleamed. The Talpa had taken it upon themselves to give their defenders everything they could, which apparently included cleansing her black and white armor to a shine that would, on this rock- and dust-covered mess of a world, last a minute or less in real combat.

Aurora stepped towards the armor, its chest and leg sections split open and waiting for her to walk in. The lower level tunnel Sever had commandeered for their own didn't leave much space to hang up the armor, so she and Gregor had taken an entire oval room for the suits, setting them up on opposite ends, a single silver light hanging down from the middle.

"Stale air, a sore back, and an impossible mission," Aurora muttered. "Feels like home."

Walking into the armor felt like pulling into the tightest, snuggest hug. The armor, calibrated to Aurora's body, folded around her legs, her shoulders and her arms, the clamps locking in and pressing to her muscles so that the slightest twitch would trigger the armor's kinetic bursts. Take a punch and turn it from a light blow to something capable of caving in these rock walls.

The visor slid over Aurora's head with a click, powering up and displaying the armor's checks in a green graph swath. Blue dots haloed the visor's edge, the armor doing its job and picking up nearby Talpa. She'd made the adjustments to consider them allies, and any human not on the Sever band a target.

With two rifles, two pistols, and enough Talpa-improvised grenades qualify as a weapon of mass destruction, Aurora clanked from Sever's caves, took the lift up to ground level, and stomped to the mine's main entrance.

Designed for loading up ore and unloading provisions, the mine's main entry kissed the canyon's end with a wide rock archway buttressed with black stone support columns on the end, those bright silver lights streaking across the ceiling, and two heavy skiffs parked on either side. One on the right disgorged the ambush crew, including a few wounded Talpa getting thrown into makeshift carts and carried by their furry fellows into the mine.

"Report," Aurora said as Gregor turned her way, his own armor marred with dust and at least three new blast scars. The big man's hammer had made the trip back, sticking up from its back holster like a devastating radio antenna. "What are we up against?"

Gregor flipped up his visor, showing off the sweat that'd made its entrance during the ambush and stuck to him since. Sai joined from directing the barricade efforts, looking small without his own power armor, but Sever had played with limited resources all its life. Today was no different.

"Locals. Paid reserves and mercenaries," Gregor said.

"Cowards looking for easy cash. These are not the ones to be afraid of."

Not surprising. DefenseCorp might be sending more, might not. Aurora figured Sever's value as deserters to be dependent on how much other action Wexer's sector had going on. Five squaddies weren't worth redirecting a fleet. Or even a contingent of regulars.

"Primary arms?" Aurora said.

"Personals," Gregor replied. "Everyone has their own collection. Like fighting in a junkyard. They are not coordinated."

"Perfect," Sai said. "Aurora, if we can funnel them here, they won't know how to break our line. I bet once we show them the Talpa aren't the frightened creatures Calico probably told them about, they'll jump back in their skiffs and run."

"Then set up," Aurora said. "Gregor, get refreshed, then come back here. This is going to be the primary point, and we can't let them break through."

Through the entry arch, Aurora could see the occasional long-range laser flash from above. Rovo kept delivering observation reports: the skiffs were closing and, thanks to that laser, were centered right on the mine's main entrance.

DefenseCorp wouldn't take on a strategy like this. The head-on was so obviously bad, and Sever would so obviously have set up to counter it. Unless Tarla and Calico thought so little of the Talpa that they expected to walk in, wipe out, and take over.

"Nothing else that you're hearing, seeing?" Aurora said. "No skiffs breaking off towards a different point?"

"Nothing," Rovo said.

Beside her, Talpa set up behind stacked mine carts and rubble piles, makeshift cover for them to pop from and deliver their snub-nosed rifle blasts. Gregor had returned, was discussing his optimal position with Sai, who stood well back from the barricade, behind one of the skiffs where he could direct Talpa reserves and trigger any explosives he needed.

Wexer's ever-present wind flipped through the archway, whistling in spurts. The bright daylight tangled with the mine's shadows to mix a washed out feel. Still, Aurora felt the tension, saw the twitching Talpa and knew she wasn't about to fight with experienced soldiers.

A citizen army protecting their home. Noble, but perhaps a mistake.

Too late to reconsider anyhow.

In front, a rising dust cloud highlighted the skiffs on approach, bustling up like a rising curtain over a stage. The reddish skiffs emerged—Calico must have emptied his lot —on a straight line towards the archway, their deck guns swiveling towards the barricade.

"Ready!" Aurora shouted, taking Sai's thunder.

Twenty rifles, makeshift and otherwise, took aim. Other Talpa scurried around the walls and ceiling, clutching sharp stones and grenades. The long-range laser took its final shot, a wide miss that fizzled into the blackrock somewhere far behind the skiffs.

On the lead skiff, zipping towards them, Aurora recognized Javelin on the bow gun. He saw her too, but when he pulled the weapon's triggers, the heavy laser swept to Aurora's left, pounding into the barricade and ionizing a cart.

"Fire!" Aurora called. "Aim for the gunners!"

As she shouted the words, Aurora realized with dire absurdity that the Talpa likely couldn't understand them. The creatures squeaked and chittered as the high energy whine from laser fire sprang up around them, so maybe someone parsed her words and sent them along, but just as likely, considering where the snub-nosed rifle shots were hitting—namely, everywhere on the skiffs but the gunners —nobody knew what to do.

Which meant Aurora had to take the defense into her own hands.

"Sai, cover us!" Aurora said into the squad band as the oncoming skiffs swerved into a staggered line across the archways entrance.

The eight remaining skiffs swept their broadsides facing the barricades, the mercenary soldiers swapping between deck guns, small arms fire, and spilling out from the skiffs in a haphazard charge towards the Talpa defense. The creatures fought back, spraying green white energy, throwing rocks and grenades towards the attackers.

Smoke and dust choked the air as Aurora kicked her kinetic boots, along with Gregor, and jumped over the barricade. The Talpa didn't have any defense beyond those stacked mine carts, and if Sever let the attackers get past the barrier, the creatures would find themselves getting roasted in horrifying fashion.

Aurora landed with a bang, the two grenades she'd tossed while loping through the air nestling into the deck of the closest skiff and exploding as Aurora hit the rocky ground. The small bombs hit a power pack in the skiff, causing a blossoming, crackling white nova that ran along the skiff's body before sending its metal bulk blasting everywhere.

Calico's attackers fell, either knocked out from the blast or ducking away from the shrapnel, and Aurora felt the ticks and tacks as metal shards splattered against her armor. Two motley Wexer mercenaries, their haphazard shrouds and modified weapons suggesting bar fight recruits, came at her, one raising a blue-lit ax and the other holding a heavy pistol with both hands.

Aurora stepped into the ax-wielder's charge, catching the man's overheard swing with her left forearm, following through with a punch to the man's chest that knocked him back a meter and sent him crashing, wheezing as breath fled his shocked lungs. Heat saturated Aurora's right side as the pistol man fired, his bolt sinking into her power armor and doing nothing more than leaving a blast stain.

"Have to do better than that," Aurora said, drawing her own pistol and hitting the man with a hard shot to the chest.

He staggered back, raised his weapon, and she pulled her trigger a second time, sending him down to join his friend.

Looking back at the skiffs, Aurora tried to get a sense of the battle's progress. Sai's reports came pouring over the comm, but in the chaos, with the chitters, the explosions, the whines and the screams, Aurora couldn't tell what the hell was going on. Only that more enemies were running through the gaps in the skiffs.

Gaps that could be filled: the first skiff that Aurora's grenades had detonated created a dead zone with its hot fires and sparking remnants. Three skiffs spanned most of the archway, and by blowing those up, the Talpa could create a fiery wall. Maybe buy a retreat from Calico and the others.

Aurora reached for more grenades, when something heavy slammed her from above and drove her to the ground, digging her visor into the blackrock floor. Reacting on instinct, Aurora kicked in the kinetic energy in her arms, restored from the block and punch on the ax man, and pushed herself over. The weight flung off her back, and, staring up, Aurora saw the cause.

Skiff deck guns laced the archway's top with red energy, burning away Talpa up there and dropping them.

The lasers also melted away the rock, sending steaming stones crashing to the ground. The rocky culprit lay next to her leg.

"Sai, Rovo!" Aurora shouted into her wristlet as she kicked away from falling rubble. "Get the Talpa off the ceiling. It's a death trap!"

Getting to her feet, Aurora felt another chunk strike her back, pushing her forward a step. Only this blow hadn't come from above. Aurora whirled, her power armor clanking along with the motion, to see a familiar face staring back at her.

"Betcha thought you got me," Javelin said, those cables still spooling around his arms and legs, grappling gun held in his right hand. "I'm a little too slippery for you, though."

"Are you?" Aurora said. "Let's find out."

Aurora twitched her neck ever so slightly and the back-mounted rifle on her left shoulder whipped around to her grip in a half second. By the full second, Aurora's left hand pressed the trigger, sending bright bolts spraying Javelin's way. He dove to her right, but caught one bolt to the cables along his abdomen, a shot that sliced through the mess and left them tangling as Javelin tried to keep moving.

Keeping her finger on the trigger, Aurora followed Javelin's move, bringing the burning lasers closer. Javelin looked her way as the shots neared, and rather than the panicked eyes Aurora thought she'd see, the man had a wicked smile.

"Too slippery!" Javelin crowed as Aurora caught the rifle up with his chest.

Javelin's left hand, still holding that grappling gun, shifted, and Aurora felt the shock, then the sudden flash as her visor blinked bright red everywhere before shunting black. Her armor locked up, legs and arms no longer responding as Aurora unbalanced, toppled over, and hit the ground.

A close-range EMP. Aurora knew about them, had fought against them, but hadn't expected them here on Wexer. Tarla had been talking with DefenseCorp, and who would know better how to counter their own power armor?

Without her suit's functions, Aurora couldn't feel anything other than the slightest vibrations making their way through her dead exoskeleton. The battle's sounds were muffled. Aurora couldn't hear Sai and Gregor coming in through the squad's band, couldn't hear the chittering Talpa cries.

But she could hear, crystal clear, when Javelin leaned in towards her helmet and whispered, "Guess who's got you now?"

TWENTY-TWO

Burn

SAI FOUND it hard to direct a fight he couldn't see. Stuck in cover behind a Talpa skiff's big butt, Sai snuck looks and the occasional rifle shot at the oncoming DefenseCorp and Calico mercenary force. They'd parked their skiffs just inside the big entryway, staggering the vehicles to give their attackers cover as they streamed towards the Talpa barricade.

Aurora's order to withdraw off the ceiling played out overhead as Talpa dropped down around Sai, some scurrying to the front lines while others fled to prep backstops in the mine. The move would save a lot of Talpa lives while sacrificing a major advantage: without attacks from above, the enemy could sit behind their skiffs and use their superior firepower to chip away at the Talpa cover.

Sai figured those Talpa lives would be lost anyway when the enemy advanced, but he kept quiet. Winning this fight was always going to take a miracle, or extreme measures.

He'd laced the archway with makeshift mines but triggering those explosives could cause half the mine to collapse. Sai would push away the attack, but he'd probably kill as many Talpa as the invaders, and possibly all of Sever too. A last ditch effort, one to use if defeat was inevitable. At least it'd buy time for all the young, old, and non-fighting Talpa to get away.

"Aurora," Sai said. "We need a change. Can I give Eponi the go-ahead?"

A heartbeat and no reply. Sai stuck his head around the skiff, saw only a giant dust cloud with lasers flashing through in either direction. Bodies lingered beneath the smoke, Talpa and otherwise, and the constant shouts and chitters echoed between the laser whines, but Sai couldn't see Aurora. Couldn't see Gregor.

"I'm not getting her," Sai said. "Anyone have eyes on Aurora?"

"Will look," Gregor's reply crackled. "Heavy out here."

"Sai," Rovo came in, his voice clear, with squeaks in the background of the command center. "If Aurora's down, you're up."

Truth. Chain of command hadn't been discussed among Sever since ditching DefenseCorp, but Sai fell next in line. The call was his to make, and he couldn't spend any more time waiting.

"Eponi, bring it around," Sai said. "Don't take too long."

"On it," Eponi replied, her voice clear and clean. "Just remember if this goes sideways, we're stuck."

"If you don't," Sai said, "then we're dead."

Bangs sounded out behind him, and the big skiff lurched, its struts grinding against the ground. Sai took another glance and saw the barricade burning away, struck by grenades, mines, or worse. Talpa streamed back by him in a retreat to the mine's tunnels, where the plan called for a delaying, guerrilla fight while families evacuated out the back.

Their defense hadn't held. Not even long enough for Sai to burn out a power pack on his rifle.

Time to change that.

"I'm covering the retreat," Sai barked. "The sooner help comes, the better."

Peeling off from behind cover, Sai broke into a strafing run towards the other parked Talpa skiff. He fired into the dust, trying to aim where he saw flashes from enemy weapons, trying to keep his shots high enough to miss any Talpa still in the fight. Lasers came back Sai's way as he moved, dodging around retreating Talpa. The bolts struck the ground, the rock walls behind him, and Sai felt the hot sting as molten pebbles blasted off into his skin, burned through his clothes.

The entryway grew hot as the continued fires, lasers, and sheer energy pouring into the space superheated the air. Sai's breaths came hot down his throat, tearing at his lungs as he hit the far skiff, keeping his finger on the rifle's trigger.

"Gregor," Sai rasped. "Position?"

No reply.

"Aurora?"

Silence.

Across the way, towards the skiff Sai had been using, several Talpa scurried by, one with burning fur. A form moved after them, running with a rifle raised and looking to take a shot. Sai raised his weapon, fired, and sent the enemy burning to the ground. The enemy hit dirt, his rifle triggering a few red lasers into the ceiling.

The dying shots drew a response from the entryway, hot fire from skiff deck guns focusing on the Talpa craft, searing into its bow and chewing through the thing until it blew apart. Sai dove to the far side of his skiff, getting the thing's plating between its sister's shrapnel. Smoke, heat, fire swirled everywhere, but Sai pulled himself up, hands burning where they touched the ground, the skiff's hot metal outsides.

A furnace, a charnel pit.

Better, then, to make sure the bad guys went with the good.

"Don't know if anyone can hear me," Sai said, because he damn sure couldn't see anything anymore. "I'm blowing the charges. If you're in the entryway, get out, or good luck."

He swiped the wristlet over to the simple program synced to the devices. A single button would blow the explosives. Take'em all out with Sai.

Not the death he wanted. Not the katana swinging kind, or the old man watching a breeze move the leaves with his grandchildren in his arms. But how often did we get to say goodbye how we imagined?

"Sai, you blow those charges, I'm gonna be so pissed," Eponi's voice sang through. "Cause you'll ruin my moment."

"What?" Sai said, and then he realized something.

He could hear Eponi. Hear her crystal clear. Sure, Sai still burned, his breath still scratched, and the entryway still crackled with burning fires and the shouts of those who'd caught the wrong ends of weapon fire, but that was it: the weapons weren't firing. The constant whine from skiff deck guns had died out. Lasers didn't flash through the smoke.

"I'm saying we're at a stalemate, and I hope you're up for some negotiating, because I'm not leaving this ship."

"Negotiating?"

"It'll be easier if you walk out," Eponi said, "though I'd

keep your hands clear when you do. Can't guarantee one of 'em won't try to blast you."

"You're making this sound like a bad idea," Sai said, saying the words as he sat on the ground, trying to process that he wasn't, actually, going to die.

At least, not yet.

"Just go before they decide to take their chances," Eponi said. "The shields on this thing seem pretty good, but I'm gonna get real upset if your lazy ass gets me shot down."

Sai started to shoot back that, instead of being lazy, he'd been fighting for his life, but wound up sighing instead. Standing, coughing and walking, Sai made his way around the skiff towards the barricade's remnants. The dust and smoke, caught in Wexer's constant breeze, thinned with every passing second. While the clearing air made breathing easier, it made seeing harder.

Sever had taken on this mission to defend the Talpa. They'd wanted to keep the creatures safe, let them run their mine in as much peace as anyone could get in this disaster of a galaxy. Now Sai saw the results: casualties everywhere, wounded and beyond. Grenades, lasers, fiery explosions as power packs and other material superheated in the mine's entry oven. Sever hadn't rescued anything, hadn't saved anyone.

If the Talpa had just taken Calico's offer and left, all these would still be alive, would still be unhurt.

DefenseCorp didn't send squads like Sever on protect and defend missions. They were an assault squad, designed to get in, get out, and destroy what needed destroying on the way. Sai wasn't used to looking at a battle's aftermath and seeing his allies on the suffering side. Wasn't used to seeing allies at all, beyond Sever's armored and super-skilled crew.

"Not a pretty picture, is it?" Tarla's voice broke through as Sai stepped over the smoldering barricade.

The Twilight Ranger captain emerged, first as a gray figure, then as herself, sporting thicker gear than before, with a particularly nasty streamer set on her back. The weapons, able to spew various deadly liquids that could burst into flame, poisonous gas, or acid, weren't too useful outside of situations like this one, with targets clustered into a tight space.

"We didn't cause this," Sai said. "You're the ones that came here, shooting first."

"Did we shoot first?" Tarla replied, coming right up to Sai's face. She looked unharmed, unbothered by the fighting. "The way I remember, your little friends there started shooting at us from a long ways away. And, lest I forget, that pop-up out in the desert? We had dead on our hands before we fired a shot."

"Not every shot comes from a rifle," Sai replied.

He tried to look past Tarla, figure out where Gregor and Aurora were. He hadn't seen their bodies anywhere yet.

"Spare me the sermons," Tarla said. "The best member of your team found a good spaceship and has us pinned outside. I don't want to shoot her down, and I don't want to lose any more of my people." Tarla tapped at Sai's wristlet. "Here's the trade. You're going to call anyone else you have hiding away back there to come out. All of you are going to climb in the skiff I tell you to and come back with us. The Talpa have the rest of the day to get their wounded and clear out of this mine. If they don't, tomorrow we come back, and I'll be looking for my bonus."

"Sounds like a terrible deal for us," Sai said. "I could have Eponi burn you right now."

"You all die if she does," Tarla replied. "We have six skiffs ready to shoot. Even if she takes out half, her ship's going down. You don't have anyone else, and while I've persuaded Calico to accept another day, he'll be too happy to have us start our clean-up right now."

Sai folded his arms, looked at the ground. Sever had wanted to help the Talpa keep their mine, but giving the creatures their lives might be the best the squad could do. That courtesy wouldn't extend to Sever, who would no doubt get tossed to DefenseCorp as soon as Tarla secured a reward.

But the Talpa would live.

"How do I know I can trust you?" Sai said.

"Simple. You want my word, you look at the cash," Tarla said, putting on her flashy smile, one that seemed so, so wrong given the ruin around them. "I'm going to make so much more handing you over to DefenseCorp than Calico would ever pay me. And DefenseCorp wants you alive." Tarla laughed, short and quick. "Guess you found out some things, and they want to make sure you weren't spilling secrets."

Dynas. That had to be it. A virus that didn't work, but that someday might take a human and turn it into whatever DefenseCorp needed for its next contract. Broadcast that around the galaxy, and DefenseCorp might find more than a few opponents among people, and aliens, that didn't like playing test tube with the living.

Sai and Sever had figured the word would get out eventually, that DefenseCorp wouldn't care all that much if it did, but maybe they'd guessed wrong. Maybe the target on their backs was big enough to find them all the way out here.

"Yeah, I see that look," Tarla said. "You know what I'm talking about. So yes or no, bomber guy." Tarla paused, made a sound like she'd just thought of something. "I forgot to mention, we already have Aurora and the burly man with a hammer. So if you're hoping for another last-second rescue, that isn't happening."

"They're alive?"

"For the moment."

Sai, keeping his eyes on Tarla, brought the wristlet up, tapped over to the squad band. With Tarla waiting, he relayed the terms to Eponi and Rovo. The rookie agreed right off, saying that while he didn't like the idea, it was better than getting the Talpa slaughtered. Eponi, though, hesitated.

"Eponi, don't worry," Tarla said, leaning in so her voice would get picked up. "I'm sure DefenseCorp doesn't need all of you."

What the hell did that mean?

"Don't think they need any of us, but I guess this squad always runs by votes," Eponi said, bitterness seeping through. "See, Sai, we could've just kicked the Talpa out before and none of this would've happened."

Tarla nodded, "Would've been the smarter play."

"We chose the better one," Sai said, "because we're not monsters. Land the ship, Eponi. Rovo, tell the Talpa to get going. Tarla, we're yours."

And with that, Sai had surrendered Sever Squad. It felt cold, harsh, free and terrible. A feeling Sai had experienced before:

When he left his family for the last time.

Cell Story

THE RAMPAGE HAD BEEN GOING strong. Gregor had charged over the barricade with his hammer whirling, catching the first attackers in wallops they couldn't take, that had Gregor laughing every time the hammer found a new mark and drove them across the entryway or slapped them into a skiff's hard side. The dust and smoke and fire only helped hide the big man as he moved, his power armor's kinetic boosts taking him past firing fields and deep into Calico's lines.

Until he heard Sai's call for Aurora, Gregor had contented himself as a wrecking ball. Other people could concern themselves with strategy: Gregor had fulfilled that requirement during the ambush. Now he could be pure id. Destruction personified.

But even Gregor couldn't reach those total mindless heights. As good as it felt blitzing hapless mercenaries, when Sai asked for help, Gregor shifted, jumped, and bounced from one enemy skiff to the next, making his way towards the barricades. Aurora wasn't like him, she wouldn't dive deep, because she had to consider things other than the next target.

He came upon his captain dark on the ground, not moving. Next to her, pinging shots towards Talpa fleeing the ceiling, stood Javelin. The man's cables, tarred with dust and rock and laser damage, looked less imposing and more like he'd fallen into an industrial accident. Gregor raised his hammer, pounded closer from behind.

Javelin would smash like any other human.

Gregor's visor lit up red on the right, a sudden flash that had the big man turning, bringing the hammer in a sweeping swing across his body to hit whatever might be coming his way. Except the attack wasn't coming at waist level.

Jumping from the enemy skiff running behind him, Gregor's enemy came in over the hammer blow and tackled Gregor on the shoulder, bearing him to the ground beneath her weight. Through the smoke and the crunch as he hit the ground, Gregor recognized Briany's white hair, and he tried to throw her off.

"Don't bother," Briany said, pressing on Gregor's side. "Toss me, he'll shoot you. Then he'll shoot Aurora, and that won't be any fun for you at all."

Gregor felt his hammer beneath his left arm, its haft squeezed against the ground by his armor. Useless. Briany had his right arm pinned, and she had her legs planted on the back side of his, away from any kicks.

The woman knew how to fight.

"This isn't fun either," Gregor replied as something exploded nearby, heat and dust washing over them.

"Right?" Briany said. "I saw you tearing through those bums over there. Calico hired them off the streets over the last couple days, once DC said they weren't sending their good guys in. Was jealous. They deserved to get smacked."

"Why are you helping them, then?" Gregor asked, trying to get a bead on Aurora, see why she wasn't moving.

"Because the pay's too good to pass up," Briany replied. "We all need cash, Gregor. We're not evil, we're just pragmatic. And, if I'm being honest, I love this."

"That's what she said?" Sai shook his head as Gregor spoke. "They're all terrible."

Sever Squad, all five, sat cramped in one of the heavy skiffs. Neither Gregor nor Aurora had their power armor on, nobody had weapons, and all looked like Wexer's dust had sand-blasted their minds. Rovo and Eponi, at least, didn't wear the scuffs, scratches, and battle scars, though Gregor preferred the sore limbs, the grit in his mouth and the sting above his left eye where he'd smacked his head when Briany tackled him: power armor helmets weren't well padded on the inside.

"They're fighters, like us," Gregor said. "She was doing her job."

"The job we should've been doing," Eponi said.

"Quit whining," Aurora snapped. "It's too late to change anything. Focus on how we can get out of here."

Escape? Gregor looked around the slit-windowed skiff as it cruised the canyon back towards the city. All five of them wore stun cuffs, the electrified metal sitting tight around their hands, ready to knock out their nerves if they tried anything. Gregor had used the tools on his own prisoners, back when he did DC police work, enough times to know the cuffs had their faults: for one, if you managed to slip some cloth or deadening fabric between the skin and the metal, the stunning didn't work.

Even if Tarla's crew hadn't cut away their sleeves, cutting the stun would still leave them bound. Gregor gave himself a lotta points in a fight, but cuffed and going against an armed, skilled mercenary group?

A fast way to wind up where they were going slow.

Nobody stood watch on the skiff. A locked door blocked Sever off, though Gregor would bet cameras kept eyes on the crew from somewhere. Besides, where would they go if Gregor could punch through the wall? Stumble into Wexer's desert, weaponless, cashless, and lost?

"They even took our wristlets." Eponi rubbed the red, pale patch on her left forearm where the computer had been attached. "Can't even watch something."

Rovo, across from Gregor, leaned his head back against the skiff. His left ear had a red, bloody trickle running down from it where Perro had torn out the Bug. They hadn't forgotten about the device from the run-up to the mine, and as soon as the rookie had made his way to the mine's exit, Perro ripped the thing from him. He'd been about to smash it until Tarla stopped the sniper, said DefenseCorp wanted anything that might hold answers.

For what? Tarla wouldn't say.

"Do you think DC will let us send goodbyes?" Sai asked the room. "I've never seen what happens to deserters."

Neither had Gregor. Sever hadn't been a hunter squad.

"You'll get nothing," Aurora said, softer now, letting her head and those brilliant red bangs flop towards the floor. "They'll mark us as KIA and keep it that way. DC doesn't want anyone to know people run away."

"Will they just shoot us?" Rovo asked, his voice as dead as he looked, as if a computer were asking the question.

"Don't know," Aurora said.

"Tarla mentioned DefenseCorp wanting to ask us questions," Sai replied. "We'll get a chance to talk, and *then* they'll stick us in the ground."

"It'll be an airlock," Aurora said. "They'll dump us

outside the space lanes or into a star's gravity well. No evidence."

"You make it sound like we're the worst people who ever lived," Eponi gave a dire chuckle. "Like we're monsters or something."

Gregor cracked his knuckles, "To them, maybe we are."

Who 'them' was, Gregor and the rest of Sever found out several hours later. Wexer's evening brought the five from the skiff, escorted by Tarla's crew while Calico's other mercenaries dispersed until the next day. The Talpa's clock had started, not that Sever needed to worry about that anymore.

"This is your new home," Tarla said, opening a large cell door in the basement of the tower, so Sai and Eponi said, they'd broken into not long ago. "Don't get too used to it."

As cells went, this one had space. Benches lined the smooth walls. A courtesy toilet and privacy shield sat in one corner, though a small device set in the ceiling above would fire a stunning shot if anyone did anything beyond their business. Sleep would come on the hard ground, a prospect not all that worrisome after spending those nights in the mine.

At least this would be flat. And quiet. There were no other cells in the basement, confirming Gregor's suspicion that DefenseCorp wanted the option to hold anyone wanted for something, but didn't think Wexer as a criminal hive worth the investment.

Tarla held the gate open as they all shuffled past, with Eponi taking a long moment, last in line, to enter. She looked at Tarla, who frowned, shook her head, and ran a single finger down Eponi's cheek.

"Sorry," Tarla said. "The people paying wanted all of

you. I couldn't catch a break." She pushed Eponi through, shut the gate and locked it. "DefenseCorp's going to be taking over from here on out. Can't say it's been a pleasure, can't say it's been a bad time. Aurora, sorry it has to end like this. Would've liked working with you."

"Shove it, Tarla," Aurora said.

"So spicy," Tarla laughed, shrugged. "Bye bye, Sever Squad."

"She talks too much," Gregor said as Tarla found the lift—no stairs, to keep things more secure—and vanished.

"Always has," Aurora said.

When the lift doors opened later, Sever looked over as one. Given the time interstellar travel required, they all expected some days would go by before a hunter squad landed on Wexer and went about their bloody business. But here stood a man all done up in his regional, crimson DefenseCorp uniform, carrying a large, royal blue case in his left hand.

The officer didn't say a word as he walked up to the door, touched his wristlet to the gate, which unlocked its black metal bars for him. Gregor sought Aurora's eyes, caught her head's slight nod. If the man came close enough to get a strike before the stun cuffs, Gregor ought to take it.

However the man didn't step through the gate. Rather, he placed the blue case just inside, laying it flat and then tapping on the upward-facing side. Like a mechanical, budding flower, the case opened. A thin chrome bar rose up from inside the case, like a stem, and when it hit a meter in height, the bar split. The thin right and left sides swung open, creating a rectangle with the chrome bar's front half forming the top and bottom, while its back kept the straight up-and-down spine.

A slight whine came from the case, and Gregor thought

he saw tiny blue sparks shimmer off the bar's edges. A faint gray, like fine mist, filled in the space between both bars, before picking up color, depth, and sound. A face filled in the center. Human, with wrinkles smoothed over through surgeries, wispy white hair at the roots passing into deep brown at the ends. Eyes that seemed to shift color even as Gregor watched, as though unable to decide what shades they wanted to be.

The face rested atop a pressed black collar, the barest hint of DefenseCorp's crimson beneath it. Behind the face, around it in the image, sat a static star field, nebula and cosmic formations splattered across the black. Gregor had seen those before: field maps for DefenseCorp, covering the galaxy and all the company's forces.

He'd never seen this man. Never once.

Gregor would've remembered the cover-ups. The coward's stain that came through even from here, from wherever the man stood all the way into Sever's cell. This one wanted to hide his past, and in doing so, had let himself be marked by it.

"Sever Squad," the man spoke in smokey rolls, a voice that'd no doubt been as stitched together as the rest of him. "I never imagined I'd say those words. I didn't even know you existed until a few weeks ago. Funny how the most insignificant people can cause the biggest problems."

The man looked off camera for a moment.

"Who the hell are you?" Rovo asked.

"It's a recording," Aurora said as the man nodded to his off-camera partner. "They'd never get a live signal going this fast."

"Aurora, Rovo, Eponi, Sai, and Gregor," the man said. "An odd collection of names, but I suppose one of DefenseCorp's many features is its diversity. Which is why I am so disappointed that you decided to leave us, and in such a sudden way. We all wished you well after your supposed deaths that we were so hurt when you reappeared, alive and healthy."

"Who's this 'we'?" Sai asked. "Does anyone know this guy?"

"No," Aurora said, echoing the head shakes around the room.

"—everyone you've been in contact with since your mission to Dynas. You will tell us, or we will assume all of your family and friends have been informed and will deal with them as we are going to deal with you." The man shook his head. "Deserters must pay a final price, of course, but you knew that. This is simply how things ought to be. Aurora, Rovo, Eponi, Sai, Gregor. Don't let your families suffer for your mistakes. Reclaim what little dignity you have left, and do what's right."

The image shimmered, faded, and the bars folded and collapsed back into the case. The officer picked up the device, turned and, shutting the gate behind him, left.

"All that just to tell us we're going to die?" Rovo said. "Really? And I still don't know why they didn't use a normal screen."

"Because," Aurora said. "That wasn't a normal message. Those cases, they're for the heaviest secrets. Dedicated bands, satellites. You're not going to catch that crawling the normal frequencies."

"Okay," Rovo continued. "Why, though?"

Aurora shook her head. Eponi shrugged and Sai looked at the floor. Gregor kept his eyes on the gate, where that too-smooth face had been shining a moment before. Rovo had it right, there wasn't a reason to record a personal message before an obvious execution. To ratchet up the threats.

Unless.

Gregor clenched his fists, "Because he is afraid."

"Of what?"

"Us."

TWENTY-FOUR

Escape Plan

THE SMOOTH-FACED VISION spoke at them, Gregor muttered something about fear, and Eponi felt the cuffs on her wrists and tried to figure out why. How. Despite a string running across the galaxy partaking in kart racing and the inevitable, legally dubious parties to that enterprise, Eponi had never found herself on a cell's wrong side.

As strange as the weight on her wrists felt, though, the image she couldn't shake, even as Eponi threw in token comments to Sever's ongoing discussion, was Tarla's look. The final one the mercenary captain had given Eponi before the gentle shove into the cell. Eponi had seen that look before, knew the burn, the embarrassment, the damn failure directed at *her*.

When Eponi had crashed out on Farlane Twelve, a beautiful world reserved for leisurely retreats and break-neck races, she'd received calls. From her manager, from her team owner, from, eventually, fans and reporters asking questions Eponi didn't want to answer. Didn't want to face from a hospital bed.

Eponi had been close, so close, all those looks said.

She'd almost won, almost achieved everything those simpering eyes, the soft frowns, the barely hidden sighs said in those goodbyes.

The last time Eponi had seen those looks, she'd lost her career. Been cut adrift only to stumble, in a hazy morning some weeks later, by a DefenseCorp office advertising a need for pilots. Low on funds, low on morale, and low on life, Eponi had figured getting shot at would provide enough of a shock to wake her up, or at least end it quick.

And now she'd found herself at hope's end again. Another lost chance. Maybe Tarla had hoped Eponi would be the Twilight Ranger's next pilot. Maybe Tarla had hoped Eponi would be a friend, maybe even more. Now, none of that. Now, she'd failed—

"Eponi, you here?" Aurora asked, and the sound of her name jolted Eponi, blinked her back to the grim cell and its . . . not-so-grim occupants?

"I'm here," Eponi offered, trying and failing to recall the conversation she'd been missing. "I wasn't for a while."

"We gathered that," Rovo said.

"But you're here now," Aurora said. "I need you to stay with me, Eponi."

"I'm here, I said."

"No, look," Aurora pointed to her sharp blue eyes. "I don't care about whatever that was with Tarla. I don't care about whatever's pulling you away in your head. I need you to focus."

You know, for all her gruff, Aurora could really be a loving, caring—nope. Eponi shrugged, kept her focus on Aurora's face like the captain wanted. The woman had zero empathy, but Eponi had lost the energy to push back on Aurora right now. The stun cuffs had a way of cutting out her will.

"All right, I'm focusing." Eponi tried, failed to keep the sarcasm out.

"So here's what we're going to do," Aurora said. "You're the smallest of us."

"Thanks."

"You're welcome. I think, with your wrists, Rovo can use his mouth to tear off some more cloth from your arms," Aurora continued, her voice as level as if she were briefing a mission, not describing a ludicrous escape strategy. "Then, we'll slip that cloth around your wrists and use it to break the stun cuffs. Then you slip out."

"Don't know if I'm that thin."

"It might cost you some skin, but it's the only way I can see us getting out of here before DefenseCorp gets us."

Eponi glanced at Rovo, who clacked his teeth together like some sick toy.

"Have you all lost your minds?" Eponi looked at Gregor and Sai. The former just kept staring at the floor, and Sai raised his eyebrows.

"Look at where we are, Eponi," Sai said. "Things are going to get a little weird."

"Can you scoot over this way?" Rovo said. "I need a better angle."

This was insane. Stupid. Eponi scooted along the bench, getting her skinsuit sleeve, currently torn off at the elbow, into as good a spot as she could imagine for Rovo to tear it with his teeth.

"This doesn't fall under my list of badass escapes," Eponi muttered as Rovo leaned in.

"Definitely on mine," Rovo said, his voice muffled as he closed on her sleeve.

The lift dinged open, spitting out two DefenseCorp squaddies. At a glance, Eponi saw their low ranks, standard, unadorned crimson uniforms and wasn't surprised:

Wexer wouldn't be a place for quality soldiers. They ran to the cell like it contained diamonds instead of five dirty deserters.

The lead, a greased-over gumbo who'd held his own at too many buffet lines, slapped his wristlet into the cell gate so hard that it dinged out. The other, shouting for Rovo to stop in a scratchy voice that spoke to more bar nights than bedtimes, lingered behind, seemingly content to point fingers.

Rovo did not stop. Eponi felt the slightest tug on her sleeve, such a mild pull that Rovo would never get any fabric that way. Either the rookie didn't actually know how to bite off clothes—understandable—or . . .

Gumbo barreled towards Rovo, sitting across from Aurora at the cell's back, and as he ran, Eponi saw his eyes go wide as the man's legs flew out from under him. Gumbo flailed forward, cracking down on the hard rock. Gumbo managed a moan, his arms slowly shoveling along the ground.

"What'd you do?" Squeaky, the other guard, demanded.

"He fell," Aurora said. "We didn't do anything. Looks like he might be bleeding though."

"What?" Squeaky said, moving to the cell's door.

"I'm saying you ought to get him to a doctor," Aurora said, authority hitting every word like a hammer. "Now."

"Uh, right. That's what I was going to do," Squeaky said, coming into the cell towards the moaning Gumbo. "You all stay still now."

Squeaky made it to Gumbo, leaned low over him, asked if the guard was all right.

Then Gregor smashed Squeaky from behind, letting the guard join Gumbo on the ground.

Sever broke into action as one, no orders necessary.

Eponi and Rovo dove down on Gumbo while Sai and Aurora went for Squeaky, checking pockets for keys to the stun cuffs. Gregor, keeping his hands low so the cuffs wouldn't trigger, went to the cell's gate and stood in its path to stop any remote systems from slamming the door shut.

Eponi's fingers dug into Gumbo's belt loops, and, sure enough, found the smooth, plastic remote that, while pressed and pointed, would short the circuit on any target stun cuffs.

"Got one," Eponi said, pulling back with the prize. She aimed it at Rovo, pressed on the light red button smacked into a pearly shell. Rovo's cuffs lost their light blue glow first, then popped off and hit the ground. "See? Much easier than biting off my sleeve."

"Indeed," Aurora said as Eponi turned to her next. "It's almost as if the sleeve wasn't the plan at all."

Yeah, yeah. Eponi had connected those dots as soon as Gumbo had played the charging card. Aurora, Sai, and Gregor, Sever's old guard, if you wanted to call it such a thing, played with these damn hand signals all the time. Eponi could read some of 'em now, and Rovo had mentioned, back on Dynas, that Aurora and Gregor had pulled a move using the fingers. Aurora's speech had probably spooked the guards, and Rovo's biting attempts had made it convincing, all while Gregor had been prepping for the ambush.

"Next time we're not fighting for our lives, you're gonna teach me all those," Rovo said.

"I think they like it," Eponi said, as she passed the button to Rovo, who zapped off her cuffs. "They think it's cool."

"It is cool," Gregor said, from the cell doors.

Freed from their cuffs, Sever left the cell and headed towards the lift, only to find its buttons dark.

"Apparently they're not all as dumb as those two," Eponi said, glancing back at Squeaky and Gumbo. She'd followed Aurora last from the cell, shutting the gate behind them and locking the two guards inside. "Other ideas?"

Squeaky and Gumbo, at least, had pistols on them. So now Sever had two weapons to work with. Not that being armed helped overmuch when they were trapped in a basement.

"They'll have to come get us eventually," Sai said. "We could wait them out."

Aurora dismissed that with a head shake, "They could use gas, set up a trap, any number of things. We can't wait."

Set up a trap. Hmm. Eponi held out her hand towards Sai, who had one of the pistols. The demolitionist stared for a second before giving over the weapon. Eponi turned, aimed, and fired once, twice, three times. Each red bolt incinerated a black, camera-hosting nub.

If this had been a true, high tech facility, Eponi wouldn't have been able to see, much less shoot, the cameras and worse watching them. Once again, Wexer's outlier status paid dividends.

"Now they can't see us," Eponi said. "Which means we get to try my idea."

"Your idea?" Rovo asked. "What, have you done a lot of escaping?"

"I've done a lot of crashing," Eponi replied, looking around the basement, hunting for what she needed. "Half the time, your kart goes down, you're not in an easy spot to get help. You take the bubble that saved you and find a way to get into the open."

Rovo did not looked convinced that kart crashing was relevant to a prison break, but hey, it wasn't Eponi's job to get Rovo to believe her.

It was to get Sever out.

"The weakest spot in the walls are going to be right there," Eponi pointed left of the lift doors, where the wall went behind the cell. "The lift shaft's on the other side. Not just rock."

"So?" Rovo continued his questioning looks, but Aurora nodded, flicked her eyes to Gregor.

The big man brushed by Eponi, sized up the blackrock wall next to the lift doors, "This will hurt."

"Sorry," Eponi said. "It'll be the best way."

"I was talking to the wall."

Oh.

Gregor backed up several steps and, with Sever all clearing back, lowered his shoulder. The charge lasted less than a second, but ended with a crunching, plastered cracking. For the fiftieth time, Eponi coughed as she breathed in Wexer's infernal dust, but as the fit subsided and the dust cleared, a Gregor-sized hole sat in the wall, leading right to the lift shaft.

"See?" Eponi said. "Just like I said."

Gregor stepped back out, his left shoulder hanging limp, "Help?"

Aurora went over, "Ready?"

"Do it."

Gregor grimaced ever-so-slightly as Aurora popped the dislocated shoulder back into its socket. Feeling a little disgusted at the sight, a little thrilled that she'd crawled some from the dark place she'd been not too many moments ago, Eponi ducked through the hole into the rubble-strewn shaft's base.

A big magnet sat on the ground, no doubt dead now. Looking up, the shaft extended several stories, the lift's dirty black underside filling it a couple floors above. A sea green maintenance ladder climbed the far side, lit up by red diodes.

"And there it is," Eponi said, nodding to the ladder as Sever squeezed in behind her. "Our way out."

As if answering Eponi, the magnet at her feet activated, its hum filling the shaft. A click-chunk from above drew Sever's eyes up.

The lift moved.

Down.

TWENTY-FIVE

Arming Up

SEVER SQUAD DIDN'T FAIL, and therefore Rovo, being a part of Sever Squad, didn't fail either. That's what'd powered his moves on Dynas, picking up Kaia and running for it, standing up for the Talpa against hard odds. Rovo ought to fight for the good side of things because he was part of an invincible squad that could only succeed no matter what stepped into their path.

And yet, while he sat in that cell with the stun cuffs on his wrists, Rovo couldn't help but brood over how he'd pulled himself to this sorry spot after, as his father put it, achieving a stable career orbiting above a pretty-if-dull planet. Sure, Rovo had cracked Helix communications, had saved Kaia, and had bought the Talpa some more time to evacuate, but was all that worth his life?

Biting Eponi's sleeve proved to be a brilliant distraction from those thoughts, and Rovo had turned to the escape attempt with a dire gusto. They were dead anyway, so why not take the most extreme plan and run with it: blast their way from a DefenseCorp base and take on the galaxy?

"The lift!" Eponi shouted, and Rovo's first instinct was to laugh at the descending metal box.

As if a lift, of all things, would be Sever's end.

Gregor pushed Rovo out through the wall's hole, the rookie stumbling backwards after Sai. Rovo's foot caught on the cutout and he fell back, Gregor stepping over Rovo, then reaching down and pulling the rookie away as the lift settled into place.

"Did you want to die?" Gregor said. "Or are you that slow?"

"Both?" Rovo said, starting to pick himself up from the floor as the lift doors opened.

Four DefenseCorp personnel, wearing office-grade vests and wielding pistols like they'd never really used them, streamed from the lift. They shouted a whole mess at Gregor, Rovo, and Sai as the trio backed up across the cell's front towards the room's opposite wall. Something about dropping weapons they didn't have, freezing, and falling to the floor all at the same time.

Every person had a certain purpose, a situation for which they are perfectly suited and that reaches out to call them when it arrives. Rovo felt that pull, looking into those four frightened faces. He was the communications officer for Sever. Now was his time.

"Hey, hey," Rovo said, sliding over and just in front of Gregor and Sai. "Slow down for a second. We don't have any weapons. We're not going to hurt you."

The leader, whether by vote or, given his wild eyes, adrenaline, gestured towards the ground with the pistol, "Then get on the floor. On the floor!"

"Whoa," Rovo said. "Have you seen how dirty this floor is? Calm down, let's talk."

"Shoot him!" said one of 'em from the back.

"I'm gonna, if they don't get down now," the lead man said.

"Careful," Rovo replied, forcing that calm into his voice. "You wouldn't want to spoil DefenseCorp's prized prisoners, would you?"

"I—" the lead man looked puzzled for a moment, trying to solve the impossible logic between killing Sever and pleasing his superiors.

Red bolts flashed. The DefenseCorp crew shouted, turned, died. Rovo winced.

Behind them, Aurora and Eponi walked from the lift, holding their captured pistols ready in case any of the targets weren't really down. Rovo looked at the bodies, sighed. Gregor and Sai went around him, picked up weapons from people who no longer needed them.

"You know," Rovo said to nobody, "I felt we were really connecting."

"Arm up," Aurora said, getting back to the lift and standing in between the doors. "Let's go."

Sever piled into the lift, each now carrying a pistol and an ID badge that'd hopefully work to let them through any other locked doors they encountered. Aurora sorted the plan as the lift doors closed:

Get out from the base by whatever means necessary.

Grab a skiff or some other ship.

Dash back to the mine, find where Eponi parked the *Prisa* and blitz off-world before anyone figured out where they'd gone.

"Then what?" Eponi asked as the lift rose to the first floor. "We keep running?"

"No," Aurora said, not turning around as the doors clunked open. "Gregor called it. DefenseCorp's scared of us, and we're going to find out why."

Dim lights met them off the lift, buttressed by the blinking alarms scattered throughout. Fire, gas, and prisoner escapes, apparently. By Rovo's internal clock, Wexer's local time had to be hitting late evening now, so there probably weren't too many people here anyway. Four had the guts to go down and fight Sever. The rest had done the smart thing and ran.

"There's only the front door," Eponi said.

"Then lead away," Aurora replied. "Eyes sharp. As soon as word gets out that we're not in the cell, we're going to have anyone hunting cash after us."

"Well isn't that awesome," Rovo cracked.

Comedy would get him through this, if nothing else.

Eponi opened the base's front door, leading them into a barren courtyard beneath Wexer's creamy twilight. The wall spread around them, the hole where Sai had placed his mines and detonated them papered over with signs declaring no entry. The main gate was shut. No guards offered themselves, no fire rained down upon them.

Sai started cursing anyway, with Gregor and Eponi joining in. Rovo followed their eyes upward, expecting to see a drone, maybe a small ship. What Rovo didn't see? Stars.

A glittering oval descended overhead, large enough to cover the courtyard. Its edges still glowed orange from the ship's atmospheric entry, the heat dissipating like a shimmering cloak. Rovo recognized the shape and its deadly purpose, and he added his own epithet to the conversation.

DefenseCorp patrol craft existed for one reason: to menace and destroy.

Rovo hadn't seen one in action, but he'd read the reports. Bristling with weapons and packed with troops, the ships were meant to annihilate any local resistance. The kind of things sent in when peace talks had collapsed and DefenseCorp wanted to show the other side their mistake.

"Don't stand there," Aurora said. "Run."

They sprinted towards the blown wall, Eponi and Aurora's speed getting them there ahead of everyone else. The two women hit the hole, went through. Sai came next, but as the demolitionist neared the gap, huge red rays lanced down. Not pistol lasers, but fatter, burning things that forced Rovo and Gregor to pull up, to fall back as they immolated the ground in front of them.

The burning beams blasted the earth, kicking up molten blackrock, setting the stone wall on fire, and nearly blinding Rovo even as he turned away. Cracks, pops, and hisses whistled out as air superheated and burst from the patrol craft's fire. Rovo felt Gregor's hand on his shoulder, pulling the rookie along back towards the base. The laser fire followed them, boiling the courtyard until Rovo followed Gregor back inside, slamming the door behind him.

Gregor whipped a shroud left behind on the rack near the door and swatted Rovo's head, buffeting it hard again and again.

"Hey! What the hell?" Rovo cried, reeling back.

The big man pulled back, looked at Rovo's incredulous face, and nodded, "Your hair was on fire."

"What?" Rovo reached up, felt stiff, charred locks, and saw bits of burnt hair drift down around his eyes. "Oh."

Guess he wouldn't be getting that modeling gig any time soon.

Gregor glanced up through the tower and Rovo followed the look. Thus far, the patrol craft hadn't opened fire on the base itself. The ship could've melted the building without much issue. For that matter, Rovo and Gregor shouldn't be alive at all.

"Why didn't it kill us?" Rovo said, turning back around, cracking open the front door, then shutting it again after seeing the molten ruin outside. He never realized that rock could burn quite that hot. "They had us in the open."

"They don't know," Gregor said, walking further into the base. "Dynas. They are protecting it."

"Still?" Rovo said. "At some point, they'll just pull the trigger on us. They've got to."

Gregor nodded, still hunting for something in that office, "We have to be ready before then."

"Sure, except we're stuck in DefenseCorp's crappiest base, without a way to contact any of the others, if they're even alive."

"I have seen worse."

"Have you, Gregor?" Rovo said, joining his squadmate in the office center. "Tell me, where have you seen worse?"

"There," Gregor said, and went moving through the desks.

"There?" Rovo flung out his arms in a shrug. "Okay, you don't like offices, but to say a desk job is worse than—oh. I get it now."

Gregor had marched up to a locked, heavy door. A sign on the outside designated the room as *Equipment*. Holding up the stolen badge, Gregor again nodded as the door clicked open. With a light push, Gregor moved the door aside and revealed, well, to use words Rovo used to read in novel after novel burned during the dull days in orbit, a treasure trove.

DefenseCorp had standard allotments for every base, targeted to the world's size and contract potential. Wexer was small, so the armaments in the equipment room weren't vast, but for two people? The half-dozen rifles, grenades, and protective gear meant to outfit an ad hoc squad for a paid mission or two were more than enough.

But the real prize hung at the back, stuffed away there

and tagged with labels not to use. Aurora's black and white power armor stood next to Gregor's, and in between?

"How is it you always find your damn hammer?" Rovo said, glancing at the rifles and trying to decide which one to take. "It's like the thing calls you."

"Maybe it does," Gregor said, moving his power armor over and stepping inside it.

Rovo looked at himself for a long second, contemplated whether he could fit inside Aurora's armor. The suit would reject him, but Rovo had Sever's override codes. It'd be tight, but maybe . . .

Not too long ago, Rovo thought he'd failed the Talpa. Failed his family and his own moral code. Now, a chance glimmered. A way to take back the momentum. To change the equation. To—

"Are you going to try, or are you going to stare at it?" Gregor said, hefting his hammer and creaking by Rovo to grab two rifles, some grenades. "I am leaving soon, rookie."

"Okay, okay," Rovo replied.

He took a long, deep breath as he stepped up to the speckled white and black suit. When he touched his fingers to the suit's wrist, the armor beeped a stern warning, telling him in clear mechanical terms that this device did not belong to Rovo.

So Rovo fed the suit Sever's override code, a series of jumbled numbers that Rovo had, during some idle time back on the *Nautilus*, cracked as Aurora's home system coordinates, reversed. The suit took the input, beeped an affirmative, and a silver-green light lanced out from the popped helmet's back. The light ran over Rovo, and as it did, Aurora's armor started to shift.

The suits couldn't change much—Gregor, for example, was never gonna find a way inside Aurora's armor—but the arms and legs let out their vents and squeezed out a few extra centimeters. The chest expanded as it might in watery missions where floating mattered.

"Maximum size reached," the armor chirped.

"Maximum? Really?" Rovo patted his stomach. "I'm not that outta shape."

"Let's go," Gregor rumbled from the exit.

"I'm going, I'm going," Rovo said, stepping into the suit.

Pinches, pokes, and pains pierced Rovo all over as Aurora's armor clasped itself too tight around his arms, his stomach, his neck. The helmet felt like Rovo was squeezing his head in a vice. But, the suit powered up and on. Rovo tested a step, found he could move. There'd be bruises, cuts, and sore muscles on the other side, but all those beat being dead.

"Now, we go find the skiff," Gregor said as they stomped back into the office.

"Wrong," Rovo replied. "I mean, we'll do that anyway, but there's somewhere we need to go first."

"What?"

"I made a promise, Gregor," Rovo said. "I said we'd help the Talpa, and I'm not leaving until we do. We're going after Calico."

"That's against orders."

"It's a detour, is all," Rovo pointed to Gregor's hammer. "Besides, you said they're scared of us. Don't you want to prove them right?"

TWENTY-SIX

Retreat

YOU WANT to be a squad leader for DefenseCorp, you had to be lucky. Survive until you managed a battlefield promotion, a singular instant where the command chain broke down and you stepped in, completed the task, kept your squadmates alive. A rare few times you'd get a retirement, with the captain throwing up a caustic single-fingered salute to DefenseCorp before walking away with whatever severance they could manage, leaving you armed and in charge of an unruly bunch hunting for cash by the bloodiest means possible.

Aurora had been one of those hunters, had spent time under squad leaders more concerned about their own survival than the mission, the mission than their squad, and sometimes, the very rarest, the squad over everything else.

That last had stuck with her, had been Aurora's own gateway into Sever's leadership. Similar styles, similar drive, and a similarly awesome skillset had slotted Aurora to be the follow-up after her last captain took the high road out, walking away while he still could and leaving Aurora in control of a squad with a newfound reputation for hard, out-of-bounds missions.

Isolated, without back-up or DefenseCorp's customary overwhelming force, Sever and Aurora had to rely on each other. Had to trust without question. Had to be willing to adapt when disaster struck, rather than huddling up and hoping for help.

But when the patrol craft immolated the wall, silhouetting Sai in its barrage so that he came through the hole burning from the laser's proximity, Aurora really wanted to hide. Really wanted to back away and run.

Instead, she and Eponi smothered Sai's burning clothes with dirt, patted him out as best they could. The skinsuit did its work, keeping Sai safe from the worst of the flames, though burns littered his neck and arms, where the suit didn't cover.

"I've seen worse after wrecks," Eponi said as they pulled Sai along the alley towards the main street, hugging the building's side. "You'll be fine."

"Good, because I don't feel that way."

"If we see someone with medical supplies," Aurora said, "we'll grab them. Until then, I need you to focus. Both of you."

The patrol craft continued laying down fire, but for now the laser blitz plastered the courtyard.

"Rovo, Gregor," Sai said, frustrated pain hissing through the names. "What about them?"

"They'll catch up," Aurora replied as they reached the street. Any crowd that would've been mixing it up in the evening had scattered, shouts to run falling away from their spot. "We have to stick to the plan."

Without any way to communicate to the others, any deviation from getting to the skiff, the mine, the ship would put Rovo and Gregor in a terrible spot. They could manage to dodge away from the patrol craft only to find themselves alone among the skiffs, or back at the mine without a way to pilot the *Prisa*.

"Glad you're so worried about Rovo and Gregor," Eponi said as the trio stuck to the building wall, staying in the alley. "Maybe, though, we think about us for a hot second here? We've got no cover, crap weapons, and a big dangerous ship over our heads."

"Do you have ideas?" Aurora asked.

"Actually," Eponi countered. "Yeah, I do." She pointed across the street, towards what looked like an evacuated restaurant, one catering to the DefenseCorp employees that'd be milling through here. "See those tanks?"

Opposite them, in another alley running behind the restaurant, sat a couple large gas tanks. Relics of a fringe world like Wexer that hadn't climbed to perfect solar adoption. The white-and-red lumps played host to explosive fuel, and sat waiting to be used for eggs, sandwiches, and whatever else the restaurant offered.

"Blow'em up and run?" Sai said. "In a civilian center?"

Those were DefenseCorp regulations talking. Burning down cities tended to ruin business relationships, so DefenseCorp took a dim view towards squads that practiced total warfare in populated streets. Sever, though, didn't need to follow those rules.

And yet . . .

"We destroy those fuel tanks, that block's going to be ruined," Aurora said. "Who knows if anyone's living in there, whose lives we'd be destroying."

Above, the patrol craft cut off its bombardment, settling lower. New lights appeared along its lower bulge, bays opening for ground troops. Aurora had made drops like that before, diving into hostile territory with a thousand guns at your back. Exhilarating to have superior fire-power on your side.

Less so when you were the target.

"Hello?" Eponi said. "This is your squadmate speaking. Now is no time to grow a conscience!"

"We've already made enough enemies." Aurora confirmed the dropping troops, the ones waiting for their own jumps. "Let's go. They won't risk shooting while they're unloading."

Eponi swore, but Aurora grabbed Sai and turned around the corner, cutting into the street and staying as close to the side as possible. Hoping that the patrol craft wouldn't fire did not, in fact, stop the ship from letting loose a laser stream. The bolts lanced down from frontal batteries at bad angles to catch runners along the ground, but the superheated energy slammed into the rock ahead of Aurora, bubbling and smoking the street.

Storefronts crackled as lasers slammed down. Over-hangs burned as stray fire struck the shrouds. The street's center buckled, shimmering in the heat as Aurora flung her hands in front of her face, shielding her eyes. She felt hands around her waist as Sai grabbed her, pulled Aurora back.

"Inside!" Sai shouted, and Eponi fired her pistol into the real estate office's front door, burning off the lock and letting them duck into the squat center Eponi had been on top of not even a day ago.

"Great idea captain," Eponi said, crouching inside the door, keeping her eyes on the window while Aurora caught her breath. "Didn't realize you wanted to get cooked so bad."

Aurora wanted to deliver the kind of hard discipline her training called for. Insubordinate talk like Eponi's could, according to DefenseCorp guidelines, corrode morale. Destroy authority. Break cohesion in dire situations where the squad needed it most.

"You're right," Aurora said, taking a deep breath. Outside, the patrol craft killed its firing spree, leaving burning shops and buildings, adding their orange halos to Wexer's night. "I didn't think they'd be that aggressive."

"Maybe Gregor's more right than we thought," Sai said, peering around the building, lit up by the fires outside. "They'll risk anything to keep us from getting away."

"Doesn't mean we won't," Aurora said. "Those drop troopers will be on us in a second. I'd rather not be here when they arrive."

The real estate building didn't offer much help, unless Aurora decided to be interested in bare blackrock patches. As for developed buildings, given the giant DefenseCorp craft outside spraying lasers around, who knew which would still be standing by morning?

Except, across the long middle section and past some offices, a door, plain and unmarked, sat in the far wall. A rear exit, and a chance.

"C'mon," Aurora said. "Eponi, take back. Sai, you're behind me."

Holding her pistol ready, Aurora led the others through the office, past the posters showcasing Wexer's creamy rivers, its canyons, mountains, and soaring starships. All parts of a planet they hadn't seen and, likely, never would. The continual price paid being a mercenary: Aurora would see everywhere, and visit nowhere.

Behind them, barked orders carried through the real estate building's few windows, all blown out by the laser fire's concussive force. The signals sounded familiar, the code words falling into a lexicon Aurora knew well: DefenseCorp opting for a containment strategy, circling through the blocks around here and falling in slowly to trap Sever in their center.

"Hear that?" Sai said as they pulled up at the back door.

"Hear it, but we're going to beat it," Aurora replied. "Ready up."

She put her right hand on the door handle—one clue the door wasn't meant for regular use? It had a literal handle—and Aurora pulled the door open, stepping back with the door itself for protection.

Sai fired. The red flashed from his pistol and, as Aurora looked at what she'd revealed, crashed into a DefenseCorp man. Stepping around the door, Aurora copied Sai's move, laying another two bolts into the enemy, who collapsed while managing to bring up his rifle. For a hot second, seeing someone in her old uniform played with Aurora's head, spun things up into a confusing mix that, with a call to the iron discipline that'd brought her this far, she clamped under control as she went outside.

The real estate building's back slammed into a broken alley nexus cluttered with trash and construction leftovers. Shrouded stacks littered the space running to their right, with the DefenseCorp's compound blocking off the left-ward route. In front sat another building's rear, its own alley exit door shut a few meters away.

"Scout," Sai said, crouching next to the downed man. "His friends are coming in the front, I bet."

As if hearing him, staccato pops echoed from the real estate building's entrance, the DefenseCorp squad firing through the door Eponi had already broken. At the same time, shouts came from the alley's near end, as two more DC troopers came around the end, rifles raised.

Sever had numbers, but no armor. Only pistols. Aurora couldn't get into a straight firefight. She dropped her pistol, crouched over the body while waving Sai and Eponi back into the doorway, which wouldn't serve much longer once the front crew went inside.

"He's been hit!" Aurora shouted towards the troops. "We need a medic!"

"Hands in the open!" the nearer soldier replied, closing the gap quickly while the second kept his distance, navigating to the alley's opposite side to keep Aurora in clear sights.

And putting him clear in Sai's. The demolitionist fired around Aurora's body, sending one then two red bolts at the covering trooper while Aurora dove to the ground. Eponi took advantage of the sudden move, popping the close trooper with her own pistol. A little bit of surprise work, and two more pursuers down.

Zero Sever casualties so far. Though, Aurora supposed, she couldn't be sure about Gregor and Rovo.

Eponi shut the rear exit door behind her as they went into the alley. Aurora wanted to grab the rifles, but unhooking the weapons from their previous owners would take seconds they didn't have.

"Let's go," Aurora said, and followed her own orders by breaking into a sprint away from the bodies, the compound, and the coming death.

The DefenseCorp patrol craft popped into view here and there as the trio ran down the long alley, using the buildings for cover and dodging between junk. After they'd gone a full block, at least by Aurora's estimate, the alleyway opened into a cross street. Before venturing into the clear, Aurora pulled Sai and Eponi to one side, sitting between two stacked crate collections in weak blue light cast from diodes lacing the building roofs.

"That went better than I thought," Eponi said,

hunkering down, her pistol in both hands. "But does anyone actually know where we are?"

A weird question to ask in a time when wristlets tied into satellites and local networks to offer exact locations, detailed maps, and, if neither of those should suffice, the option to call someone to ask.

"Honestly?" Aurora said. "I have no idea. I said we should make for the skiffs, but I'm not sure how to get there."

"Head to the docking bays," Sai said, his voice tight with burns that probably weren't helped by the run. "If we can get there, we know the way to Calico's skiff yard."

Not direct, but it would get the job done. Might also confuse anyone trying to guess Sever's trajectory.

As for how to find the docking bays?

Easy.

There'd been one constant sound since the patrol craft showed up, a humming rumble underpinning everything else on Wexer: spacecraft, fleeing for their lives.

TWENTY-SEVEN

Trick Play

AFTER THE REVOLT BEGAN, when the insurgents pressed up against the people, Sai's father included, suppressing them on his home planet, the streets emptied except for those willing to bring violence with them. Sai's megacity turned quiet, the crowds once shifting from store to store, drinking their coffees, disappeared as roving bands took their place, demanding concessions, demanding a better place. After his father died in the crash during their would-be rescue, Sai and his mother retreated to their apartment, where Sai would spend the next days breaking through his neighbor's places, hunting for food, for hope.

And trying, at all costs, to avoid the fighting springing up below as DefenseCorp began their sponsored, contracted purge.

Wexer felt familiar, the suddenly-deserted blackrock paths lingering in the night while DefenseCorp squaddies hunted for the enemy. Lights flickered from inside squat homes and small apartment buildings as Wexer's population hunkered down for a war it had no part in causing.

"Anyone ahead?" Aurora asked Eponi as they huddled near the docking bay's first berths.

The space port had been crackling as ships took to the stars, but the bursts had slowed down as Sever came closer and the bays emptied. Sai looked up now and counted all the bright points that were very much not stars, but ships small and large sitting in Wexer's orbit, waiting for an all-clear for the disaster on the ground.

At least the patrol craft wasn't there. Aurora made the guess that it was dealing with Rovo and Gregor, though nobody knew how the two could be either free or alive at this point. They'd been trapped back in the DefenseCorp compound, surrounded and without much in the way of weapons, armor, or anything else.

"Clear," Eponi said.

"Then let's keep moving."

Sai winced as he lurched up to his feet, holding his pistol tight and following Aurora's crouching run through the bay's entry. The curving spaceport bordered one side of the city, and if they made it to the bay's opposite end, they'd pass right by where Sai held his street fight approximately a thousand years ago. Beyond that lay the communications center and the outskirts where Calico kept his skiffs.

Now that they'd passed beyond the patrol craft's fire, Wexer's chill breeze had settled in with the night, feeling at first comforting on Sai's singed skin, but now pressing in and chilling the sweat that'd come rolling out during the escape. Adrenaline still ran high, but in this strange limbo, Sai found his teeth chattering as he ran, blackrock crunching beneath his boots.

They passed by a robot-manned bar, still open for business and empty. The screens crackled through galactic sporting highlights and news clips. His face haloed in the bar's happy lighting, Sai wondered if, for a brief moment, the assault on Wexer would make any clips anywhere.

Not likely. Nobody cared about anything this far out.

"Wait," Eponi said as they passed by the bar, holding up her hand. "I hear something."

"Cover," Aurora ordered, seeing as they were all standing in the open.

The bar stood out as the closest option, so they retreated back to the stools and the shelves coated with booze bottles. The robot rotated in their direction, but stayed quiet. The machine likely would until and unless Sever took their seats.

"What'd you hear?" Aurora whispered as they crouched low.

Sai couldn't see anything looking around his side, just the well-lit bay and its berths sitting still. Without any cargo to load or unload, bots clustered in their holding places against the stone walls, their silent eyes staring out at nothing while their batteries charged. Shipping crates lay beside the bots, waiting for something to store.

"Sounded like an order," Eponi said.

"An order for who?" Aurora replied.

Sai leaned around his end, pistol ready. Not that he didn't trust Eponi's ears, but they were on something of a timetable here. DefenseCorp might be distracted with Rovo and Gregor now, but they'd eventually come hunting Sever's other three, and Sai would prefer not to get caught from behind. Would really prefer not to get caught at all.

The bolt screamed by and blew into the dirt at Sai's feet, the bar offering just enough cover to keep the demolitionist from losing toes to the attack. Sai jerked back behind the bar as Aurora and Eponi looked his way.

"Sniper," Sai said. "Someone knows we're here, and doesn't like us very much."

"So, half the people on this planet?" Eponi said.

"Quiet." Aurora held up a single finger. They waited for one long breath, listening to see if anyone was trying to approach. No sounds came. "Okay. They're going to wait for us to get impatient. Can either of you see a distraction?"

"You mean like those fuel tanks you didn't want me to shoot earlier?" Eponi said. "Or is it okay now that we're getting shot at?"

"Not the time," Aurora said.

Aurora never failed to keep Sai impressed with her icy calm. Eponi was going after the captain's buttons tonight. Sai wouldn't say so, but he found himself agreeing with Eponi here. They were, and had been, pinned down. Getting soft about collateral damage wasn't going to keep Sever alive.

The people fighting back home certainly hadn't cared how many of Sai's friends died to make their point. Nor had the DefenseCorp response, which had torn through the city with vengeful abandon. Sai and his mother had left as soon as they could, but Sai bet the world was still being rebuilt.

Wexer could handle a burnt building or three.

Targets didn't present themselves for Sai's pistol, though. No spare fuel tanks lingering here. Maybe in the berths, but not in the conduit. Shooting a random bot might get some sparks, but nothing to throw a sniper off his game. They'd have to find another way, try and—

"I've got an idea," Sai said. "When I stand up, try and spot them. Take them out."

"When you stand up?" Aurora asked.

"Trust me," Sai replied.

Never gets easier, risking your life. When it happens by accident—getting caught out in a firefight or having to

make the in-the-moment reaction to go into harm's way—
the choice went on instinct. Actually choosing, as Sai did
now, telling his legs to send him standing and out beyond
the bar's curve, sent his heart cold, sent the back part of his
mind racing through a last message to his squadmates, his
family.

But if Sai had this figured, if he had the right suspi-
cions about who could possibly be waiting out here, ready
to take a sniper's shot at the trio as they outran the
DefenseCorp forces, well, they wouldn't want to kill him.

No profit in it.

Sai stood as he went, tossing the pistol out in front and
holding his hands up. If the sniper wanted to kill him right
out, now would be the time. No cover, no counters.

Nothing came at him for a heartbeat, and Sai could
count those because his heart had itself hammering.
Beyond his eyes, the bay stretched dark and quiet. The
sniper held his fire. The bot swiveled behind the bar to
look at its potential customer.

Aurora and Eponi ought to be moving now. Advancing
beyond the bar and hunting for a way around the sniper.

"Don't even think about shifting," Tarla's voice came
from the berth across from the bar, to Sai's right, as she
walked out. Her modified pistols in both hands and leveled
towards Sai. "You're pinned, and if the other two don't
step out from behind that bar, you'll be dead."

"Tarla," Sai said, keeping his hands raised and turning
towards her. "Can't say that I'm pleased to see you."

"No doubt," Tarla replied, closing with Sai, though he
noticed her eyes flickering past him. "But I'm very pleased
to see you. Sever squad keeps throwing cash my way."
Tarla stopped with two meters between her and Sai.
"There's a bonus for catching all three, but if your two
friends don't join you, I'll take the pay cut."

Sai took Tarla's threat to mean Aurora and Eponi had used the seconds Sai had bought. If Tarla and her crew relied on the sniper to observe, Perro's scope would've limited the view. Kept, maybe, Aurora and Eponi out of sight while he zeroed on Sai. A chance, then.

"Sorry," Sai said. "Don't know who you're talking about."

Tarla shook her head ever so slightly, "DefenseCorp never did teach its people to lie." She raised the pistol, centered it right on Sai's head.

"You shoot him, I shoot you," Eponi said, curling around the bar enough to see Tarla, but to keep herself out of the sniper's fire.

"There you are," Tarla said, moving her left pistol to cover Eponi. "That makes two. And what a second player. Eponi, after all we shared, you wouldn't hurt me, would you?"

What did that mean? Sai tried to clamp on his confusion and failed, but Tarla wasn't watching him anyway.

"Tarla, it's going to take more than a couple drinks to make me fall in love," Eponi said. "Nothing's charming about threatening my friends."

"That's too bad," Tarla replied. "Guess we'll just have to—"

Sai went. Broke into a diving tackle. Tarla's reflexes kicked in and she fired, the shot grazing Sai's already-singed hair en-route to a disabling blow to the bar bot. Sai hit Tarla's ankles, pulling her off-balance before she could get a second shot off.

Tarla hit the rock hard, kicking up dirt as she tried to get the pistols aimed at Sai. The demolitionist had done enough wrestling in the *Nautilus* with other DefenseCorp soldiers, enough fist-fighting in the dragging days after the revolution on his home planet, to know staying still in close combat is the worst move. He pulled himself up as Tarla fell, expecting Perro to shoot him any second, but the shot never came. Sai stuck a grip on Tarla's arms as she faced the pistols his way.

Sai jerked himself to the side as Tarla fired, the two bolts streaking to the sky where Sai's head used to be. He slammed her arms together, the bashing forcing Tarla to let go even as she scooped her knees beneath Sai's chest and kicked him off.

Sai hit the dirt and rolled with the move, curling towards the pistol he'd tossed aside earlier. Still no sniper shot, but where was Eponi?

"Give it up!" Tarla shouted, anger cutting into her cool composure now. "You're only hurting yourselves."

Sai found the pistol, wheeled around with it, expecting to be facing Tarla's double barrels. Instead, he saw her brushing dirt off herself. Saw Eponi behind her, on the ground. A bright chrome cable wrapped around Eponi's shoulders, pinning her arms to her sides. The cable trailed back along the ground towards that berth, to where Javelin stood holding its ends.

A heavy weight slammed onto Sai's shoulder, pushing him back to the dirt. Briany's hand reached down and wrenched the pistol from Sai's hand and threw it away.

"You're done," Tarla said. "Totally done. And now I've got a lot more laundry to do, thanks to you assholes."

"I'm not sorry," Sai replied, and Briany buffed him across the head hard enough to set his ears ringing.

"I'm so tempted," Tarla said, "to just shoot you right now and screw the bonus, but my team's worked hard. So I'm not going to deprive them. Instead, I'll be happy knowing what DefenseCorp's going to do to you." She picked up her pistols, put them in her waist holsters. "You know, I'll even do you a favor, Sai. You've got family, right?

I'll make sure to tell them where DefenseCorp kicks you out, so they can find your frozen corpse."

Time was, Sai might take offense to that. Time was, he'd get angry, enraged, throw every insult he had Tarla's way. Now he just smiled, a tired smile that came easy when Sai had nothing else to do, no way to break free from Briany's grip.

"You know what, Tarla?" Sai said. "At least my family would come look for me. Who'd give a damn about you?"

Tarla rolled her eyes, glanced over Sai at Briany, "Knock him out, would you? He's annoying."

Sai closed his eyes, waited for the strike, for the small bit of peace that would wait in the unconscious oblivion.

But the blow never came.

TWENTY-EIGHT

High Ground

So the rookie wanted to protect the innocent. Gregor had been there, on the comet and plenty of times afterward. Hell, Gregor had done that on Dynas, launching himself right into a bad fight to save the little girl Kaia from obliteration. The girl had survived, Gregor had nearly died. Now Rovo wanted to punch through a patrol craft to hunt down a businessman that wanted a mine Calico had legally acquired?

Not quite the same.

And yet, as Rovo settled into Aurora's power armor, holding Sai's katana awkwardly in his hands, the new custom scythe latched into Aurora's waist slots, Gregor figured the rookie had earned the right to make his own choices. He certainly packed the power to act on'em.

"We go out that door," Gregor said, "that craft's going to blow us apart."

They stood in the DefenseCorp office, looking out the front door into the courtyard beyond. Laser flashes splashed into view; the patrol craft shooting at something, or several someones, out of sight.

"So we need a distraction," Rovo replied. "I can make one."

"Can you?"

"Watch this," Rovo said. "They're gonna come running, and that's going to be your chance. Get up top."

An opportunity to dive down and hammer-blow some squaddies? Gregor could get behind that. He lumbered to the stairs while Rovo went to the wall and slapped the compound's emergency alarm. Ear-piercing noise sprang out from interspersed speakers, while the lights began to flash white every other second. At first, Gregor didn't understand why Rovo would do something so annoying, but his power armor picked it up.

A local broadcast on DefenseCorp's frequency buzzed in his ear. An automated request for assistance from DC personnel in the area, followed by the base's coordinates. A way to get fast action, a way to, maybe, draw in the patrol craft and its teams. All they knew was that Sever had run from the base, not whether any of their other members still lived inside.

Gregor kicked up his opinion of Rovo another notch. Aurora had done a good job drafting the kid into Sever.

As Gregor hit the second, then third level, he glanced down to see Rovo positioning himself inside the central room, hiding as best he could along a wall parallel to the entrance. The DC flunkies would run in, hunting for hostages, and Rovo could go to work. But the patrol craft would have to buy into the bait first.

Gregor went around the second level to an office above the base's front door. Inside, he slapped at a wall panel to shift the windows from automated screens showing, sensibly, a beautiful jungle view to Wexer's purple-white twilight. Outside, the patrol craft dipped closer to the base.

Its lasers had stopped firing, and yellow squares opening on its base showcased Rovo's move had worked.

Or they'd decided a man-to-man approach made more sense than burning down the city. Though, now that Gregor had the thought, he saw fires aplenty off to his left. Hopefully Sai, Aurora, and Eponi weren't caught in those blazes.

Like on Dynas, Sever had been separated. Like on Dynas, they'd either come together fighting or die apart. Either way, Gregor would be swinging his hammer.

Below, crawling through the courtyard, a full dozen-man squad advanced towards the front door, rifles raised. Above, the patrol craft swooped in closer, those open doors filling with reinforcements. They'd wait until the squad on the ground called for the forces, or, if they weren't needed, the patrol craft would jet away and drop them elsewhere.

Gregor and Rovo were outnumbered and, despite the power armor, outgunned. Much as he loved his hammer, Gregor didn't like the odds against that many troops, against a patrol craft that might, should its on-the-ground forces get toasted, decide to raze the building from above.

No. When you had your back against the wall, when you were outnumbered, you had to pull a major move. Change the battlefield.

Gregor left the office as the first troops closed on the front door. Their shouts to put down any weapons, to let go any hostages, went unanswered.

"Ready?" Rovo said, his voice coming through the narrow band tying the two suits together.

"I'm going higher," Gregor said. "Hold them."

"What?"

"You wanted to play bait. Do it."

Rovo uttered something that made Gregor grin as he looked up. The roof sat above Gregor without any obvious way to get up there. A problem, but with a potential solution.

Gregor shifted sideways, outside the office door on the balcony ringing each level and hefted the hammer behind his back. Gregor threw up the hammer as, on the first floor, the incoming troops fired their first weapons through the front door: flashbangs bursting with loud pops, amplified when Gregor's hammer crashed through the thin ceiling with a crack.

The power armor handled the flashbangs without an issue, filtering out the sudden light and muting the noise enough to keep things stable. The suit took the crashing destruction from Gregor's hammer with less composure: Gregor's visor flashed red all around as rubble rained from the blow.

Gregor ignored the sensitive suit, marching through the falling blocks—several bouncing off his armor—to pick up his hammer from the balcony. Flowing down around him through the brand new hole, Wexer's twilight mingled with the flashing lights and buzzing alarms.

"You're crazy," Rovo shouted.

Gregor glanced down to the first level as he picked up the hammer. The attackers had paused at the crash from above, but as the rubble found its places, they swarmed in through the door. Rovo waited till three had gone past him before opening up with his rifles, the katana planted in the floor at his feet. The shots, more a spray than a precisely-aimed affair, laid out the group in a burning red and yellow cascade.

"Careful," Gregor said. "You'll burn out your power packs fast like that."

"Thanks for the tip. You helping any time soon?"

"Yes."

Gregor looked up at the hole. Not quite wide enough

for a clean jump, but the roof didn't look all that stable anymore. He could punch through. While Rovo broke into his next firefight, Gregor slotted the hammer back into its holster, crouched in the armor, and activated its boost jumpers.

Really, the damn things were the most fun.

The boots kicked in when Gregor bent his knees and jumped, the instant propulsion shoving Gregor upward and through the hole. His arms and shoulders jerked—that dislocated one definitely wasn't thrilled with his choices—as they crunched through dangling remnants from the hammer strike, but the boots brought Gregor high enough to land on the roof. He took a quick, leaning step forward to keep from falling backwards, settling into the open air.

And what a magnificent view to have before getting shot to pieces.

Up here, Gregor saw the city's edge lay out before him, squat homes dying away beneath the dwindling twilight to the vast blackrock desert and the shimmering cream rivers beyond. Turning towards his target, Gregor felt the snapping breeze buffet his armor, like a hundred invisible hands pushing him towards the building's right edge. A command he couldn't follow, because his target sat huge before him.

About as long as a city block and half as wide, the oval patrol craft had its bulk hovering over the DefenseCorp base's courtyard. The ship's maneuvering jets pulsed blue-white towards the ground, keeping the ship a few meters above the base's roof, but close enough for its soldiers to rappel down. Gregor had done that a few times himself, holing up with the fifty-odd soldiers the patrol craft could carry en route to devastate some sucker planet.

This close, the doorways for the dropping troops loomed large, their yellow backlights seeming almost golden in the ambient Wexer light. Gregor saw two more drop down the thick cables to the ground, but nobody filled their spots. He had to act fast, or the craft would shut its doors, head up to a safer altitude, and again play the part of a god, sending lasers to smite Sever from above.

Gregor's left and right hands went to his waist while he spoke the keyword for his power armor. The armor took the command and opened two slots Gregor had stuffed back in the base's armory. Grenades, these ones the most basic explosives you could get for a cheap price, popped out and into his waiting palms.

As they did, a red light washed over Gregor. Fuzzy lines coming from bright dots on the patrol craft's port side, the one staring right at him. Scanners, learning whether Gregor needed to be destroyed.

Perhaps the DefenseCorp-branded power armor bought Gregor some time. Perhaps the patrol craft was paying more attention to Rovo below: the rookie's fight kicked laser noise, shouts for help, and smashing furniture up through the roof.

"Enjoy," Gregor said, throwing the two grenades at the craft.

The little balls arced through the air, and slapped right into the closing doors as the patrol craft proved itself smarter than Gregor hoped and sealed its entries. The two bombs fell towards the ground, exploding out of Gregor's sight, but drawing a whole lot more shouting.

Gregor sighed, reaching up to draw his hammer, "Guess we're doing this the hard way."

He took two long steps towards the roof, charging up those boots just enough so that on the third, when Gregor hit the roof's straight edge, his foot planting on the lip, he kicked in the boosts. Gregor launched off the roof as the patrol craft finally overrode its own targeting systems and sent lasers crashing towards him, towards the base.

Gregor flew through a neon tunnel, a laser-hot barrage that filled the air around him with deadly energy. His suit screamed as at least one blast grazed the armor, melting the plating, burning Gregor's skin inside, but lasers didn't pack physical force. The bolts didn't knock Gregor back, didn't stop his momentum even as they turned the base's rooftop into a blazing wreck.

The hammer struck first, Gregor swinging it as he jumped, twisting the haft to activate the weapon's stored kinetic energy. Like the boosts on Gregor's boots, the weapon discharged the energy on impact, amplifying its bang into the patrol craft's side and turning the strike from a denting blow to a rending one. The ship's bent and broke as Gregor's hammer pushed through and caught on the ship's inside, with Gregor holding on to the hammer's handle.

Whistles and cracks sang from inside the ship, as systems not designed for it suddenly dealt with the rattling hit from Gregor's hammer. While the big man dangled over the courtyard, the patrol craft listed right, its jets sputtering as the ship's pilots, engineers, tried to keep it afloat.

Gregor tried to do the same with himself, fighting through rippling, fiery lines along his arms and legs, and a suit that filled his visor with alarms about broken systems. He didn't have his boost boots anymore, and most of his compensators were fried, meaning moving with the armor on would rely on Gregor's strength alone. No help to shift hundreds of kilos in extra weight. All that heaviness bore down on him now, pressing on his grip to his hammer.

Falling to the ground from this height in working power armor wouldn't be a threat: the armor would suck in the energy from the impact and shunt it to the boosters. With his armor dead, Gregor would hit the ground and get mashed.

"Zero free." Gregor issued the key command, and the armor's independent, tiny discharge system went to work.

Blowing small charges meant for exactly these situations, Gregor's armor disintegrated. The coatings along his arms and legs that'd kept him safe through so many missions popped and flew off, spinning down to the dirt. The helmet split apart over his head, each half falling away to its side and letting Wexer's breeze finally blast Gregor's face with cool wind.

But Gregor kept his hold on the hammer's haft, and as the patrol craft weaved away, he began to climb.

TWENTY-NINE

Dessert Fights Back

EPONI WOKE up looking at a smoothed-over face. The hospitals on Farlane Twelve weren't at the galaxy's pinnacle, but they still had robots nearby when the sedation wore off. The bot spoke to her in calming tones, designed through countless testing and iterations to hit the pitch most soothing for those that had undergone extreme trauma.

Eponi thought it sounded like lavender-scented pillows.

The bot started with simple suggestions. Could she feel her toes, wiggle her fingers, smell the sterile air? When Eponi passed all those, the bot encouraged her to look around, see where she happened to be. While Eponi did this, the moments flashed: Farlane's glossy saffron meadows under its beet red sky, the twisting along the tight sculpted corridor. Five karts all fighting for the lead, clustered entering the final stretch.

She'd seen an opening along the right side, narrow but viable so long as Eponi could engage her right landing jets at the perfect time to pop her kart vertical. The saffron course leveled out for the final straightaway and Eponi pushed, angled towards that gap as everyone sped up, more conscious about how close their blistering craft sat next to each other.

Going vertical would kill Eponi's drag, give her the slightest edge. She drew up close to the leader, then popped her right jets, the sudden jolt sending Eponi's world view askew. The flight stick juddered, the kart trying to compensate for its switch in relation to the ground below. Eponi killed the racer's stability systems, stopped the kart from doing anything except respond to her slightest twitch.

She didn't realize it, but she'd stopped breathing.

Ahead, the finish loomed with its green smoke soaring into the sky. Twenty seconds of arrow-straight blitzing to get there. The move kicked up Eponi's speed, and she saw the leader drifting by as she passed him. She had the kart level, like a blade, blazing through. In another few moments, Eponi would be in the lead. Could level out and seal her place.

Her replay, there in the hospital bed, stuck on the face. The lead's glare as his cockpit started falling behind her's. There were too many kart racers to really develop rivalries, but Eponi felt the slightest chill at the sheer anger in those eyes, etched into a youthful face that must've been a new entry into the league.

She remembered thinking he'd learn something from this one.

Until he nudged his kart right, its wing clipping Eponi's vertical tip. His kart, level and flat, compensated for the bump. Eponi's?

"You flipped," her manager said, voice coming from the comm in the bot. "Went right over and nosedived into the dirt. The bubble kept you from dying, but your head still hit hard."

"Why am I here?" Eponi asked. "Where are you?"

"I'm gone, Eponi. Off to the next race," the manager didn't even sound sympathetic, hurt, or at any loss. As if she was telling Eponi she'd gone shopping. "You knew the terms. One more needless crash and you're done."

"That wasn't my fault." Eponi struggled to sit up, to glare at the bot because she needed something to do, but the hospital had strapped her down. Supposedly, so the bot said, to keep her neck and spine stable. "He hit *me*."

"Because you made the move," the manager said. "If you'd taken your place, you would've been fine. You had the points. It was a show, and too late in the track to do it."

"Isn't winning the goal?"

"Cash is the goal, Eponi. Always has been. And right now, you're costing us with your wrecks. Too much to keep afloat." This time, at least, the manager had the grace to sigh. "Sorry, but you're out. We've sent you a severance that should get you through till you find something else. Good luck, Eponi."

Good luck. That was it. A click and a dismissal. A career dead in a moment.

Eponi wouldn't let that happen to her life.

With Tarla heading over to Sai, Eponi saw that same dismissal, that same cancellation at what could've been a promising partnership. Those minutes at the bar, swapping stories, had opened a door to a private mercenary life steadily shut by every subsequent encounter with Tarla, where that hope had been murdered by the very same damn thing that'd killed Eponi's first love.

Cash.

The laser shot from the dark distance and hit Javelin, whose coils had closed around Eponi like a suffocating cage. The mercenary shouted, pain and surprise coming more than any word, and fell back. The coils, chromed things tied to a net gun meant for hunting animals, tugged on Eponi as Javelin pulled them with his fall. A second sound followed, the hard thud as Javelin's net gun hit the ground.

Eponi rolled towards her captor, feeling a little stupid as she dipped her shoulder into the dirt and pushed. That, though, was a hidden secret about so many fights: what looked ridiculous at the time seemed brilliant when it worked out.

Javelin's gun, the source holding the netting together, touched Eponi's legs as more lasers flashed behind her. Tarla shouted for cover, to fire back, to get Javelin help, but nobody paid any attention to the bound pilot as Eponi squeezed her legs up to her chest, bringing the net gun with it.

The coils kept her arms wrapped in tight, but Eponi could move her wrists, her hands, and once she had the gun close, Eponi managed to find the release. Pressing the light green indent on the silver weapon popped the netting free from its center, the coils relaxing and giving Eponi a chance to take a full breath as chaos erupted around her.

Sai looked to be tangled up with Briany, fighting to get loose from her grapple while she, with a strong lock around his neck, tried to keep him facing the darkness from which the lasers kept coming. Tarla poked up from behind the bar counter to squeeze a couple shots into the dark with her pistols, bolts that had no chance to find their target. Either she'd lost her senses in desperation, or the attacks had another purpose.

Javelin groaned as Eponi crawled free and she confirmed the mercenary's injury would keep him out of the game: the sniper bolt had burned a hole near the man's stomach, not a good place to get hit. Eponi would've felt more sympathy if the man hadn't just wrapped her up for what would be a summary execution at DefenseCorp's hands.

As for who had saved her? The sniper?

Aurora actually coming through on her promise. She'd ditched into the dark while Sai served up his distraction, leaving Eponi to serve as dessert to Sai's dinner platter in drawing out Tarla and her Rangers. Eponi had given it even odds whether Aurora would actually overtake Perro, who had to be the one taking the shots, but apparently Sever's captain had succeeded.

Which meant Eponi couldn't let Tarla keep firing with those pistols. She might not kill Aurora, but Tarla might be trying to serve up a similar distraction. Sanje was out there somewhere.

"Hey," Eponi said, climbing over the bar counter and grabbing some fun along the way. "Tell your friend to back off."

Tarla whirled, bringing around those pistols, so Eponi smashed a bottle into Tarla's face. The glass shattered and Tarla stumbled back into the bar shelf, dropping the pistols as her hands flew to a brand new cut along her forehead.

"Ask you again," Eponi said, picking up the dropped pistols. "Tell Briany to let Sai go."

Tarla shuddered, tried to stand and fell back against the bar counter. She wiped blood away from over her eyes, then gave Eponi that same smile, one that'd once been enticing, mysterious even. One that now seemed all too menacing.

"Think you have it played, little racer?" Tarla said. "I'll let you change your mind. Right now. Put the bottle down, and we'll tell DefenseCorp you didn't make it."

Eponi took a step closer, squatted down to Tarla's level.

"Give it a couple days," Tarla continued, watching Eponi. "They'll forget about you. I'll make another spot on the Rangers and you can hop in. You're a better pilot than Sanje anyway."

"Yeah," Eponi said, getting up close. Another red bolt flashed outside, as Sai and Briany continued to fight, their curses becoming the background noise. "I am. If you'd told me that a few days ago, I might've taken you up on it." She put a pistol barrel up to Tarla's throat, and finally that smile went away. "You're just like all the others. You wanted to use me."

"Oh, don't be naive," Tarla said, the leaking red dancing around her lips now. "Everyone's using everyone. At least I'm honest about it."

Eponi shook her head, "Not that cynical, sorry. Sever kicked your ass, Tarla. Better learn that lesson tonight, because next time you won't get another chance."

With her left hand, Eponi swatted Tarla's temple, and the Ranger's captain crumpled over. All that swagger, all that talk, and Tarla looked like any other bum that'd taken Eponi for granted.

Sever's pilot stood over the bar and aimed at Briany, still struggling with Sai, who hadn't figured out a way to break the woman's headlock. Sniper fire had left smoking black burns in the ground around them, where Aurora must've felt like chancing a shot.

"Hey," Eponi said. "Let him go."

Briany glanced up at the command, finding Eponi and then hunting around for Tarla. When Briany noticed the weapons Eponi held, she froze and Sai took advantage, delivering an elbow to Briany's ribs and pushing away.

Without her hostage, Briany didn't do anything except raise her hands and glare.

"Here's what you're gonna do," Eponi said while Sai recovered his pistol. "You've got at least two partners in bad shape, so go find whatever passes for a hospital on this miserable rock and find them some help. Then you're going to forget we ever came this way so that I don't have to put a laser bolt in your head."

"Big words for such a little woman," Briany replied.

Eponi narrowed one eye, pulled the trigger on the right pistol. The bolt snared through the gap between Briany's left arm and the woman's hair, singeing the edges.

"Don't make me repeat myself," Eponi said.

Briany, thankfully, didn't. With one last curse, she glanced at her wristlet and broke into a lumbering run towards the city. Feeling heat in her hands from the laser bolt, Eponi glanced at the pistols in her hands. Modified, the weapons had Tarla's stamp. Eponi could leave them with their owner, or consider them a debt paid.

"We should probably go," Sai said.

"Yep." Eponi climbed over the bar, sliding the pistols over the surface before grabbing them when she hit the other side. "Still don't know where Sanje is, and I don't see Aurora."

Sai, though, looked past Eponi towards the bar, "Did you kill her?"

"Tarla? She's just taking a nap. One she won't like waking up from."

"I didn't expect you to stay," Sai said as they broke into a run towards where the sniper shots had come from. "But thank you."

"Don't thank me," Eponi said. "It was Aurora's idea."

"And yet, you pulled it off," Sai replied. "Don't know how many others could've managed it."

"I'd say about four."

Though Aurora's silence might bring that number down to three.

Back And Forth

A DOCUMENT SENDER. A rubber stamper. A way station for notes about this and that to get to here and there. Rovo's career had been laid out from the moment he took the desk job with DefenseCorp from the start of his life to a natural end, potentially centuries later, doing the sort of work that doesn't lead to legends, but to, as his parents continually put it, a stable, happy life.

Stability died for the thousandth time as Rovo fired at the incoming DefenseCorp troops. They'd approached the base with the hesitant, tactical motions of a force intent on capturing lightly-armed adversaries, not someone wearing power armor. Not someone holding multiple rifles, a strange scythe, and, placed in the floor before him, a diamond-sharp katana.

Gregor's work above rained rocks around Rovo as he planted himself square in the entry, lighting up the door and turning its glass and frame to molten ruin with red and yellow bolts. He held down the triggers, felt the rifles heat up with the constant stream. They'd short out soon, but Rovo had to hope Gregor was doing something worthwhile. Had to hope that, by buying time, Rovo could give the big man a chance to change the equation.

His enemies dragged the couple bodies away, arms reaching out from behind the outside walls to drag the two Rovo had hit into cover. The rookie's fire wasn't striking anyone anymore, but Rovo held down the triggers anyway. Gregor shouted something about burning out the power packs, but that was okay.

This wasn't going to be a slow shootout.

His sisters, in the usual way siblings did, reacted to Rovo taking the communications position with laughter. Their brother, the one who'd always obsessed about action movies, about adventures and stories that took him away from the staid existence on an ideal planet, was choosing to shuffle papers. At least, they said, Rovo would be able to focus on his love life, because the work wouldn't take much attention.

And yet, Rovo tasted the exhilaration when he launched up to the space station that would serve as his home and office. He'd never left the planet before, and the pull shoving him back into his crash couch as the Defense-Corp shuttle took off, the moment when his stomach flip-flopped as gravity fell away, infected a disposition mellowed by time and low expectations. Rovo floated off that shuttle, kicking with his pack towards the small quarters he'd be living in for the next few years, tasting the recycled air and dreaming, again, of adventure.

The rifles fizzled out slow, their bolts firing slower and with fraying edges, a spray rather than a tight strike. The shots scored the walls around the door, struck scattered artwork and lit the posters aflame. The DefenseCorp soldiers had apparently decided to let Rovo work out his frustration, and when the last spark died, Rovo waited one long count, then threw the rifles towards the door

Two DefenseCorp soldiers spun around the corners, raising their own rifles, only to find Rovo's tossed weapons smacking them in the face, in the chest. The spent rifles glowed orange with heat, burning the two soldiers and buying Rovo the distraction he needed to step to the side and away from the firing line.

Now he had to choose: he had pistols in the power armor. He had the scythe. Sai's katana sat nearby too.

Rovo had won the scythe on Wexer. It seemed fitting to use it.

Inside the office, the scythe felt comically large. Rovo held its dark metal handle, his right hand gripping the upper third beneath the hooked, blue-chromed blade. He listened, waited for footsteps, and instead heard the rolling, clanking sound belong to grenades. The soldiers had already tried flashbangs, so when Rovo glanced down and left and saw the real things this time, he wasn't surprised.

Kicking in the armor's boosters, Rovo jumped hard right. He broke through desks, computer screens, and furniture as he flew, crunching into the ground and completing an awkward roll with the scythe. Rovo faced back the way he'd come as the grenades went off, their blue-fire, crackling explosions mixing both the traditional burning death of conventional explosives with an EMP's shorting power.

The blasts didn't make it all the way to Rovo, but the office's furniture lit up at the heat, while electronics sparked and broke as their components fried. The blinking, squawking alarm dwindled out a last, mournful cry before falling to sputtering silence. Another bang came from the roof, and Rovo looked up to see the beige ceiling blacken and start to crumble.

Either Gregor was getting shot at, or he'd started the roof on fire.

From the very first day, Rovo redirected wild stories handling disasters and far worse. DefenseCorp dealt with escorts, insurrections, and wholesale wars between planets, systems, and clusters. One sad missive to an annihilated squad's families that Rovo copied and redirected to all the appropriate worlds would be followed by an action report showcasing a squad's assault, destruction, and eventual takeover of an enemy hold. Rovo would tally up the damage and route the invoice to the proper account, but while his fingers crunched up the numbers, his imagination would be following along on the escapade.

The DefenseCorp troopers followed up their grenade fire with a tactical charge, walking into the first floor as Rovo picked himself up and began a lumbering run towards the entrance. Despite the armor, Rovo wouldn't survive concentrated fire from too many rifles. Chaos was his ally, here, and Rovo embraced it.

A few strides gave his boosters enough charge for a short jump as the first trio came into the smokey office, rifle flashlights glowing, searching for their mark. Rovo's visor punched through the haze and highlighted the troops in a beautiful crimson, so when he flew threw the air, swinging the scythe as it was meant to be swung, Rovo knew exactly where to aim.

No scythe that looked like this one had been meant for farm work and the hook did an admirable job slicing the DefenseCorp troopers. Rovo screamed as he jumped, broadcasting and amplifying the noise through the armor's speakers, a wordless roar that followed his swing as the scythe slit its way through the three bodies.

Rovo landed as the troopers stumbled back, fell to the ground, looked at their torn chests. They wouldn't be fighting anymore today. Flashes and burning lasers came at

Rovo from his left, showing plenty more troopers willing to take their place.

They didn't even give Rovo a chance to enjoy his move.

The rookie stumbled back from the onslaught, his left arm hot and the suit telling him not to take another shot there unless Rovo wanted to lose the arm entirely. As Rovo back-stepped, he tripped on rubble that hadn't been there before, falling backwards as more chunks fell from above. Some collided with the mezzanine, crunching through its balcony and tearing it apart.

Rovo dropped the scythe, put his hands in front of the visor to try and block the debris as they came crashing down towards him. Fires flickered through the smoke, and while the visor cut unnecessary sound, Rovo could hear the panicked calls from the troopers to grab the wounded, to get out.

To run.

Two months into his time on the station, Rovo had seen the first notice. A free overview of what it took to be on the DefenseCorp front lines, offered up by a larger squad transferring through the station. The twelve members stood in full regalia, power armor, weapons, and all when Rovo and his fellow spacers came floating into the station's primary hangar bay.

"There are a trillion more that can do your job," the squad's commander said at the session's start, shoving a pitying look over Rovo and the rest as they hung out in their collared shirts and poorly-fitted slacks. "In a squad like ours, you are unique."

There were grades, but everyone started at the bottom. DefenseCorp's peerless algorithms and assessments would set anyone interested in making something from their lives into their ideal slots, all of them with potential for greatness. Some very few would make it into a squad like the one Rovo saw, the most elite, the ones able to handle any situation and make it out, mission accomplished.

For the first time, Rovo's imagination had found a key, and it unlocked an obsession. Not just with joining DefenseCorp's literal ranks—Rovo could've done that from day one—but to find himself on a squad like that. With power armor, with comrades that oozed deadly skill. To take on the work that made the legends, that made the movies.

Another block crashed against the visor, sneaking by Rovo's hands and leaving a long scratch on the glass. Not all the way through, but with his left arm pinned by some gray-metal utility box that'd made the plunge, Rovo couldn't do much about it. His right wasn't much better off, snared by tangled wires that'd trapped him like a spider's nest when the base's right wall had collapsed.

At least the smoke had started to clear, showcasing Wexer's wide open night. Through the beat up glass, Rovo could see the hazy cream rivers reflected far above, and maybe a star or a spaceship engine. The troopers were still shouting, but they'd gone off in some other direction. Maybe they assumed Rovo had died in the collapse.

Maybe Gregor had pulled them away.

"Hey," Rovo said, trying out Sever's narrow band. "Anyone out there?"

Static.

He had the power armor rerun its checks, see how bad things looked. Most systems came back yellow, damaged but workable. Rovo could move, could probably dig himself out from the disaster. The question, though, was when?

Too soon and the troops would return, put lasers through his face before Rovo worked his way out. Too late, and Sever would be dead or gone.

He tried another comm check. Nothing again. Above him, the view changed. The creamy reflection disappeared, replaced with something else. A fuzzy, hot blast swept over Rovo's armor as the sky vanished, covered by the dark bulk of the last thing Rovo wanted to see: the patrol craft. Red targeting lights splashed down towards Rovo, highlighting his visor, ready to fire.

No getting out of this one.

When the acceptance came through, Rovo spent the whole morning staring at the message. Reading it over and over to confirm he hadn't missed anything. DefenseCorp had received his application, had evaluated it, and, pending a successful skills test at an outpost several lightyears away, there was a potential spot waiting for him.

Aboard the *Nautilus*, in a squad called Sever.

THIRTY-ONE

From A Distance

AURORA RAN EXPOSED beneath the midnight sky, a hard sprint carrying her through the shadows between Wexer's few lights. The berths and the bar lay to her right, far brighter than the dim warehouses she hugged on the opposite. Dead-eyed bots stayed stone as she went, watchers to a story they'd never tell. Her footsteps scattered packed dirt, and with every footfall, Aurora waited for a shot that didn't come.

Sai's shouts echoed through the space, serving their purpose. Keeping Aurora alive as she tried to look ahead, tried to figure out where the sniper had plugged himself. The bay curved around the city's outskirts, and as it wrapped left, potential positions faded in. There were stacked crates near berth doors that would serve, or even the structure's roof; more a thin stretch serving to anchor the walls splitting each berth from the next.

Experience bled its way into the possibilities. Aurora, Sai, and Eponi had been running continuously since leaving the DefenseCorp base. Any ambush like this one wouldn't have had much time to pull itself together. A sniper would've had to pick a position that gave him options, but also one near enough to take at a moment's notice.

Aurora saw the spot and almost dismissed it. Too obvious, but there it was, the rifle's long barrel extending over the railing and catching light. The sniper had taken a cargo loader and ran the flat slate up to its max height, four or five meters, and placed it near enough to the bay's curving roof to give him a great shot at anyone coming from, well, anywhere.

The important thing, as Aurora slipped between two big fueling bots?

The rifle pointed towards the bar, not Aurora. The sniper didn't realize she'd made the escape.

Taking a breath, Aurora counted the stacked containers at the loader's base. She couldn't make a running jump to get up to the sniper's platform, but if she could get to that base without getting detected, Aurora could bring the bastard down to her level.

To do that would mean an open run straight towards the sniper. Even if Sai did his best performance art back there near the bar, and Aurora adopted cat-like stealth, the sniper could glance to his right and see her. Shoot Aurora before she had a chance to get where she needed to go. Unless Aurora went fast.

The sniper moved, adjusted his aim; the weapon sliding along the rail to settle on something new. Aurora had left Eponi behind. Maybe the pilot had played her trick, maybe she'd started a fight. Maybe the sniper had friends back at the bar.

Regardless, Aurora didn't have explosives. Didn't have any lovely targets to blow up with a precise shot from her pistol.

But Aurora had speed.

Ditching stealth for a run, Aurora sprang away from the bots and, arms pumping, raced across the sand in long strides heading straight for the loader and its lift. A square meter platform, the sniper's perch clanked as the shooter heard Aurora's footfalls. She caught the rifle turning towards her, but Aurora had made it halfway across the concourse. Too close, too low for the sniper to catch.

The loader's railings that he'd been using to level the weapon didn't give the sniper the angle he needed, and Aurora almost laughed as he tried to back up in the tight space, angle the weapon down. By the time he managed to drop the barrel, she slipped underneath, slapping away at the loader's base and the big, sea-green down arrow.

The loader didn't fight with Aurora's orders and dropped, a grinding descent that Aurora spent directly beneath the stand. The platform would squash her, but Aurora wanted to keep hidden from the sniper as long as possible, keep him guessing as to where she'd come from. Aurora heard him turning, footfalls vibrating through the metal.

The prey trying to find the predator.

Aurora rotated, crouched, and as soon as the platform fell to her standing height, Aurora back-stepped to come out on the side opposite the sniper's original position. She rose up, aimed the pistol, and saw the sniper looking sideways, dressed up head to toe in a purple-black outfit that would've, in a more normal nighttime shot, provided good camouflage.

"Hey Perro," Aurora said. "Mind dropping that rifle?"

Perro froze, did not drop the rifle.

"Has the little leader lost her mind?" Perro replied, turning his head to look at her. "Your friends are surrounded, trapped like mice in a cage. Hurting me will only hurt them, if you understand."

"Could say the same about you," Aurora said. "Hands off. I won't ask again."

Perro let go of the weapon, the rifle clattering to the platform's floor. In the same motion, the sniper reached for a holstered pistol, trying to duck away from Aurora, get back to the loader and find some cover.

Except Aurora wasn't some rookie soldier. Some new kid that'd get distracted by an obvious play. She fired once. A yellow-red bolt that lanced out and hit Perro in his upper right chest. Above where his heart ought to be, but close enough to take him down. The sniper fell back against the loader's bars, and Aurora climbed over the ones on her side, keeping her pistol trained on Perro the whole time.

"Stop cursing, save your energy," Aurora said as she reached Perro and pulled away his pistol. "If you're lucky, that shot won't kill you. If you keep being stupid, I'll add another one that will."

Perro didn't offer much more than a wheezy curse in reply. Aurora pressed him up against the loader's railings and took a long look back towards the bar. Without the sniper scope and on ground level, she could make out Sai and several others—Tarla, looked like. And Eponi towards the back with something wrapped around her? Either way, it didn't look like Sever was on the winning end.

"You all plotting an ambush?" Aurora said, holstering her pistol and picking up the rifle.

Perro, perhaps taking Aurora's advice, didn't say anything.

Aurora wouldn't consider herself much of a sniper: Sever had always been more of a smash-n-grab squad with little use for fixed ranged support. Any sniper traveling with them would be left behind as the squad tore their way to the objective and then off-world. But she could fire a weapon, and it didn't look like she'd have time to make the run back to the bar.

Slapping the loader again sent the platform trundling skyward. Aurora set the rifle on the rail, just like Perro had and leaned into the scope. Losing peripheral vision should've bugged Aurora more, but the power armor visors did much the same thing—though the sniper scope wouldn't warn her of an enemy approach like the visor would: surviving with Sever meant getting used to operating with trade-offs.

Here, Aurora traded sensing her surroundings for a close-up look at the bar, at Eponi coiled and pinned down while Sai struggled against Briany. Tarla, cocky as ever, looked to be saying something to Sai. Having already downed Perro, seeing the Twilight Rangers taking Sever's other two wasn't all that shocking.

Though how they'd known to set up here bugged Aurora. Maybe DefenseCorp had been talking. Maybe Tarla really was just that good.

Briany stopped Sai's struggle, holding him tight. Tarla had her pistols out now, aiming them Sai's way. An interrogation going wrong.

Time to put a stop to that.

Aurora centered the scope as Tarla worked her mouth. The woman always talked, an annoying flaw, trait, whatever you wanted to call it. She had to hold attention, and she'd left DefenseCorp, declared an early retirement, with a splashy message to some soldiers stating her intentions to form the Rangers.

Ditch the mothership, join her squad. Make more cash, leave behind the bullshit.

Why DefenseCorp hadn't gone after Tarla for that was a mystery. She'd pulled some people with her and vanished. Her name never appeared on a targets list, a bounty roster, or anything else. As if Tarla had left on good terms.

Aurora pulled the trigger, compressed the gas and energy together in the barrel to send a bolt streaking towards Tarla. The shot came close, but missed high, hitting the dirt right over Tarla's shoulder. Aurora hadn't registered the scope's settings right, and she cursed as the scrambling started below.

Sai reacted like he should, using the interruption to get back to his struggle with Briany. Tarla dove behind the bar, leaning out and peering towards Aurora. She spoke into a wristlet, and Aurora heard Tarla's voice coming out of Perro's, asking what the hell was going on.

"Answer her and you die now," Aurora said to Perro, whose pallor, sweaty forehead, and weak breathing told a dire story. "Be smart."

Perro groaned. Aurora went back to the scope.

Tarla would figure it out if she hadn't already, but every second counted.

Aurora squeezed off another shot, this time striking Javelin, giving Eponi a chance to get away from the man's coils. If she could. With Javelin down, Aurora tried and failed to get a clean shot at Briany.

Bolts lanced her way from the bar, wild and wide, striking the containers, the docking bay roof. Tarla taking pot shots. Nevertheless, the more times Aurora pulled the trigger, the better chances Tarla could track the laser and hit its shooter.

Aurora pulled back from the scope, noticed Perro had gone quiet. Four Rangers accounted for, which meant the fifth, their pilot, had to be somewhere. Still on their ship, maybe?

A chance Aurora didn't want to take. The sniper's perch had run out its game. Aurora could sprint back to the bar, help Sai and Eponi up close. Taking out Briany with a solid fist to the face would be less dangerous than risking shots from afar.

The platform trundled to the ground. Aurora took out her pistol, aimed, and shot once into the sniper rifle's housing, slagging its ability to fire another laser. She pressed two fingers to Perro's throat, caught a weak pulse. He needed help, but the man wasn't dead yet. Another bargaining chip for Tarla.

"Move, I fire," Sanje said, stepping around the crates at the loader's base with a normal, assault-style rifle in his hands. "What did you do to him?"

The pilot must've come from one of the bays right here. Aurora had kept a look on the concourse, checking back and forth often enough that a running sprint like the one she pulled wouldn't have worked.

"Shot him," Aurora said, keeping her hands on her pistol. "What do you think I did?"

"He's alive?"

Sanje didn't have a killer's look. Even in the dim light, wearing light clothes that suggested Tarla hadn't planned for him to take part in this ambush, Sanje radiated nerves. He might be a decent flier, might have some skill with that rifle, but the man didn't want to put himself in harm's way.

"For now. You keep talking to me instead of getting him help, that might change," Aurora said.

The words triggered a shift in Sanje, from weak and wary to panic. The pilot brought the rifle up to his face, took a stuttering aim at Aurora.

"Help him, then!" Sanje said. "Or I'll kill you."

Oh, how the desperate give themselves away.

"Sanje," Aurora said, flattening her voice to the same tone she used on any Sever member that lost themselves during a mission. "I can't help him. He needs a real medic."

"Then pick him up," Sanje replied. "Help me carry him to the ship. Now."

"I can't carry him alone." Aurora didn't know, actually, if that was true. Perro wasn't a large man, but that didn't matter. She needed Sanje to come closer, drop that rifle. "You'll have to help."

Sanje hesitated. Always a bad sign when your enemy started thinking.

"Drag him. Now," Sanje said. "If he dies, I'm putting a laser through your skull."

"I'm sure you will," Aurora said, holstering her pistol and looking back towards the bar. She could make out figures there, but couldn't tell who they were, whether Sai and Eponi had turned things around, or if Aurora's squadmates were dead in the dirt. "Lead the way, killer."

Aurora to grabbed Perro's wrist and pulled the unconscious man from the loading platform and onto the dirt. Tugging with her legs and a double-grip, Aurora dragged Perro along, following Sanje into the dark.

Towards a docking bay, towards a chance.

THIRTY-TWO

Detective Work

In desperate moments, take the obvious path and work out the details later. Sai's father had laughed after dropping that little pearl, then returned to making the haphazard meal. The man loved to cook, had been terrible at it, and often took to cobbling together foods in any way he could imagine, leading to countless meals supplemented by late-night deliveries secretly placed by Sai's mother and devoured by her and her son once her husband had returned to work.

But the axiom remained, one light guiding Sai's life among many others. Most weren't all that applicable on a deepening night on a fringe world where, pursued by mercenaries and all-powerful organizations alike, Sai had to find his captain.

"Follow the dirt," Sai said as they approached the loader and the melted sniper rifle laying on its platform. "Something heavy moved across here."

With true night taking hold, the white lights lining the bay washed out the blackrock color, turning the ground into a ghostly gray, as if they walked on a firm storm cloud.

Dust kicked up with every footfall, hanging in the air until Wexer's breeze picked up again and sent the stuff flying. Dust coated Sai and Eponi, as it did everyone on the planet, and their recent close encounters with the ground had left large dirt patches on their skinsuits.

In short, Sai itched everywhere.

"Aurora's body?" Eponi went over to the rifle, her frazzled hair falling around her head. Normally she kept it tied, but in all the running, it'd come loose. "Someone shot the weapon. Nice one, too."

"C'mon. You can play detective if Aurora's not at the end."

Following the sand, a ragged trail without, say, a crate's defined path, led the two Sever squad members to the next docking berth back towards the bar. Unlike most, the doors to this one were wide open, the security lights shining a happy green. Sai went to the wall just outside the doors, hugging the crusted metal and beckoning Eponi to do the same.

"Weapons ready," Sai said. "Who knows what's in there."

"Who knows?" Eponi replied. "I know. It's Perro and Sanje, the only two we didn't beat up back there."

"I said you can play detective later."

"Uh huh."

Rather than continue letting Eponi prove herself right, Sai raised his pistol and curled around the wall. Sai looked for targets, fully ready and willing to demand a surrender or snap off a bolt. Instead, he saw running lights, a bold orange, lacing a craft that Sai could only describe as a gourd.

Broadly circular, the ship appeared to suffer from some sort of disease, with metal lumps growing off in various places where someone had added on additional rooms, weapons, or devices. The theoretical cockpit stuck off facing Sai and the berth exit, a flattened end that at least used its shape to give a top-to-bottom window the chance to shine.

And through that window, Sai saw Sanje, raging into the ship's console, hands waving and mouth working through its entire range.

"He's distracted," Sai said, continuing forward. "Let's go."

Sai kept moving forward, passing beneath the cockpit and heard Eponi's footsteps behind his own. The ship's ramp, lowered the short distance to the dirt ahead of them, sat open and ready. The trail they'd been following led right to it.

"Uh, Sai?" Eponi said, behind him. "I think Sanje saw me."

Sai didn't reply, just broke into a dead sprint towards the ramp. A hissing noise coupled with white steam signaled the hydraulics kicking into play and the ramp shunted up. Sai threw the pistol towards the rising ramp. It clattered up the metal board, and Sai, hands free, jumped.

His fingers caught the ramp's rising edge, and Sai started to pull himself up as the ship's hull came close. Red lights at the ramp top started flashing, a warning to anything on the slanted surface to get off or get in or get crushed.

"Sai!" Eponi shouted. "Let go!"

He couldn't. Not with Aurora in there. Not knowing where Sanje might fly this ship. Sai managed to get his left elbow over the ramp, pressing it into one of the raised grooves meant for traction. With a heave, Sai pulled his right arm over. Risked a glance up to see how much time he had.

Zero. Zero time.

Sai winced, tried to let go of the ramp before it crushed his arms, his skull into the ship's base. The ramp, though, froze. As Sai's moves to loosen his grip worked, a hand shot out and grabbed Sai's right wrist, holding it steady.

"Hey there, bomber man," Aurora said, lying on her stomach, arm outstretched and holding Sai's wrist. "Don't give up on me yet."

With a pull, Aurora heaved Sai onto the ramp and they crouch-crawled into the ship's central room. The gourd craft's middle held a wide platform, clearly meant for cargo or other large gear. Around the edges, sloping ramps led to upper and lower modules, with handgrips along the sides for easy zero gravity travel. Yellow light, the kind meant to mimic life-giving starlight, shone from a hanging globe in the center.

Perro's apparent body lay beneath the globe, dirt marring the bronzed tile everywhere else.

"Never realized how useful emergency stops could be till right now," Aurora said, nodding towards the ramp's local control panel.

"Do we have one?"

"We don't have a ship, Sai."

"Oh, right," Sai said, leaning down to pick up his thrown pistol. "Well, when we do."

"Hey!" Sanje shouted, running over from the gourd's cockpit, holding a rifle and trying to decide who to aim at. "Get off—"

Sai shot him. Raised the pistol and blasted Sanje straight on before the man could make a choice. The bolt hit Sanje in the gut, and the pilot dropped his rifle, looked at the charred mark on his clothes. Little flames burned for a hot second in the light fabric before dissipating as Sanje collapsed.

"Nice shooting," Aurora said, slapping the lower button for the ramp. "Hope you didn't kill him though."

"Why?" Sai asked, holstering the pistol and going for the rifle instead. Never miss a chance to upgrade: another of his family's principles. "Do you have a soft spot for Tarla's team?"

"Tarla understands debt," Aurora said. "If she knows we kept her crew alive, she won't come after us."

"Which she wouldn't do anyway if they were all dead."

"Sure," Aurora said as Eponi climbed up the ramp, looking bewildered at seeing her captain, Sai, and two bodies on the floor. "But then any friends Tarla had, or anyone she owed something to, might come after us. We have DefenseCorp on our asses. That's enough."

Sai didn't quite get Aurora's reasoning, but if the captain wanted these two alive, then Sai wouldn't question it.

"Eponi," Aurora said. "Get to the cockpit and see if you can fly this thing. If you can, I want us in the air and swinging back towards the base to find Rovo and Gregor."

"You want to go back?" Eponi said slow, giving Aurora a chance to rectify her words.

"I want to cover our path, see if we find them," Aurora said. "DefenseCorp shouldn't know we have this ship. And if they get in the way, it looks like this thing might have some teeth."

"I'm gonna be real upset if we made it out of there just to die in a ship as ugly as this one," Eponi said, but she went by Sai and Sanje's moaning self towards the cockpit.

Sai helped Aurora unload Perro and Sanje into the dirt close to the berth's entrance while Eponi worked at the ship's controls, powering up the vessel's jets.

"She has a point, Aurora," Sai said while the moved

the bodies. "We could take this ship and break for the stars. We'd be long gone before anyone knew we left."

"And leave Gregor and Rovo?" Aurora's defiance matched her dirt-filled hair, the way her green eyes flared in the ship's orange lights.

"They were getting blitzed by that patrol craft, Aurora," Sai said. "I'm not happy about it either. I hate it, but I don't want to die looking for the dead."

Something changed in Aurora's look as Sai said the words. As if her spine had been severed, her energy drained. She dropped Perro's wrist and started back towards the ramp. Sai waited a second for one of Aurora's patented turnarounds, where she'd burst back at him in a fury about how she was the captain, they had to follow orders, and she knew what was best and so on and so on as Aurora had done a million times before.

But Aurora didn't say a word as they went back up and into the ship. Eponi raised the ramp behind them, and the ugliest ship Sai had ever seen started its rise into the Wexer night. Sai followed Aurora right to the cockpit, a four-seat, stadium-style affair that gave everyone great views as Eponi guided the craft over the berth's surrounding walls.

Wexer's city spread out before them, lights aglow save for one section off to their right. There, no artificial halo touched the dark. Instead, raging fires burned, their flames towering up as a growing drone fleet, red and white lights flashing, sprayed suppressant.

"Guessing that's where we're going?" Eponi said.

"Eponi," Aurora said. "Sai says looking for Gregor and Rovo is a stupid risk to take. That we ought to turn skyward and leave. Right now." The captain took a long breath. "I ordered you otherwise minutes ago, but that was wrong. This isn't a dictatorship. You're not my subordinates any more. I can't fly this ship myself, so it's up to you to choose where we go."

Aurora sat back into her seat, looking ahead at those fires, "You know where I would take us if I could. What I would do. I can't make that choice for you anymore."

What the hell was that? Sai looked at Aurora like he might a strange insect, a confusing equation, a bomb that didn't go off when he'd timed it to. Some things just didn't fit right, and Aurora letting the reins fall from her hands? That didn't fit at all.

"I. . . " Eponi said, then she pointed to an incoming order from Wexer's flight control. "They're telling us to land. They're saying DefenseCorp is seizing the planet's air space, and no ship gets to leave. That means more than one patrol craft."

"We can't outrun them?" Sai asked.

"Don't know if you looked at this ship," Eponi said. "But it's built for cargo and crew, not speed."

Sai joined Aurora, sank back into his chair, "Then we're dead."

The thought sank in, the future playing out. Capture by DefenseCorp forces, a quick declaration of desertion and its punishment, and out the airlock they'd all go. After all this work, all the running and fighting and hoping, they'd wound up right back at the start: a hunted band that'd be caught.

"So what do you want to do?" Eponi said.

"You know," Sai replied, the despair leaking into another feeling, one a little crazier, a little exhilarating. "If we're going to go out, I'd rather do it looking for friends."

Silence, but when Sai looked left, saw Aurora sitting there, he could read the slight smile on her face.

"Can't argue with that," Eponi said. "But if I'm flying

into that mess, I'm going to need some help. This thing's got weapons, and I'd appreciate you two using them."

Sai scooped out from his seat, heading back from the cockpit. He heard Aurora's own clanks join his, doing what Sever ought to be doing: running into the fight, not fleeing from it.

THIRTY-THREE

A Brawler's Creed

THE FIRST YEARS off the comet came hard. Mining those icy rocks went slow, a deliberate process meant to make sure your valuable extraction didn't collapse the whole comet and send everyone spinning out into vacuum. Rolling away from a strict society into the relatively open world handling civil security contracts for DefenseCorp meant Gregor had to find a morality that wasn't defined by a company's code of conduct.

He could follow the DefenseCorp example, where helping people was fine and encouraged, so long as those people could pay. Or Gregor could side with those preaching a similar, less capitalist proposition, like the pacifists on his first assignment, and abstain from seeking cash altogether. Gregor found various shades as he went from world to world, contract to contract, finding and fighting corruption or, depending on the terms, supporting and securing it.

Good became evil from one day to the next, it seemed.

Gregor found a simpler answer when, bored of bar fights and suppressing protests, he switched to DefenseCorp's military division. There, he found the clearest code Gregor could ask for: support the squad. Since then, he'd known wrong, right, and who to hit.

Unarmored, Gregor climbed into the patrol craft, the burns across his arms and legs running together into a pain-filled backdrop as Gregor stood up inside the drop trooper bay. Outside, shouts to evacuate punctuated the air. Ash blew in behind him, riding smoke from the base, which must have caught fire from the laser barrage. Gregor's eyes teared up without the visor keeping them clear, and he blinked the water away while reaching for his hammer.

Seats stretched away before Gregor, filling out spaces for all the drop troopers and their weapons. To Gregor's left, beneath the flight deck, screens showcased the intended drop zone and the objective. The base glowed an orange on a top-down Wexer city map, while Sever Squad's DefenseCorp photos hugged the next screen's edges.

Those clean, close-cropped mugs looking back at Gregor hadn't spent nights deep in a mine, trudging through a swamp, or rocketing off a building with a little girl in their arms.

"Who the hell are you?" asked a hard voice from Gregor's right, and through his stinging eyes, Gregor picked out the drop commander, standing near the panel controlling the bay doors, the go lights, and all the stuff that made an assault like this one work. "And what's that hammer?"

Gregor didn't see a weapon on the man, so he started walking his way, letting the hammer's head drag across the patrol craft's floor. The ship itself, maybe reacting to Gregor's attack moments ago, veered up and away from the base, putting distance between itself and the fire.

"I asked you who you are," the drop commander said.

"Gregor," the hammer man replied when he made it within range.

"Who?"

Gregor's hammer answered that question. The hit knocked the drop commander out of his own bay door, dropping him to the ground below. Behind the drop commander, a ladder went up to the patrol craft's flight deck. Holding his hammer in his left hand, Gregor started up one rung, two, and with a jump, made it almost to the top.

Orders flew through the air as Gregor went up, frantic calls for system statuses mingling with asks if anyone had eyes on Sever. The frustration in the latter flushed Gregor with a little hope: that much anger must mean Aurora and the others hadn't been caught yet. The captain had always been smart. Not surprising that she'd managed to get away.

And now he'd make sure Aurora didn't have to run anymore.

Nobody up top paid attention to the opening at the craft's aft end, much less to the man climbing up through it. Only when Gregor's hammer thunked onto the flight deck did a few faces turn, catching Gregor's wide, murderous smile.

Not that Gregor felt happy, not that Gregor felt thrilled to be here, but throwing your opponents off their composure played a key part in his game. Gregor had to get close with the hammer, and the longer these confused fools took to realize his dangerous aims, the better.

Four people helmed the patrol craft, likely a minimum after all the troops jumped to the surface. One sat at the far end, hands on the ship's flight controls and paying no attention to Gregor at all. Beyond him, a swooping view laid out a burning cityscape as the ship advanced, hunting Sever.

The other three sat at various monitors, screens showing turret controls, scanners, and communications data. Those faces looked Gregor's way, their looks going from irritation at the interruption to confusion to, when Gregor started towards them, straight up fear.

"Who're you?" the closest one, manning the turrets, managed to say before Gregor came within range.

The spry guy fell back from his chair as Gregor swung, the hammer crashing through the monitors. Sparks flew, the turret man screamed, and the patrol craft's emergency lights shifted to their panic spectrum, blazing through the flight deck with screeching sounds. The communications officer grabbed his gunnery friend and dragged him back as Gregor recovered his swing.

The last of the trio, a tired-looking woman who'd been staring at the scanners, managed the most coherent response: standing and reaching for her pistol.

"Shoot him!" the turret guy cried, offering sound advice.

Blasting someone with any accuracy required a stable environment. Steady footing, a target that wasn't moving all that much, and the ability to keep the weapon straight while you pulled the trigger.

She wouldn't get any of those.

Gregor swept the hammer in a long, low swing, twisting the handle as he moved to activate the weapon's kinetic energy. He let go near the hammer arc's end, arms reminding him that they weren't in the best condition for such a move but, because he was Gregor, dammit, doing it anyway.

The hammer soared, spinning through the flight deck's

center and crashing through the diving pilot's chair, right into the patrol craft's controls. With a crackling, shredding sound, as if a billion flight systems cried out in fear, the entire console blew apart. Wexer's open air flew in as the patrol craft lurched hard into a dive, and the scanner's shot, fired in wild desperation, buzzed well behind Gregor, adding a blast mark to a panel that'd soon be burned to nothing.

Even Gregor had to admit, that'd been a damn good throw.

DefenseCorp built their ships to handle damage, to take catastrophe and survive it as best they could, so while the patrol craft started its sudden dive, throwing everyone on the flight deck towards the ragged opening—Gregor's hammer had disappeared on through, no doubt making its landing somewhere on the ground below—the ship's jets kicked in a second later, trying to find some way to stabilize things.

The pilot, closest to the opening, fell out and vanished in the first second. Gregor pitched forward, tumbling across the flight deck's open center while the other three reached for their own handholds. The hammer man tucked his shoulder into the tumble, trying to pitch himself towards the scanners. Sparks continued to fly as Gregor fell, as the patrol craft's broken flight computer tried to stabilize itself.

Most people would panic in an uncontrolled ship, surrounded by shattered computers, screaming flight crews, and a fiery death below.

Gregor had been through DefenseCorp's hardest simulations. He'd been through battles outnumbered and outgunned and outsmarted, where survival came more by luck than skill. He ought to have died a hundred times over, but Gregor still lived.

And he kicked off the floor like he planned to continue doing so.

That final push brought Gregor into the craft's left side, crumpling into the patrol craft's forward end just outside the hole his hammer had created. In vacuum, the sucking force would've pulled Gregor out, but here, in Wexer's low altitude, the breeze blew back in. Broken metal sliced into his skin suit, cut up Gregor's arms and legs, but the hammer man stayed in the ship.

A thud hit Gregor's chest, and he looked down, his arms and legs spread to keep stable while the patrol craft slowed its dive. The scanner's pistol, dropped by its owner, who had both her hands clinging to her bolted workstation. Her eyes met Gregor's as he picked up the weapon.

"Bad luck," Gregor said.

He rolled, dropping through the broken hole in the patrol craft and falling all of a meter before landing on the loose, dirt building roof below. The ship whirled above, struggling to stabilize itself. Gregor laid there for a long moment, pistol in his hand, and watched the craft veer, its jets popping on and off. Wexer's breeze kissed his skin with cool lips, and the big man was content to let it. Content to lie there for a long time.

When he'd dished out his last fight on the comet, when the company's security had wrestled Gregor into one of two holding cells on the icy ball, Gregor had done just this: laid out and let the moment wash over him, knowing that his life would never go back to what it was. He'd just fought his way onto and disabled a DefenseCorp patrol craft. They'd shoot him for that, forever.

DefenseCorp soldiers joked they didn't have a real home. They were sent from place to place, picked up and put down according to whims beyond their control. So, inevitably, the company became your home. Your squadmates, the vessel that carried you from place to place. He'd never be able to go back to that, to the *Nautilus*.

Aurora would say Sever ought to be Gregor's home. Now, Gregor didn't have a choice.

If Sever even existed anymore.

AFTER TOO LONG LAYING ON the roof, a new whine interrupted Gregor's dark musing, the characteristic low vibration claimed by spacecraft humming along at power meant for atmospheric flight. Overhead, the few stars strong enough to poke through the haze from the nearby fires died as the ugliest, most bulbous ship Gregor had seen trundled on. Orange lights crossed the craft from front to back, giving it a pumpkin look. At first, Gregor thought the ship might be Wexer's idea of an emergency craft, coming to put out the fires or offer medical support.

Then a green laser cascade launched from turrets Gregor hadn't been able to see in the dark. The bright bolts found the reeling patrol craft, burning through the hull, the engines, the jets, and sending the vessel plummeting into the DefenseCorp courtyard. Gregor sat up as the patrol craft spiraled to a low-speed, fiery smash, noticing that the base building itself had fallen apart.

The remaining troops around the building scattered like roaches as their craft crashed, breaking away through damaged walls into streets and alleys. Gregor made his way to the roof edge and looked towards the base, looking for Rovo and seeing no signs.

Power armor could get you through a lot, but an entire building collapse? Gregor hadn't seen that before. Or maybe Rovo had made it out, maybe the rookie had turned Gregor's distraction into an escape.

Spotlights hit Gregor hard, and he looked up, wincing

at the ugly ship as its humming jets brought the craft alongside the building. The ship rotated, and Gregor caught a look through the clear windows blanketing its cockpit.

"Eponi?" Gregor said, not quite believing what he saw, though that definitely explained the offensive salvo on the patrol craft.

"Looks like you lost your hammer, big guy," Eponi said, her voice coming through the ship's broadcast. "Don't know if we can let you back in the squad without it."

Adrenaline could do a lot. Gregor ran on the drug, his body kept him pumped full of it whenever the excitement picked up, but the crashes came fast. He felt it now, presented with Eponi's safe smile and a total lack of enemy fire. The burning pain along his arms and legs kicked in, and for a second, Gregor felt like he might fall off the roof.

"Whoa," Eponi said, apparently seeing something. "Just joking, Gregor. Hang in there and I'll get the ramp lined up."

By the time Aurora and Sai had him into one of the cockpit chairs, a painkilling shot stolen from the ship's medical supplies and jammed in, Gregor had circled back to the same question the other three kept asking him:

Where the hell had Rovo gone?

The New Deal

THE KATANA BLADE hovered near his eyes and Rovo started. Or, rather, tried to. The situation slammed back into his consciousness, a freight train railing his arms and legs into their locked places. The visor, cracked and dim, added no details to glaring light outside. Rovo heard his heartbeat and nothing else: the power armor's carefully crafted audio design, meant to discard irrelevant noise and keep the focus on the important, had died out too, leaving the rookie in a silent, surreal world.

Passing out had come both slow and fast, in that Rovo knew that he'd eventually fade to black given the suit's weight, his inability to move, and the piled on damage from the collapse. All the same, the onset had been like an invisible hand, reaching out and snatching his consciousness away. No gentle slide into oblivion.

The katana moved, rolled up and away as its owner crouched down and waved at the visor. Rovo blinked once, twice to confirm Sai really was staring at him. Behind the demolitionist, a bright orange light washed out everything else. The orange didn't make sense. Had Rovo actually died? Was this some strange afterlife?

The helmet shifted around his head, a dull grinding noise echoing in Rovo's ears as someone cleared rubble away. A pop sounded, cracking some as caked in debris worked itself out. The helmet twisted against Rovo's neck for a half-turn before, with a strong pull, lifting off and exposing Rovo to some fresh, delightful, dust-clogged air.

He coughed once, twice, and on the third time Aurora replaced Sai and slipped an oxygen mask over Rovo's face. The filtered goodness hit Rovo's lungs like holy water, cleansing away the pollution.

"Don't work yourself too hard," Aurora said. "Sai and I are going to dig you out. Might take a minute, but you'll be fine."

Rovo couldn't really talk with the mask on, so Aurora filled him in while she and Sai worked with their hands and some random objects definitely not made for clearing debris. Every so often, Aurora would ask Eponi to fire a targeted blast from the ship at a particularly nasty chunk, melting it away. Rovo always twitched, figuring they'd miscalculate the blast strength and burn off a limb, but by the time they'd excavated the power armor, Rovo still had all four.

"You owe me a new suit," Aurora said back in the ship, the damaged pieces of her black and white armor littered across the central room. "Now that DefenseCorp isn't buying new ones."

Rovo looked for the joke in Aurora's eyes, found none. Gregor shared the space with them, looking torched and tired as he laid on one of the couches. Gregor's hammer, recovered from the rubble, sat on the floor. The big man's adventure with the patrol craft reminded Rovo just how new he was to this game: the rookie hadn't been able to beat back a few troopers without getting crushed by a building, even with power armor.

That armor, though, had kept Rovo alive. Had let Aurora and the others find him with its low-powered distress beacon firing away on squad frequencies.

"You don't get time to relax," Aurora said. "Defense-Corp pulled its troops into the city after we downed the craft, but they're going to bring in more once it gets here."

"So we're going to take Tarla's ship and run?"

"Not exactly," Aurora said, then she glanced towards the cockpit. "Eponi, what's the ETA?"

"Almost on point," Eponi shouted back. "You still have energy for this?"

Wexer's night had crept along, and Rovo counted at least twenty hours since they'd slept. Not counting his knockout. Sever had defended against an assault, been arrested and trapped in a cell, escaped and fought across the city for its own freedom. Every neuron in Rovo's brain screamed for him to take a back seat, to let his bruises heal.

Eponi's vote had been to zip back to the *Prisa*, a ship she felt was far more suited to the running they'd be doing than the lump Tarla called home. Rovo had vetoed the move. Had pushed for one last effort.

"I made a promise," Rovo said, standing up and checking his holsters. "You don't have to come with me, but I'm going."

Aurora put a hand on Rovo's shoulder, talked back towards Eponi, "Tarla said we'd need to make our own reputation out here. That starts by keeping those promises."

The power armor had kept Rovo's skinsuit safe during the collapse, and he'd attached the scythe, found in the rubble right next to him, in its two-piece mode to the belt around his waist. A pistol sat there too, with a rifle—all courtesy of the Twilight Ranger's armory—slung over his shoulder.

Sai came in from the cockpit, the katana ready and a fresh, if not-quite fitting black combat outfit on. Skinsuits were designed for fast-moving power armor play, but Sai's uniform made more sense for their mission:

Get into Calico Max's compound, find the man, and make sure he wouldn't touch the Talpa again.

Finding the vested speculator wasn't difficult: like any good businessperson, Tarla kept all the contract details on the ship's computers. Calico's address, contact numbers, and other details were attached to the contract file that'd brought Tarla and her Rangers to Wexer in the first place. Rovo found it very fitting that Calico's attempt to destroy the Talpa would wind up torching the man in the end.

That is, if they could get to Calico at all.

"Looks like our man doesn't take chances," Eponi said over the ship's intercoms. "He's put up a wall just like DefenseCorp did."

"And we can't fly over it?" Sai said.

"Oh I'm going to," Eponi replied. "I'm just letting you know it might not be Calico alone in there, curled up and waiting for you."

"Doesn't matter," Aurora said, stretching a look between Rovo and Sai. "We're going to get in and deal with this fast, okay? If Calico doesn't play, we back out and torch the place, him included. There's no time for negotiations."

Eponi blew the ship in, settling the craft down into a courtyard that, while still mainly blackrock, at least had enough random junk to give it personality. Rovo counted a couple tight courts for games, and what looked like a heavily scarred shooting target, sticking up from the ground like a red metal tombstone.

Calico's house, a three-story affair, stood solid and quiet in the orange-white dawn wrapping its way across the city. Smoke from the night's fights fuzzed the air overhead, now punctuated by sirens as Wexer's bot emergency crews went to work cleaning up the damage. No spaceships bothered to descend: DefenseCorp's order to clear the planet still held.

With Gregor on, as Aurora put it, forced medical leave, the Sever trio ran down the ramp as it lowered. If anything, the Twilight Ranger's ship, with its battered creamsicle color scheme, looked uglier in the daytime. Rovo would never consider himself a spacecraft connoisseur, but if he had to fly around in the lumpy tumor all the time . . . well, he'd probably still stick with Sever, but he'd complain a lot.

Moreover, the ship showed Tarla must pull in plenty of cash to keep her crew coming back to that thing.

"Sai and I go first," Aurora said, rifle in hand, grenades and pistols on her waist. "Rovo, you're covering."

"Why?" Rovo said as they broke towards the front door, a single-paned, gray metal slab. "Isn't this my idea?"

"Because you just spent a couple hours unconscious in power armor," Aurora replied. "I need the first shot to hit the target."

Okay, fair. Rovo's muscles definitely weren't doing their best work in the run towards the door. His arms felt floppy, his legs loose, and the headache coming on wasn't doing Rovo any favors. Regardless, he sat center as Sai went to work on the door, plastering a gelled explosive to the entry. Nobody popped out and started firing, so Rovo didn't get to test his accuracy before Sai's big bang rippled through the dawn air and sent Calico's door flying inside.

Aurora followed up the entrance-making pop with some Twilight Ranger EMP flashbangs, nifty bombs that took their knockout tendencies and coupled them with the electronic-shorting blue lightning. They had no intelligence on Calico, so best to assume the man was a panicked, heavily armed brute with a thousand drones at his disposal.

Drones that could've, should've dismantled the Talpa if Calico actually had them. Sai had presented that logic on the flight over, when Aurora and Rovo raided the Twilight Ranger armory, and Aurora had shut down that approach by saying she wasn't getting outgunned again.

Sai hadn't pushed back, and now they stood inside what looked like a gentle family room. A solid entryway desk had caught the metal door, its legs snapping and collapsing to the floor. Digital pictures lay cracked around the space and, to the right, the big living space had the couches, the sedate lamps and end tables Rovo would've expected in, well, his parent's home.

Hardly the domain of a crazy, vest-sporting madcap miner.

"What is this?" Sai said, echoing Rovo's mind. "Do we have the right place?"

A little scream came from above, a voice like one Rovo had heard not all that long ago. He went forward, pushing past Aurora and Sai to look up and see a woman not all that much older than himself holding a girl and looking both very afraid and half asleep.

Aurora and Sai looked totally lost, so Rovo dug into his training, his negotiating tactics, and went for broke.

"We're looking for Calico, miss," Rovo announced, parsing out a lie as he spoke. "We have reason to believe he's in danger."

"You blew apart my front door," the woman said, clearly hoping this was all just a bad dream.

"Sorry," Rovo said. "You can bill DefenseCorp for the damages. Do you know where Calico is?"

Across the floor, on the other side of the sofas and the pleasant decor, a normal door opened, knob turning with a satisfying click. Sporting a warm-looking pajama outfit, Calico Max, hair hanging over his ears and wide eyes, walked out from the bathroom and reached for a coffee mug steaming nearby.

"Uh," Calico offered as Aurora, Sai, and Rovo turned their heavily armed selves his way. "What are you doing here?"

"We're going to keep it simple," Rovo said. "You're going to remove your claim on the mine with the Talpa."

"What?"

"You heard me," Rovo continued, and was about to go into a series of threats on the man's life and livelihood, but a second, soft cry from above brought another look to the little girl, peeking out from around the woman's legs. Maybe, maybe now wasn't the time to take the aggressive approach. "You're going to let the Talpa keep the mine. They were going to pay us to protect them, but you're going to do it instead. You'll get some good cash, the Talpa will get a good home. Deal?"

Calico hesitated, and Rovo dropped his hands to his weapons. Subtle enough that, hopefully, the little girl wouldn't guess what was going on. Overt enough that Calico Max would understand.

"Isn't DefenseCorp after you all?" Calico said.

"They tried," Aurora stepped up. "They failed. Think about what that means for you."

"WHAT A LINE," Sai said as Eponi coasted the ship through Wexer's sky, in the broad expanse outside the city. "What that means for you? Aurora, you're learning to speak with something other than your rifle."

Aurora laughed. Rovo sat back in the seat, watched Wexer's black landscape carve away beneath him. They'd extracted the promise from Calico, and Rovo would have to hope Sever's potential threat would keep the man in line. If nothing else, the time should give the Talpa a chance to prepare. Calico would have a harder time dislodging them with another random mercenary band.

"You happy, rookie?" Eponi asked from the pilot's chair.

"I'm hurt and exhausted," Rovo said, "but yeah, I guess you could say I'm happy."

"Good. Because we just picked a fight with the big boys, so take your smiles when you can get'ed."

From one battle to the next, the Sever way.

But he'd savor this little victory.

Into the Jaws

STARSHIPS, just like karts, had personalities. You felt them when the engines powered up, when they slid through the air as you nudged the control stick, as you sent them up to brush the stars and leave gravity behind. Flying Tarla's tumor over Wexer's city had been like steering a rock: no aerodynamics, all raw power from the ship's engine banks. No grace, all brute force.

The *Prisa*, though, brought joy. She'd unlatched the bulk cargo container back at the Talpa mine, donating the thing to the furry creatures, and losing the rectangle brought the stolen ship to life. With Sever aboard after a short rest and Rovo-led reckoning with the Talpa, they were heading up and out from Wexer's blackrock desert.

Eponi, hands wrapped around the single silver flight stick, began the ascent with a slow lift, feeling the ship judder in Wexer's breeze as it rose over the Talpa gathered to see them off. The mine mountain hung starboard, blocking some early afternoon light. Eponi could see the shade cutting across the *Prisa*'s twin prongs on the cockpit's sides, the very tips sparkling as they escaped the mountain's shroud.

Three sharp screens spread before her, swappable with finger swipes or spoken word to show whatever Eponi wanted. Now she had the *Prisa*'s systems sitting front and center, the green bars showcasing a craft that'd been well-maintained. To the right buzzed a communications panel, one picking up Wexer's air traffic control and its continued warning to avoid the planet. DefenseCorp maintained its blockade, and the details showed on the left screen, set to the *Prisa*'s scanners.

Short-range showed nothing nearby, save some energy leaking from the mine. DefenseCorp hadn't pressed in on Wexer yet, perhaps still trying to figure out what'd happened the night before. How a captive squad of five managed to destroy a patrol craft and escape.

"Think Tarla will know where to find her ship?" Eponi asked Aurora, who joined her in the only other chair the *Prisa* offered in its narrow cockpit.

"She's not going to get it back," Aurora said. "I sent its location to the woman that owned this one. Made a trade."

"Yeah, except this ship's way better."

"For us," Aurora replied. "Tarla's has more cargo room, more weapons. It might be slower, but they'll get by."

"And Tarla?"

"She lived," Aurora frowned. "That's enough."

"Cold, captain."

"Tarla will understand, and if she doesn't, I don't care." Aurora leaned in, looked at the scanner. "No fighters yet?"

"Don't think they've seen us," Eponi said. "I'm not flying flashy here, but in a minute or two Wexer's going to pick up that we're in the air."

"Then we run. Follow the plan. We don't want to get into a fight."

The plan, carved out over noon coffee in the mine, came down to Gregor's words from the cell. DefenseCorp, and whomever that general happened to be, were sending more resources after five deserters than made any sense. The question, though, came down to what scared DefenseCorp so much.

"Knowledge?" Sai had posed over lunch in the mine, wearing burn-salving bandages all over his arms, much like Gregor. "They think we're going to spread what happened on Dynas?"

Eponi would've jumped in on that explanation, except there were too many people that had the same intel as Sever.

"Dynas had a city with thousands," Eponi said. "Like, way more people than DefenseCorp could contain. Everyone that delivered a shipment to that world would have a chance at learning what happened there."

Aurora stared into her mug, as if answers might be hiding in the soft smoke curling up and out. Gregor ate the warm, grainy mush the Talpa kept offering up, though Eponi thought it tasted like sand. Rovo hadn't joined them yet, the rookie was off on a call between Calico and the Talpa leader, finalizing terms with the suddenly-reasonable businessman.

"If it's not the virus, then what?" Sai said. "That's the only thing that makes sense."

"I didn't say it's not the virus," Eponi replied. "Just, like, not that alone. Or maybe something totally different. Maybe they want your sword."

Sai laughed, "They can try to take it."

"We keep running until we know." Aurora looked up from her mug. "We'll get more remote. If DefenseCorp follows us out to the absolute fringe, then we adjust. I don't want to fight them head-on."

"More remote than Wexer?" Eponi said. "Goody."

But that's where they were going. Eponi already had the coordinates plugged into the *Prisa*'s computer, ready to spin up their engines once they'd broken away from Wexer's atmosphere to send them further from the core, into galactic space where the only thing that mattered was how dangerous you happened to be.

With only one damaged suit of power armor, Sever wasn't all that dangerous anymore.

The communication screen lit up with the first incoming hail, a call from air traffic that Eponi ignored. When Aurora asked why, Eponi pointed to the dark sky they hurtled towards.

"They're going to ask who we are, where we're going," Eponi said. "I don't really feel like talking. Do you?"

"They'll tell DefenseCorp."

"If our former employers don't have constant beads on anything moving on Wexer, then they're being lazy," Eponi said. "We're not making a stealth getaway from here, Aurora. The question is how much fire we're going to take before we jump."

The answer came in the next call, the small screen lighting up with an ID neither Aurora nor Eponi expected to see, possibly ever again.

Nautilus.

The screen blinked at them, while Eponi glanced at Aurora.

"Answer it?" Eponi said.

"I . . . ," Aurora trailed off, causing Eponi to twitch an eyebrow.

Wasn't like the captain to be unsure. Eponi had her own reservations about the *Nautilus*, of course. That the ship could find and hail them, meant their former home was in system, which meant Deepak, their commander, had sent the big rock after Sever days ago. Maybe even before Sever had reached Wexer.

Aurora reached out and tapped the screen, accepting the hail as the *Prisa* began its bumpy jaunt through Wexer's atmosphere, the outside view turning bright and orange as heat built up over the glass.

"This is the *Prisa*," Aurora said. "Captain speaking."

"Captain of the *Prisa*," Deepak said. Eponi could identify that voice in a heartbeat, she'd heard the man's almond chocolate tones delivering instructions so many times that Eponi had to fight away the urge to obey. "I believe, last time we spoke, you were flying one of my ships."

"Don't know what you're talking about." Aurora tapped the mute button, halting her words from going through to Deepak. "Eponi, can you figure out where the signal's coming from? I want you to fly the opposite way."

"Even if that throws us off our trajectory?"

"Yes. We'll pick a new planet once we have an escape," Aurora said. "We can't get caught."

"—wasting both our time by denying the obvious," Deepak said when Eponi returned her attention to the commander's words while reading what the *Prisa* could pull together for a direction. "Aurora, you and your squad deserted. There's a cost for that, but apparently you've managed to make yourselves valuable at the same time. I've been asked to bring you in alive, and I hope you'll allow me to do so."

The *Prisa* punched through the atmosphere into starlit space, crowded with ships arriving and waiting for a chance to drop cargo and re-supply on Wexer. Even among all the craft, the *Nautilus* stood out on the scanners, and to the naked eye. A big round rock moving towards them, the *Nautilus* and its asteroid origins were nothing if not easy to pick out.

If not easy to fear.

"What happens after we surrender, Deepak?" Aurora shot back. "You drop us in cells and wring us dry, then kick us out an airlock when we're done? No thanks."

"You helped DefenseCorp for a long time, Aurora," Deepak replied. "One final act on our behalf, and I would fight to discharge your squad. No black marks, a clean break. I've offered the same to my superiors, and they agreed."

Eponi wondered if that negotiation happened before or after Sever had toasted a DefenseCorp carrier, wounded a bunch of troops, and caused the base on Wexer to collapse.

With all the traffic, Eponi turned the *Prisa* left, aiming it away from the *Nautilus* and towards the most empty spot she could find. As she angled, Eponi started having the *Prisa* find destinations they could jump to in that direction: somewhere, anywhere that wasn't here.

"You sent us to Dynas without any warning," Aurora said. "Why should we trust you now?"

"I knew as much as you did about Dynas," Deepak countered. "You and I are alike, Aurora. We're fighters. We complete the missions, do the work. I was as frustrated as you when I found out what had happened."

"Sure."

"I'm telling you the truth," Deepak said. "And I'm telling you that if you don't turn your ship around now, you'll never have another chance. We will not rest until we find you, and we will. I don't know whether you'll make one more jump or ten, but you'll run out of cash and food somewhere, and then you'll be caught. My offer won't exist anymore, and that will be the end."

A grim conclusion. The *Prisa*'s computer lit up. A nice space station, not too far away but not important either. An easy place to stop, grab some provisions and find a better place to disappear.

"Found a spot," Eponi said, hitting the mute button again. "Should we go for it?"

Aurora hesitated, unmuted.

"Deepak, why do they want us?" Aurora said. "What do they want to know?"

"If I tell you, will you come back?"

"Can't promise that."

Deepak's sigh came over speakers, "Aurora, I don't know the details, but I know it's about a girl. They know you left Dynas with a child. They want her. I don't know why, but they want her."

Kaia. The only one that'd survived Anaskya's virus for years. Eponi knew Rovo had seen the girl head off with her father, Kashmal. How long the two could keep themselves a secret, who knew.

New blips popped up on the scanner, closing fast. Small ships, launched from the *Nautilus*. No doubt meant to deliver a more forceful message to Sever.

"We have to make the call quick here," Eponi said. "Either side starts shooting and this gets ugly real fast."

Aurora looked out through the glass, as if she could glean some answer from the stars.

"Aurora?" Deepak said. "The fighters will escort you in, if you accept."

What they'd do if Sever declined, he didn't really need to say. Eponi tapped a few adjustments on the systems panel in front of her, charging up the *Prisa*'s shields. She hit the mute button while Aurora chewed on her bottom lip.

"Hey," Eponi said, broadcasting through the *Prisa*'s

intercoms. "If you could all grab a turret or find a spot to be useful, we might have company coming quick."

"They want Kaia," Aurora said, more to herself than anything. "We don't know where she is, and once Defense-Corp realizes that, they'll just kill us."

"Makes sense."

"But they'll find her eventually," Aurora continued, ignoring Eponi's injection.

"Not our responsibility."

"It should be," Aurora said. "Eponi, slow down. Don't start a fight. We're going in."

Eponi hesitated, didn't touch the systems, "Aurora, didn't you talk a while back about how this was supposed to be all of us, together? Not you giving the orders?"

"You're right," Aurora said, then unmuted the call. "Deepak, call off your fighters. We'll stay put while we decide what to do. Give us a little time."

The *Nautilus* commander agreed, and while Sever gathered in the cockpit, Deepak's fighters put themselves to a stop nearby. Ready to spring should Sever make a run.

But Sever wouldn't be running. Eponi wasn't surprised to see the vote turn hard one way. Go back into DefenseCorp's jaws. Figure out who wanted Kaia and why, then persuade that monster to change their minds.

"You realize this means we're going up against the biggest, most dangerous organization in the galaxy, right?" Eponi said once the other four had tallied up their votes. "Down on Wexer, that was, like, a nothing attempt. We go to the *Nautilus*, we'll be the ones with nothing. We'll get destroyed."

"No," Aurora said. "They'll be letting us inside, where we can find the source and stop it."

A boast. A bold statement. Eponi thought it sounded like something she would've said before a kart race, with the cameras and the mics in her face, reporters asking her what the competition would mean for her.

But the words didn't matter. The performance did, and as Eponi powered up the *Prisa* and set a course for the *Nautilus*, she didn't like Sever's odds.

READ *on for an excerpt from* HOME FRONT, *available now!*

An Excerpt from HOME FRONT

SEVER SQUAD BOOK FOUR

Fabricated food filled Gregor's tray, all grown by spinning together proteins in the *Nautilus*'s food banks. After setting the tray down on the cool sheet-metal table, painted over in waving blues in a concession to the *Nautilus*'s inspiration, Gregor stared at his feast, watching as the solid, real meal before him obliterated the last weeks spent guzzling powdered calories.

The mess hall, too, bubbled with constant conversation. The big space, on the *Nautilus*'s lowest level, could seat thousands in its multi-tiered arrangement and offered up several creations at all times for those on the ship to indulge. The wide room, like the table, played up the watery vibe, with preferred walking paths painted out with strange fish and sections denoted by otherworldly coral drawings.

The way Gregor had heard it, the *Nautilus*'s lead chef at the ship's christening had declared he wouldn't serve in a mess so devoid of spirit. Needing something for the troops to do en route to their first contract, the Defense-

Corp squads spent their time turning the mess into a place unlike any other on the ship, on any ship.

For all his gruffness, Gregor may have let his lips turn up when he saw the place.

"You going to eat that?" Rovo said, sitting across from him. "Or is the nice woman's generosity going to waste?"

"I'll eat it," Gregor said. "I appreciate my meals."

Before Gregor could take a bite, the nice woman Rovo referred to set her own tray down next to the big man, claiming a seat on the long bench nearly touching him. She'd been behind them in the line and offered to cover Gregor and Rovo when they realized that, without wristlets and their DefenseCorp accounts, they couldn't actually buy the food they'd picked up.

"Me too," the woman said, her build, her attitude, suggesting hard times spent for DefenseCorp. She wore the company's classic crimson too, through the black stripes up the sides marked a division Gregor didn't recognize. "You never know when your next might be coming, or what you might have to do to get it."

"Like ask for charity from a stranger," Rovo said. "Thanks again."

"We're all DefenseCorp here," the woman said, "Not a problem."

Gregor nodded and they all commenced with a bite or two or seven. The food was both as good and as solid as Gregor remembered, though the bites did have that flavorless tinge that came with lab spun protein. As if, with every chew, Gregor went a little further behind the curtain to see the nothingness at his food's heart.

"I'm not sure where you two come from," the woman said as the munching continued, "but I like to know who I'm sharing a table with. Name's Zaydi, and while it's been a long time, I'm from Poppyseed Nine."

Gregor's eyes sparked at that name. Not Zaydi, which he couldn't care less about, but Poppyseed Nine. The Poppyseeds and a few other similar-named sectors had earned a reputation for their perfection. Multiple planets in habitable ranges, life everywhere. Those with means, with DefenseCorp backing them up, had taken the sectors for their own. Anyone born on those planets had no business eating in a DefenseCorp mess.

"I'm Rovo," the rookie said, covering for Gregor's silence. "And, uh, I'm not really from anywhere important. Did you say Poppyseed Nine?"

Rovo, such a smooth talker.

Zaydi set a smile that said she'd answered this question a thousand times, "You're wondering why I'm not eating with the admiral and telling him how I'd like to buy his ship?"

"Frankly, yeah?"

"Because I didn't like it," Zaydi crossed her arms, leaned her elbows on the table. "Care to hear a secret?" That little grin widened. "The Poppyseeds are where the galaxy stashed all its awful people."

Zaydi, having opened the door, went on while Rovo and Gregor devoured their meals. Whipping up stories about this and that awful person, beats that sounded much like the corrupt worlds Gregor had parlayed into a Sever position. What a non-surprise to learn yet another sector suffered from human problems.

"So what're you two doing after this?" Zaydi asked in the relative silence after her last story. "Big plans for your first day on the *Nautilus*?"

"Waiting for our captain to decide whether we live or die, basically," Rovo said, and Gregor grunted an agreement.

"How's she going to do that?"

Gregor stopped, spoon halfway into his mouth. Rovo started answering Zaydi's question, and Gregor resumed eating, covering up the pause. Neither Gregor nor Rovo had mentioned their role with Sever, had mentioned Aurora, yet Zaydi hadn't seemed surprised at Rovo's words.

The big man took a closer look Zaydi's way as Rovo finished a blurred over description about why they were here, a potential mission to find someone that would be dangerous. Gregor had to give the rookie credit: the man could make up plenty on the fly, where Gregor would rather shake his head and say nothing.

"What's your outfit?" Gregor said, the black lines on Zaydi's uniform unwilling to be forgotten.

"My outfit?" Zaydi asked.

"Your squad."

"Oh," Zaydi looked at her own uniform, as if discovering it for the very first time. "I'm with an inspection team, running a tour on the *Nautilus* to make sure it's going right."

"Is it?" Rovo asked. "The *Nautilus*?"

Zaydi sighed, "Honestly? There's some problems." She looked between the two of them. "I can trust you both, right? No sharing?"

Gregor wanted to say that no, Zaydi had just met them. She shouldn't be trusting them with any secrets, small, large or in between.

"There's nobody for us to tell," Rovo said.

"Okay, well, apparently someone's been working in the armory here," Zaydi said. "They're putting together new suits that go against our policies." Zaydi tapped her lips, came to a discovery. "You use power armor, right? On your missions?"

"We do." Rovo looked like a lap dog, all in on Zaydi's question.

"Then maybe you can help me out," Zaydi said. "Nobody on my team works with heavy weapons, and we need to decide if the modifications are too dangerous. You said you're new here, right? So you'll be able to keep an open mind?"

"We don't work for Deepak," Rovo replied. "I'd love to help you."

Gregor felt the slightest tap on his ankle. On the front. Gregor shifted his elbow, knocked his knife off the table to the floor, where it bounced with a sharp clink. He bent down to grab it, gave a look Rovo's way as Zaydi gave more details about the armor question, and caught Rovo's right hand lingering below, offering up hand signals.

Rovo didn't quite have Sever's hand signs down to an art yet, but he managed the gist well enough. The rookie would lead, Gregor should follow.

Lead where, follow how? That remained a mystery.

At least it seemed like Rovo understood something about Zaydi wasn't right.

"You have time now?" Zaydi asked at the end of her description. "It shouldn't take long."

"Do we?" Rovo asked Gregor. "Don't think the captain wanted us back to the ship till late."

Gregor shrugged. Because the whole squad had lost their wristlets, Aurora had gone back to the stone age and set a post-dinner time for everyone to head back to the *Prisa*. The *Nautilus* had clocks on screens all over the place, so time tracking wasn't an issue, and right now they had hours yet to burn.

"There's your answer," Rovo said to Zaydi. "Lead on."

Zaydi took them from the mess hall towards the bow, eschewing the lifts to keep them on the *Nautilus*'s lowest level. Gregor hadn't spent all that much non-mess time down here, as the spaces were dedicated more to engineering, cargo storage, and analysis.

Few hammers, and fewer targets to smash than the other levels.

The mess hall bisected the lower level's central concourse, and leaving the hall put them back in what, up a level or two, would've been a packed section. The bow-ward hall should've been replete with bots and squaddies running this way and that. Messages should've been playing overhead.

Instead, leaving the mess hall through heavy double doors—Gregor noted these were blast shielded, unlike the mess hall's other exits—brought the trio to a quiet concourse. The sides here, rather than bearing motivational posters and DefenseCorp sayings, were plastered with safety guidelines, reminders about form requirements, and hard red warnings that the work could endanger the whole ship.

"Looks like a fun place," Rovo said as they walked along. No moving walkways speeding things up here, maybe due to crowds, maybe due to the hazard. "You ever come back here, Gregor?"

"Once," Gregor said. "A long time ago, to get my hammer."

"Hammer?" Zaydi asked, honest curiosity in the question.

"My favorite weapon," Gregor replied. "Most prefer rifles. I find them too easy."

"I . . . see," Zaydi said, clearly not seeing. Instead, she pointed at a yellow-clad door, one sporting an ID scanner. "Here's the lab we're using."

The label over the door marked what lay beyond as *Weapons Three*. Further down the concourse, then, would be

Weapons One and *Weapons Two*. The latter had been where Gregor earned his hammer, bought with most of the DefenseCorp cash in Gregor's account at the time, and very much worth it.

"Remember," Zaydi said. "Not a word of what you see in here."

The door whooshed to reveal . . . another doorway with a slight, featureless hallway in between. A control gap, meant to keep anyone peeking in from seeing inside. The trio bundled into the space, Zaydi tapped her ID on the second door, and with a chirp, their way back shut and their way forward opened.

Weapons 3 wasn't much larger than the *Prisa*'s central gathering space or the living room in the pod Gregor had lived in on the comet. Not that it needed to be: the ceiling crawled with mechanical arms and other devices, all slid into brackets that could be released by the massive control center opposite the door.

The room's middle, though, held the star. While the outside floor mirrored the polished silver seen throughout the *Nautilus*, a hard yellow-painted steel circle claimed center stage. That yellow paint bore scratches and burns from trials long since over.

Though, given the huge power armor suit resting on that circle, perhaps ready to start again.

Gregor had worn his fair share of the suits, had destroyed enemies aplenty with their kinetically-charged arms and legs, their holsters for a hundred different weapons. The older suits, though, had been designed with movement in mind, with giving the body a shell that would move with its owner's demands.

This one looked more like a tank that would surround the user and render them a slow-moving death machine. Arms and legs stuck out from the dense crimson metal, but surrounding the limbs were numerous other, well, limbs. Most sat empty, attachments waiting for an enterprising owner to decide which deadly implements they wanted to take today. Some looked set up for *Weapons 3*, holding a tube-like rifle, a spiked ball plugged into a narrow launcher, and one bearing a big case with a white cross on the suit's back.

"Big one, isn't she?" Rovo said, and Gregor grunted an agreement.

"Right?" Zaydi said. "We were a little surprised to find it here. Your Deepak has a sense of adventure, certainly."

Not the words Gregor would use to describe a man who hid from the front lines and sent squads to do the work, but fine.

"What did you want us to do?" Gregor asked.

Zaydi went further into the room, all the way to the control panel and started tapping away, "See, you two said you use power armor. I haven't. So I'm not sure whether this is working or not."

Something Zaydi did had an effect, and the power armor lit up. Gaskets across its body released, causing the armor's front to swing out and away. Ready for its next user.

"You want us to get inside it?" Rovo said.

"One of you," Zaydi replied. "Unless you think you both can fit."

"Power armor is solo," Gregor said. "Rovo, this one would match me."

"Go right ahead." Rovo rubbed his own shoulders. "I'm fine staying outta power armor for a while. Bad memories."

"Oh?" Zaydi asked, crossing back to stand by Rovo as Gregor moved towards the suit.

"Building fell on him," Gregor rumbled. "Tough break."

Approaching the armor, Gregor positioned his face near the visor and stood still. The power armor picked up on his stance, and a slight blue light shot out from within the suit as it measured Gregor's size and shape. The big suits couldn't completely morph themselves, but by tightening and loosening various bolts and bands, they could hit as good a comfort as possible.

The light blinked green and Gregor stepped forward. As his feet closed into the boots, the armor's back swung into place, sealing Gregor into the suit. Hisses and clicks rattled around as the armor settled itself into Gregor's size.

The visor clicked on, flooding what had been a black nothing into a clear view of the control center. Flashing yellow words in the upper left indicated the armor was in trial mode. No weapons enabled, so Gregor couldn't go around destroying the ship because he'd had a bad day.

Rovo and Zaydi came into view, the latter going back to the control center. Rovo waved at Gregor's face, and Gregor waved back, the slow hand sluggish and heavy. Whomever was designing this suit would have to tweak those settings, because having to heave an arm just to wave would get tired fast.

"What's it like in there?" Rovo said. "Feel like the future?"

The future? Gregor started to say that it felt like a prototype when the blinking trial mode in his visor changed to a hard red *LOCKDOWN*. Not a mode Gregor had used before, but old training had told him its purpose: keep the suit from doing anything stupid while you made changes.

Through the visor, Gregor saw Zaydi stand away from the control center, her movement answering who could've put the armor in lockdown. The suspicion Gregor had felt in the mess hall flared into full-on danger.

Zaydi wasn't moving like a flouncy inspector anymore. She had a professional's sure stance, carrying out her mission.

"You hearing me, buddy?" Rovo said, leaning in towards Gregor and laughing. "I know you're in there!"

Gregor tried to move. Spoke the keywords that should've triggered an emergency release from the suit. Nothing worked. If the arms had been heavy while the suit was on, in lockdown mode and without any assist, they were immovable.

Rovo rapped a hand on the armor's visor. Behind him, Zaydi reached into her uniform, pulled on a set, hard face, and drew out a small pistol.

Gregor heard his shouts.

The rookie did not.

Continue the adventure in HOME FRONT, available now!

Acknowledgments

This novel is the product of my family and friends refusing to let a dream die. My wife Nicole, for letting me write in the early mornings and making sure I don't starve. My brothers and parents for their continual comments, support, and enthusiasm.

Evan Aaseng, for being a constant sounding board and reeling me back in whenever my ideas went too far.

And, of course, you, the reader, for giving me a reason to write.

About the Author

A.R. Knight spins stories in a frosty house in Madison, WI, primarily owned by a pair of cats. After getting sucked into the working grind in the economic crash of the 2008, he found himself spending boring meetings soaring through space and going on grand adventures.

Eventually, spending time with podcasting, screenplays, short stories and other novels, he found a story he could fall into and a cast of characters both entertaining and full of heart.

Sever Squad has more adventures to come, along with new plots, settings, and stories in the future. From there, A.R. Knight plans on jumping through to other worlds and finding new stories to tell in the limitless borders of our imagination.

Thanks, as always, for reading!

For more information:
www.adamrknight.com

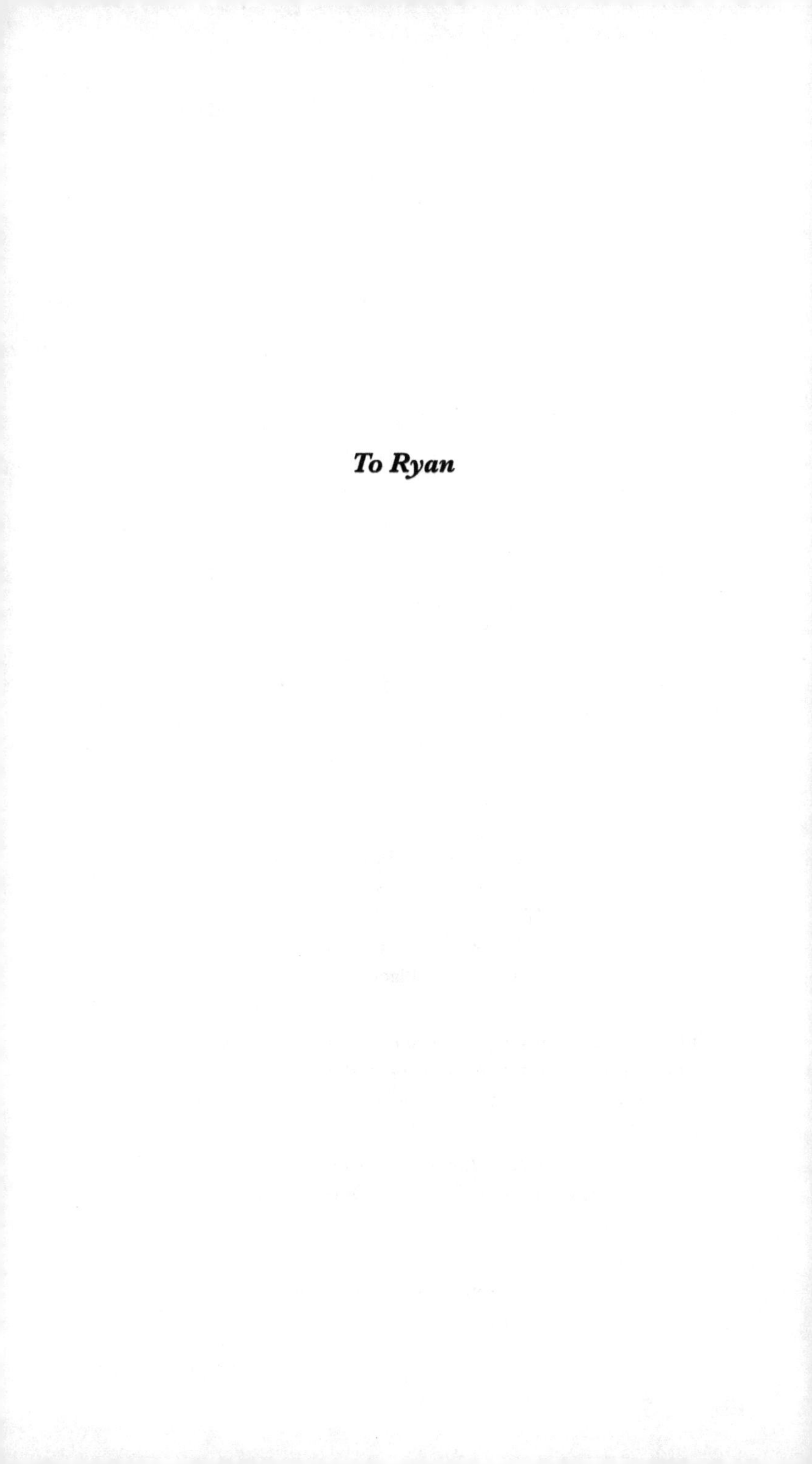

To Ryan